The soun   y
feet away, a   -
den move, h   -
lessly, but instead of falling, he crashed against something.

Cold stone, but not a wall, for there was a top to it, his fingers told him. And an end.

He froze as the scraping sound came again, echoing more loudly through the mausoleum. Then abruptly the deafening sound of something as solid and massive as a boulder crashing to the floor.

And then different sounds, not the scraping of stone on stone but a rustling, a scratching, so faint as to be almost lost in the constant background of featherless wings.

And finally footsteps—footsteps that began by shuffling, then striding, seemingly directly toward him. For a moment he could see two faint dots of reddish light almost at eye level moving toward him like a pair of dimly glowing embers. A stench of decay added to the foul odors already assaulting his nostrils. . . .

Ravenloft is a netherworld of evil, a place of darkness that can be reached from any world—escape is a different matter entirely. The unlucky who stumble into the Dark Domains find themselves trapped in lands filled with vampires, were-beasts, zombies, and worse.

Each novel in the series is a complete story in itself, revealing the chilling tales of the beleaguered heroes and powerful, evil lords who populate the Dark Domains.

BOOKS

BOOKS

Lord of the Necropolis

Gene DeWeese

For Pat Elrod,
for ex-Strahdinary cooperation

LORD OF THE NECROPOLIS

First Printing: October 1997
Printed in the United States of America.
Library of Congress Catalog Card Number: 96-60802

9 8 7 6 5 4 3 2 1

ISBN: 0-7869-0660-X

U.S., CANADA, ASIA,   EUROPEAN HEADQUARTERS
PACIFIC, & LATIN AMERICA   Wizards of the Coast, Belgium
Wizards of the Coast, Inc.   P.B. 34
P.O. Box 707   2300 Turnhout
Renton, WA 98057-0707   Belgium
+1-206-624-0933   +32-14-44-30-44
                Visit our website at http://www.tsrinc.com

 **PROLOGUE**

Barovia
735, Barovian Calendar

When the mists cleared, the lone Vistana found himself
in a place he had never been, yet a place that he instantly
recognized.

Looming high on a mountainside less than a mile distant stood the castle of Count Strahd von Zarovich, Lord
of Barovia. Though the Vistana had never seen the castle
itself, had never even been in Barovia, the massive structure with its hundred-foot curtain walls and towers at
least thrice that height was unmistakable, as was the
sheer rock face directly beneath the nearest of the walls.
So smooth and sheer was the rock, and so close to the
base of the curtain wall, that it was impossible to tell
from a distance where the wall ended and the mountain
began. And there, jutting out from between the two
halves of that wall, overlooking the valley far below, was
what looked for all the world like a massive balcony, its
occupants protected from the depths by nothing more
than a waist-high stone wall.

He had heard it described a hundred times around the
campfires when the story of the exodus from Barovia was

told, and he had seen it in his dreams, dreams he had always suspected were visions given him by his many-times-great grandfather, whose brief imprisonment in the castle's deepest, most spell-guarded dungeon had sparked the Vistani exodus. In his mind's eye now, he saw the mists roll in from the borders as they had on that long-ago night, saw them sweep across the villages and roads and forests of Barovia and finally envelop the castle itself. And he saw Strahd raging futilely along the predawn battlements when the mists had cleared and the vampire lord had discovered that not only was his prisoner gone from the dungeons but all Vistani were gone from all of Barovia, not to return for more than half a century.

But why? Why was he now here of all places?

He had entered the mists, as had countless Vistani before him, in search of a vision, a vision that all hoped would point the way for the Vistani to return to the Home Forge, to the land their ancestors had left and lost centuries ago.

And visions had come. From almost the moment the mists closed about him, his senses had been assaulted endlessly by nightmarish chaos. Desperately he had tried to make sense of even a tiny fraction of the images that were burned into his memory.

But he could not. He could only wonder if the gods who supposedly spoke through visions and dreams were being purposely malicious, still punishing the Vistani for their ancient sins. Or perhaps the gods were so different, so removed from those who inhabited the mortal planes that they—and the messages they sometimes delivered—were simply incomprehensible, the way a Vistana's words would be incomprehensible to a buzzing insect.

And yet now that the mists had finally released him, there was the feeling—the conviction, even—that there was meaning, dire meaning, hidden in the visions if only he could find it, particularly in those of an ancient-seeming scroll that had appeared again and again, as if being thrust at him by an impatient tutor exasperated by his slow-wittedness. But even though the words were indelibly etched into his memory, their meaning, if meaning they had, was . . .

A motion glimpsed at the edge of his vision drove the scroll's cryptic words from his thoughts at the same time it sent an icy shock colder than the mists themselves through his body. His eyes darted once again to the distant castle, where a speck—a body!—fell silently down the face of the curtain wall, then down the sheer rock face beneath until . . .

. . . it vanished into the shadows and the rising fog as if it had never been.

Straining his ears, he could hear nothing but the faint sigh of the wind. And he realized it had not been real. The silently falling body had been a tiny fragment of the incomprehensible visions that had clambered at him as he floundered through the mists, and now, like the scroll, it was being thrust upon him again.

But then Castle Ravenloft itself seemed to fade from view, not enveloped in billowing clouds of mist as had happened the night of the exodus but becoming misty itself, as if the solidity of stone and wood were being transmuted into vaporous illusion. A mountain peak behind it swam into view, as if seen through an obscuring haze. But then the mountain on which the castle stood began to fade as well, as if whatever gripped the structure were spreading out like cancerous ripples in a pool, until in a matter of seconds not only the castle and the distant peaks beyond but the very ground he was standing on was taking on the same ghostly form. He was afraid to look down at his own body, for fear that it, too, would be fading out of existence.

For a moment he felt himself falling, as if the ground had indeed vanished from beneath him, but as he tumbled down through nothingness, a voice from his visions echoed through his mind: *Is not the end of this land what most your heart desires?*

And it was over.

The ground was once again solid beneath his trembling legs, and Castle Ravenloft once more loomed darkly but clearly in the distance.

Just as clearly, he saw the meaning in his nightmare visions. He still could make no sense of individual images, nor of the cryptic words inscribed on the scroll, but in the moment of insight triggered by the voice's question, he realized that, taken as a whole, they meant only one thing: The end, the dissolution of this strange land to which the Vistani had been exiled for centuries.

And if this land did indeed vanish into the mists, then those outcasts who now inhabited it would—or so he desperately hoped—be returned to the lands from which they had come.

For an instant, a crystal clear vision of a gathering of a thousand colorful Vistani wagons, their passengers laughing and dancing about a hundred joyous campfires, filled his mind, and he knew it was a vision of home—a home no Vistana had seen in a dozen generations, but a home that would welcome them back with open arms and hearts.

And hidden in the chaos that still swirled and bubbled in his mind, hidden in the enigmatic words on the scroll he could still see clearly in his mind's eye—hidden there, he knew, were the means to reach that distant land of his ancestors.

If only he could fathom their meaning . . .

PART I

INTO THE PAST

ONE

Darkon
740, Barovian Calendar

High in the uppermost tower of Castle Avernus, Lord Azalin paused on a rough stone landing and looked stoically at the door before him. An unadorned slab of discolored timber suspended on massive iron hinges, it was protected by no spells, not even by a lock. Only a simple latch that could be lifted by anyone, mortal or sorcerer, held the door closed.

As always when he came to this place, he abjured the magic that silently and effortlessly opened all ways to him. Instead, he physically lifted the latch and pushed the door open. Its hinges creaked as loudly as they had when first he had heard them more than a century and a half ago.

With grim determination, he stepped across the threshold. To ordinary eyes, the musty, moth-eaten tapestries that concealed every square inch of the walls were featureless in the faint light from the single ceiling sconce. However, to Azalin's vision, unneedful of light, the tapestries' ornate and intricate patterns were clearly visible, and he wondered once again if the patterns held any meaning, any power. But if a message was indeed embedded there, his blindered mind was kept from seeing it.

Directly beneath the sconce stood a massive granite sarcophagus, its every surface as elaborately carved as the tapestries were woven. Hovering over it, as if to protect what lay within—or perhaps to escape from it—was the flowing mist that was the manifestation of his only son, Irik Zal'honan, who had long ago died beneath an executioner's axe—an axe wielded by Azalin himself.

Lying within the sarcophagus, as it had lain for more than two centuries on two different worlds, was the time-ravaged body of that son, still reluctantly awaiting the threatened resurrection and redemption.

Gradually the mist took shape but not solidity. It floated silently in the air for a moment, then drifted toward the cold stone floor on which the sarcophagus rested.

Azalin watched, waited, as he had thousands of times before, until the face and form of his son stood, wraith-like, before him. Once again, as he was every time he entered this cursed room, he was not Azalin, undead Lord of Darkon, who could raise the dead and make them do his every bidding, but Firan Zal'honan, father of Irik Zal'honan. Firan's illusory form was not that of the decaying corpse that had been Azalin's only true reality for over two centuries, nor was it any of the plush-robed forms he regularly presented to his subjects and his enemies. Instead, it was that of the sorcerer, the mortal man he had been before his nightmare of undeath had begun: slender, hawk-nosed face, gray eyes bitter with the frustrated determination that had kept him going in the face of one disappointment and betrayal after another.

"What is it you wish, Father?" the wraith asked. "Have you come this time to set me free?"

Azalin—Firan—didn't answer. He hadn't answered for—the last hundred visits? The last thousand? For there was no suitable answer, no answer the boy would understand, no answer that Firan himself hadn't tried and found wanting countless times.

But this time something was different. This time the wraith, instead of waiting silently, accusingly for the answer that never came, grew more solid until the ragged tapestries behind him were barely visible through his thickening substance.

"What if *you* were to be set free, Father?" he asked. "Would you then allow me to share that freedom?"

The image of Firan Zal'honan, meticulously and almost automatically maintained, frowned in sudden puzzlement to match the surprise that gripped his mind. "Is this some new game, Son?"

The wraith smiled, an action that struck Azalin as no more genuine than the puzzled frown he himself had created a moment before. "I am in no position to play games, Father."

"Then what is it you are saying? Have you suddenly become capable of accomplishing such a feat?"

"If only that were true," the wraith said with a mockingly mournful sigh. "No, Father. I still have no power to affect so much as a dust mote beyond the walls of this cell in which I am confined. But I listen, I listen carefully, for there is nothing else for me to do in the long hours of your absence."

"Listen? Listen to what?"

"To those who, of late, relieve my loneliness with their words when no others will."

Instinctively Azalin looked about, extending his senses in all directions, searching for an intruder, for any trail an intruder might have left.

But there was nothing new, only the legions of the undead who inhabited and guarded Avernus, only the spells that made a structure of stone and timber and mortar invulnerable to assault both physical and magical.

"Who are these visitors?" he asked.

The wraith rippled and shimmered, as if shrugging. "They have no names, Father, nor faces. They speak invisibly from the shadows, as you say voices have often spoken to you."

A dozen memories, each more devastating than the last, leapt into Firan's mind. If these voices were the same that had spoken to him over the centuries, offering one treacherous reward after another . . .

"If there is one thing I have learned in the years since your death," he said, "it is that such voices mean me only evil and ruin."

"But, Father, was it not they who gave you immortality?"

"They gave me *this!*" The illusion of Firan Zal'honan fell away abruptly, revealing the rotting corpse that was Azalin's true form, had *been* his true form for two centuries. "And they placed me here, in this prison of a land."

The wraith laughed soundlessly. "Is it worse than the prison you have given me?" The wraith gestured at the sarcophagus, where his own moldering body lay hidden, and for a brief moment, the wraith himself was transformed into that same hideousness. "At least you can cloak yourself in illusion, Father. At least you can move freely about your vast prison, doing what you wish, where you wish, bending others to your will, punishing those who resist, even perhaps enjoying that punishment. I, on the other hand, have no such alternatives. I have been chained to this cell, utterly powerless, for a century and a half, alone except when you deign to bestow your presence upon me. Would you trade with me, Father? Would you trade your prison for mine?"

With an effort, Firan restored the illusion of his once mortal shell. "Very well. Tell me this miracle your voices have whispered of."

"It is no miracle they speak of. It is the end of this land."

"Of Darkon? The end of Darkon?"

"And the end of Barovia and all the others—the end of all lands held prisoner by the mists."

A mixture of hope and puzzlement gripped Azalin. "When is this destruction to take place? And how?"

"I do not know. Perhaps in the same way the lands were created and imprisoned by the mists."

"And how was that? I have searched for an answer to that question for a century and a half and know little more now than when I began."

"The voices have not said. They are not overly talkative."

"What *have* they said? And why, this time, have they chosen to speak not to me but to you?"

"They did not speak of reasons. But why must these voices be the same ones who you say have tormented you for two centuries?"

"Are they not?"

"I have no way of knowing, Father. Nor, I suspect, do you. You do not even know the true identity of your so-called tormentors." A touch of derision had entered the wraith's voice.

"Did they speak with familiar voices of the dead?" Firan asked, remembering bitterly the mocking voices of his brother, his father, his long-dead mentor in sorcery Quantarius, even his son.

"The voice was yours, Father, though not as unfeeling," the wraith said, smiling translucently.

"What I feel—" Firan began in sudden anger but broke off as the futility of his protest silenced him. "What I feel matters not," he continued. "What these voices have said to you is all that matters."

"As you wish, Father, but they say precious little. They speak of Vistani visions and prophecies, which they say you would do well to heed."

Firan's interest began to fade. "Visions and prophecies are Vistani stock-in-trade," he said dismissively. "They cloud the air around every campfire. Were I to pay heed to every mystical pronouncement those charlatans make, I would have time for little else."

"I make no judgment on such matters," the wraith said. "I am merely the messenger for those who spoke to me."

"Then deliver the message and have done with it. Does it explain why I should pay heed to one particular prophecy among thousands?"

"The voice—*your* voice, Father—told me of a Vistana who has had visions of things even other Vistani cannot see. When certain events have come to pass, this Vistana says, these mist-bound lands will vanish as if they had never existed."

The words abruptly rekindled Firan's interest, sending his mind racing back to his own research, stretching back a century and a half, both here in Darkon and in Barovia. Time and again it had led him to the forlorn conclusion that he would gain his freedom from this land only when the land itself was destroyed. Time and again he had searched for a way to bring about that destruction, but never, in any tome of science or magic, had he found anything that held even the slightest promise.

In some small way, however, each failure to find a method of destruction had been a relief. For if he succeeded, if he found a way to destroy these lands, he would then have to make a decision he didn't want to make. Because that destruction, even if it gave him his freedom, might also take from him the very reason he most desired that freedom: his son.

Two centuries ago, Irik's weakness had demanded his death. Firan had had no choice, no choice at all but to wield the axe with his own hands. But even as he brought it down on Irik's bowed neck, he had vowed through the pain that it was not the end. Irik's failings were in part a result of Firan's own failings as father and mentor. The boy, barely nineteen, deserved a chance to redeem himself, and Firan's every action since that time had been directed toward that goal: the preservation of Irik's body, the attempted resurrection, the endless search for new and more powerful sorcery, for a means of gaining his freedom from this land.

But freedom would be meaningless if it did not bring with it at least the chance of gaining redemption for his son. And if the land were destroyed, would his entombed son be destroyed along with it? Would Irik be lost to him forever? Forever beyond redemption?

"What events?" he asked. "Are they events I can influence? Events I may myself cause or prevent?"

"Those are all things that you must learn for yourself, Father, for the voice was always silent in that regard." As the wraith spoke, his mistlike form began to fade. "But surely one blessed with powers such as yours should have little difficulty in getting at the truth of the matter," he went on, his voice fading as well until his final words were barely a whisper. "Surely no mere Vistana can escape your reach."

And then he was gone, leaving Firan to puzzle over his words and wonder about their source.

Again he sent his senses ranging throughout Avernus. Again there was no trace of an intruder.

For a long time he stood silently, gazing at the sarcophagus, wondering, mistrusting everything he had just heard and seen, even the image of his son.

For there was no treachery his tormentors were not capable of. When he had been an aging mortal sorcerer, they had offered him eternal life and given him eternal death. When that had not been torture enough, they had offered him eternal hope and given him eternal damnation in this Mist-bound land that tantalized him again and again with the prospect of new and more powerful sorceries, only to steal them from his very mind if he should ever attempt to use them. Decades later, they had offered him a "second chance" and had condemned him to the even deeper hell of Darkon. And they had watched and laughed at his misery more times than he could remember.

Was that what they were doing now? Watching and laughing as he reacted to their reported words? What new horror did they hope to draw him into now?

Or was this voice—this voice that Irik said mimicked Firan himself—indeed from another source? Was that why it had spoken to Irik rather than to himself? Was there another force at work in this nightmare world? If one force had created these lands and imprisoned them in the mists, might there not be another force that opposed this creation?

It was a possibility he had considered countless times for countless reasons. In all things, he knew, there were opposing forces. Without them, his long-ago mentor Quantarius had patiently explained, the world itself—the only world Quantarius had known—would not exist. The forces of creation and the forces of destruction were at constant war in that natural world, in all natural worlds, maintaining a constantly shifting balance in all things: light, dark; life, death; growth, decay.

In magic, the power of the sorcerer was pitted against the power of the creatures he called up from their own dark planes of existence. Even the planes themselves were pitted against each other: those dark planes of pure horror against those inhabited by mortal beings. Unopposed, each would seep through the unseen barriers and distances that separated them, and all would soon be meaningless chaos.

Surely, therefore, the forces that had taunted and tormented him down through the centuries and imprisoned him in this mist-bound land, whether or not they were the forces that had created it, could not exist unopposed. Surely other forces—forces far greater than he—struggled against them. Surely . . .

But the voice that had spoken to Irik, the voice that had spoken of the destruction of these lands—did that voice represent those opposing forces? Or was it simply yet another face of whatever power it was that tormented and imprisoned him?

And could he learn the truth of it? When those who spoke the lie, if lie it was, were as far above him as he was above the lowliest hedge wizard, how could he determine the truth or falsity of their words and visions, let alone their reasons?

There was, he thought grimly, one possible way, a way he had always known he must use if he were ever to succeed in his quest for a way to destroy these lands. It would at least enable him to learn more than he could by normal means. But it would also inflict on him more pain than even he could bear, more than he had ever inflicted on others, even the most deserving.

And in the end, when the agony was receding into memory, he would likely still not be certain. The only certainty was that, regardless of what he learned, he would continue. Even if he found evidence indicating he *was* walking into another of Strahd's traps, he couldn't afford simply to withdraw and do nothing. As long as the evidence wasn't absolute and irrefutable—which in these lands it would never be—as long as there was even the slightest chance that what Irik had told him was genuine and could lead to his freedom from this place, he had to continue, no matter what the outcome. It could, after all, be little worse than what he now endured.

With one last regretful look at the sarcophagus, Azalin began laying his plans even before the room's massive door creaked shut behind him. The first and most obvious step was to locate and speak with the Vistana in question, to learn the Vistana's words firsthand, and then . . .

 **TWO**

Darkon
740, Barovian Calendar (continued)

Learning the seer's name proved remarkably easy, requiring only a few pointed inquiries of Azalin's barons by his dreaded secret police, the Kargat. Barely a week had gone by before four of those barons found themselves being delivered roughly into Azalin's glowering presence. As always, to keep his true nature hidden whenever subjects of any rank, from peasant to noble, were granted an audience or called to task, Azalin wore the usual illusion of a mortal sorcerer in kingly robes.

"I am given to understand you have knowledge of one whom I seek," he said without preamble as the four were ushered, trembling, into the throne room.

As their Kargat escorts withdrew with perfunctory bows, Azalin's glare swept across all four before settling on Baron Durn, whose finely clad and obviously well-fed form brought back unpleasant memories of Ranald, Azalin's own gluttonous brother, who had eaten himself into an early and oversize grave while his lands and subjects had nearly perished from neglect.

Durn swallowed nervously as beads of sweat popped

out on his forehead. "You speak of the one who calls himself Hyskosa, my lord?"

"As you well know, Durn!" Azalin snapped. "Now, what do you have to tell me other than his name?"

Durn managed a nervous shrug. "There is little to tell, my lord. He is a minor nuisance and no more, certainly not a threat worthy of your attention."

"So you have taken it upon yourself to determine what is or is not worthy of my attention?"

Durn blanched at Azalin's tone, and the other three inched backward as if to dissociate themselves from the corpulent baron. "I would never be so presumptuous, my lord, but—"

Azalin waved a hand dismissively. "I have no time for your pointless ramblings, Durn. Just tell me what you know of this Hyskosa person."

"Of course, my lord. As I said, he is a nuisance, nothing more, constantly preaching to any who will listen, more like a street-corner beggar than a Vistana." Durn halted, a self-consciously thoughtful frown touching his brow. "Although he never asks for coin or food, as if such things were beneath his attention."

"But he is entirely harmless and most likely mad in the bargain," Baron Wencel put in when Durn fell silent. "Each of us has had occasion to deal with the witless fool. To call him a Vistani seer is to insult the true seers among them. This one does not ask recompense for his 'wisdom,' nor does he limit his pronouncements to the campfire or the town square, but spouts his nonsense openly to Vistani and giorgio alike, haunting our villages, our roads, and even our farmsteads, until in the end he tries our patience too far, and we must send our guards to expel him from our territories."

"And what is this message he spreads so widely?" Azalin asked. "I have been told it has to do with the destruction of this land. Would you consider *that* a mere nuisance? Harmless?"

"Not if he were a true seer, my lord," Durn said hastily, "but as Baron Wencel has said, to call him such is to insult the true Vistani seers. He speaks of things that must happen, things that will bring this destruction upon us, but they are pure gibberish, my lord. Bodiless spirits, he speaks of, journeys to other times. They have no meaning, no meaning at all."

"You see, my lord? Complete foolishness," Baron Hilg said when Durn once again stumbled into silence. "And in any event," he added, a touch of smugness entering his tone, "the fool is no longer in Darkon. My own men drove him out some months ago, and he has not dared return. He will not trouble—"

Azalin's scowl silenced Hilg in midthought. "And to what land did you exile him, Baron?"

"Falkovnia, my lord, but travelers tell me the Falkovnians had even less patience with him than we." Hilg smiled weakly. "He was sent on his way rather quickly and eventually made his way to Barovia, where he makes his madness even more manifest."

Durn nodded earnestly. "That is true, my lord. He is said to have been preaching his nonsense virtually in the shadow of Castle Ravenloft for weeks, accosting even those who have business with Count Von Zarovich himself, whom I doubt will have been as lenient as—"

"Is that the latest news?" Azalin cut Durn off sharply. "This Hyskosa is in Barovia? Near Castle Ravenloft? So say you all?"

Four heads bobbed as one as they chorused their agreement.

"Then I thank you for your service, gentlemen. You are free to go."

Even as the four exchanged startled glances of relief and scurried from the room, Azalin's mind was racing. Strahd was as desperate to escape these lands as Azalin himself, so how was it that the vampire lord had not immediately seized the Vistana and wrung him dry?

Or had he? Such news as the barons might have was many days old at best. It was probably also woefully incomplete and almost certainly second- or thirdhand.

There was also the chance that this Hyskosa was merely a pawn of Strahd's, designed to trick Azalin into some action that would eventually redound to Strahd's benefit in their never-ending conflict.

But he could not ignore the possibility that Strahd was either unaware of or had ignored the Vistana's antics, as Azalin himself would have most likely done had Irik's words not called the seer to his attention. Or perhaps Strahd had already investigated the Vistana's words and found them to be as worthless as the barons claimed.

But it mattered little. The one thing that mattered was the chance, no matter how slight, that all was genuine and might somehow lead to his freedom from this eternal prison.

And the only chance of learning the truth of the matter lay in bringing this Hyskosa back to Darkon and Avernus, which meant stealing him from within the shadow of Castle Ravenloft itself. He only hoped that, if Strahd were indeed unaware of the Vistana, the theft could be accomplished without drawing the vampire lord's attention to him. . . .

*　*　*　*　*

Tendrils of mist drifted up around the lurking men as if it were being squeezed out of the forest floor. Icy moisture beaded on their skin, their night-hued clothing, and their charm-blackened weapons as they crept forward through the darkened clearing. To their right, Castle Ravenloft loomed above them, a vast shadow dominating the moonless night sky, chilling even these experienced Kargat agents. A hundred yards ahead, if Lord Azalin's spies could be trusted, the Vistana they sought slept by the embers of his campfire, as he had done for weeks.

Captain Janos had little doubt that the disguises and charms Lord Azalin had cast over him and his men would shield them from any normal mortal, but the lord of Barovia was at the very least a sorcerer nearly the equal of their own master. In addition, capturing and subduing the Vistana would almost certainly be difficult, primarily because of Lord Azalin's own orders that he not be unduly harmed. Any injury to the Vistana, they had been warned, would be visited upon his captors many times over upon their return. Under these conditions, their only chance to go unnoticed long enough to escape Barovia was to be sure that Strahd's attention was elsewhere.

Fortunately Lord Azalin had provided for that, in the form of a second, expendable band who—

The sound of distant shouts cut through the night from the direction of the castle, and Janos realized with a start that Miltyr had either launched his attack early or had been discovered. Either way, his own situation was suddenly even more precarious.

"Quickly, men!" he hissed, but even as he spoke, another sound brought silence to his lips. Directly ahead, something moved through the darkened underbrush. Had they been discovered as well as Miltyr?

As he drew his own short sword, he heard a half dozen others being drawn as well. If they had been discovered, they would make good account of themselves!

Above them, torches flared along the battlements of

the castle, their light penetrating dimly to the forest floor. Janos squinted into the shadows as the sound came nearer. His men moved silently forward, fanning out to surround the makers of the sounds as they emerged from the thicket. Their swords at the ready, they waited as the shouts from the direction of the castle grew louder and more numerous. But the time to worry would be when silence came, when Miltyr and his men had all perished at the hands of Strahd and his guards, who could then turn their attention to—

The undergrowth parted, and a lone man in black robes, a monk's hood thrown back from his head, stepped into the clearing, empty hands held before his chest, palms out.

"I am Hyskosa," he said, as calmly as if he were greeting them in his own home. "It is good that you have finally come to take me to your master."

*   *   *   *   *

When Azalin saw that the returning party was barely an hour distant, he made his way once more to the uppermost tower of Avernus. But this time it was not to speak with his son. Instead, uneasily, he made his way past the rough-hewn door behind which the boy's body and spirit were imprisoned and continued twoscore steps beyond until he came to another of the coarse stone landings, this one facing a darkly glowing bronzelike door.

For a long time he stood there motionless, soundless, knowing the agony that awaited him beyond the door, yet knowing that he must cross the threshold at least this once, most likely many more times. For here, of all places in Avernus, of all places in Darkon, he had the best chance to learn the truth. In this room, his powers were enhanced, not just modestly but to a degree that, when he had first discovered it, had both startled and puzzled him.

But he had also discovered there was a price: agony so great that even he could bear it only for brief moments. That price, however, which was extracted every time he dared enter, quickly removed the puzzlement. The room, he knew then, was just one more "gift" from his tormentors, one more reminder—as if the cursed land itself were not enough!—of their whimsical malevolence.

A century and a half ago, the last time he had entered, he had been able to use those briefly magnified powers to restore his son to true life, to return his son's body to its original uncorrupted state and to reunite it with the boy's spirit. But he had been unable to maintain that life and that union once the agony forced him to flee the room. His powers, outside the room's confines, were simply insufficient. And he had been unable, to his shame, to bear the burden of the pain for more than a few minutes.

But now . . .

Now the Vistana was less than an hour from Avernus, and the time Azalin had dreaded had come. Since his failed attempt to restore his son to life a century and a half ago, he had not had sufficient reason to enter this room. Even now, bombarded by the excruciating memories of that other time, all his senses rebelled at the very thought.

But he could delay no longer.

The darkly glowing door swung open. Despite his vow to step through without hesitation, Azalin paused on the threshold.

The barren room had not changed in a hundred and fifty years. A sickening greenish yellow glow still seeped from the very walls, casting a pale, shadowless light on the bare plank table that was the only furniture—the only object of any kind—in the room.

Cursing his own cowardice for delaying, he stepped stiffly across the threshold.

As they had a century and a half before, the walls, the ceiling, the floor, all began to shift and warp around him the moment he entered, as if the very air was a constantly moving, distorting lens.

As it had been a century and a half before, his body was instantly saturated with pain. Its long-dead nerves, incapable of any sensation, be it pleasure or pain, were suddenly overloaded, as if the flesh that had long ago decayed and fallen away had been regenerated, only to be set aflame by a hundred torches.

Somehow he repressed the overwhelming and purely reflexive urge to lurch backward out of the room, out of the sea of agony.

Bracing himself against the nearest wall, reassuringly solid behind its wavering, sickly green image, he sent his Sight soaring out through the castle walls as if they didn't exist. Even through the pain, he felt a sudden freedom and exultation. This was as it had been on Oerth before he was trapped in this cursed place, and he wondered again why this power of all his powers had been so severely stunted here. His other abilities, his entire arsenal of sorcery, had been untouched. They were as effective here as on Oerth, except for his Sight. But here, within these walls, it was restored, even enhanced, as were all his other powers.

But even that was not sufficient for him to endure this agony, and the worse that he knew was yet to come, for any length of time. Only the possibility of escape from this land or the destruction of the land itself was sufficient.

Or the restoration of his son to true life.

Though it was still several hours until dawn, the land and everything in it were crystal clear to his Sight: The mansions and hovels of Il Aluk a dozen miles distant, the city straddling the Vuchar as that dark river made its byzantine way to Lamordia and the Sea of Sorrows. The patchwork of farm and forest and mountain, their mortal inhabitants fearfully, if not safely, ensconced in whatever they called home.

And there, just leaving the main road between Nartok and Il Aluk, turning onto the narrower road that led directly to the gates of Avernus, was the party returning from Barovia, the captive Vistana at its center. The only light was a lantern held by the leather-clad lead rider. The Vistana was dressed uncharacteristically in black, a monk's hood covering his head in place of the colorful bandanna favored by most Vistani men.

The pain assaulting Azalin's body still held at bay, the undead sorcerer sent his Sight swooping down to hover close over the party. He was startled to see the Vistana throw back the hood and look up into the starless night sky.

"You are the one who has summoned me here," the Vistana said. His escorts darted looks in all directions but of course saw nothing.

I am, Azalin said into his mind, and the Vistana nodded.

"Who are you talking to?" the nearest rider asked sharply, suspiciously.

"Your master is with us," the Vistana said simply.

The entire group, except for the Vistana, shivered and hunched down, their eyes searching the darkness as their knees gripped their mounts more securely.

Azalin sent his Sight even closer until it was hovering only inches above the Vistana's head. Even through the haze of his body's pain, he could see the aura of strength that enveloped the man. He had seen similar auras in the past, but none so strong.

But there was no trace of Strahd or any other sorcerer

lingering about him, no indication that this Vistana's mind or will was influenced by anything or anyone other than himself. Certainly not by Strahd. A half dozen times in the past, without having to resort to such extreme measures, he had detected Strahd's influence in seemingly innocent travelers, just as Strahd had detected Azalin's time and again. No matter how skillfully Strahd worked, he could not remove all traces of his sorcerous spoor.

But this time, with this Vistana, there was no hint of the vampire's meddling.

Except . . .

For just an instant, there was *something*, not the spoor of another sorcerer but something else, something more obscure, something . . .

"You sense the traces of those who spoke to me in the mists," the Vistana said, wringing another uneasy shudder from those around him.

Azalin knew the Vistana was telling the truth, but there was nothing to indicate the identities of those speakers. Were they the same ones who had spoken to him over the years? His mysterious and seemingly omnipotent tormentors? Or perhaps they were those who had spoken to Irik, his son. Or perhaps they were neither.

Abruptly he withdrew, his Sight pulling back and away like a swooping night bird, then soaring back toward Avernus. He had learned all he could, at least for now. There would be time enough for further delving when they were face-to-face and the Vistana told his story.

As his Sight descended toward the towers of Avernus, all he could think of was escaping the torture being inflicted on his body. At any moment, he knew, it would escalate from clean, searing pain to a nausea even more sickening than that which had gripped him when he had downed the loathsome brew that had ended his mortality two centuries past.

But even as his Sight swooped through the stone walls and protective spells of the tower and his body was within reach, he was brought up short.

From somewhere within Avernus, he sensed the same aura he had detected hovering over the Vistana. But here it was stronger, and he wondered how, even in his normal state, he had not detected it before. His tormentors? Or something else? Had something accompanying the Vistana ranged on ahead, the way his own Sight ranged ahead, and already established itself in Avernus?

Even as he felt his body succumb to the second stage of the agonies that besieged it, he remained concentrated on his Sight, homing in on the newly detected aura.

Within moments, he found himself hovering over his son's sarcophagus as he had hovered over the Vistana. It was there that the aura was centered, and it was indeed identical in texture to the one that hovered so lightly around the Vistana. How, he wondered, had he been blind to it before?

But before he could delve further, his body, two floors above, was suddenly gripped by convulsions he could no longer control from a distance. Like a maddened animal, the body overrode all his efforts at control and thrashed itself about blindly, smashing against a wall, crashing into the table, reeling backward until . . .

. . . it lurched from the room and collapsed like a deflated balloon onto the rough stone landing outside the door.

Two floors below, Azalin's Sight faltered and grew dim, showing him no more than it had when, as a child, Firan had first tentatively experimented with the faculty. He let it go, and he found himself once more fully and solely within his own body.

For a long moment he lay where he had fallen, but

then the memory of what his Sight had found sent him struggling to his feet. For another moment he was distracted by the startling sight of his own hands as he pressed them against the floor to force himself upright. Instead of bones half covered with a patchwork of bits and pieces of decayed flesh, they were whole once again. And it was not an illusion, not one of the countless images he presented to the world, but reality. The skin was not clean and smooth as it was in the illusions but splotchy and discolored, as if about to fall away. But it was once again complete, as it had not been in reality for two centuries.

But before he could examine it more closely, before he could bring his fingers up to touch his face in sudden hope, the discolored splotches darkened and the flesh beneath disintegrated, just as it doubtless had done far more slowly when his body had first died and lay rotting while it waited to be reanimated with the parody of life his tormentors had bestowed upon him.

Another illusion? Or the momentary results of being within that room?

But it didn't matter, not in the face of what he now feared.

Racing down the steps, he threw open the door behind which the sarcophagus lay. The wraithlike figure of his son was already fully formed and floating down toward the floor, as if anticipating his arrival.

Instead of keeping his distance and staying just inside the door as he normally did, Firan strode across the floor until he was within inches of the sarcophagus.

And the translucent form of his son.

He felt nothing, no indication of the aura his Sight had sensed so plainly. Had it truly been something detected by his enhanced senses? Or simply his own fearful imagination?

He reached out, not bothering to reestablish the illusion of his appearance. One half-fleshless hand penetrated the wraith's form without resistance, while the other came to rest on the cold, carven surface of the sarcophagus.

And he felt it.

It was impossibly faint. If he hadn't known precisely what he was searching for, he would never have sensed it. But it was, as he had feared, the same chilling aura his Sight had detected hovering about the Vistana.

He jerked his hands away and stepped back. "Where is my son?" he asked.

The wraith rippled as if caught in a soft breeze. "I am your son," he said, "as I have been for a century and a half."

"And the son I had before that?"

"The son you slew, Father?"

"The son I will someday give the chance to redeem himself!"

"The son you wished only to bend to your will? The son you could not accept unless he fulfilled *your* warped expectations?"

"They were proper expectations for any who would rule! In such matters, there is no room for weakness! Nor will there ever be!"

The wraith only smiled, infuriating him all the more.

"*Where is my son?*" Firan repeated.

"The one you slew is at rest, beyond even your reach. He has been at rest since last you tried to force him into stealing the body of another."

"*You had no right!*"

"Nor did you, Father."

"*Stop calling me that!*"

"As you wish. But I *am* your son in all ways, except that I do not suffer the torments you forced him to endure."

And the face of his son was gone as the mist fell into shapeless tatters and began to seep silently into the sarcophagus.

Azalin grasped helplessly at the last wisps and screamed in wordless fury as they fluttered, unheedful, through his fingers and vanished into the carven surface of the sarcophagus.

Finally, silently, he turned and left the room. For the first time in a century and a half, gaining his freedom from this godforsaken land meant nothing. But also for the first time in a century and a half, he had not the slightest doubt what his decision would be if a way to destroy this land—this foul prison!—should come into his hands.

With his son no longer hostage, no longer subject to destruction along with the land, there was no reason to hesitate. And all the more reason to hate this land, all the more reason to see it wiped out as if it had never existed!

And the power to do precisely that might well be within his grasp before the night was out.

*   *   *   *   *

The Vistana, still clad in black, sat waiting in the shadows of the dungeon cell. Despite a face that was lined with age, his eyes were sharp and young. The soldiers who had escorted him back from Barovia stood uneasy guard outside the cell door. When Azalin approached, once again cloaked in the middle-aged, black-clad image of Firan Zal'honan, they lowered their eyes, and when he dismissed them and told them they could return to their families, their relief was as obvious as their haste.

"As you wish, Lord Azalin," their leader said, and they all hurried up the gritty stairs away from the dungeons before he could change his mind. When the sound of their footsteps faded into inaudibility, Azalin stepped inside the cell. The protective spell woven tightly across the door shimmered as he crossed the threshold.

The Vistana shivered involuntarily as Azalin's chill aura enveloped him, but he recovered quickly and even managed a weak smile as he glanced at the door. "There is no need for such elaborate precautions, Lord Azalin, magical or otherwise. I have come willingly. Willingly I will remain."

"I gathered as much from what my men reported," Azalin said. "They did not, however, venture an opinion as to why that might be so. People are rarely eager to be brought to Avernus, least of all the Vistani."

"Nor am I, but I fear it is necessary."

"Necessary? In what way?"

"For years I have sought the true meaning of my visions, and it is said that you are the foremost sorcerer in the land, able to penetrate to the heart of matters that would seem hopeless to others less skilled and less experienced."

The Firan image frowned. "You have been preaching these visions for years, and yet you say you know nothing of their meaning? Even though you have proclaimed that a number of them have come to pass?"

"Others have proclaimed it, Lord Azalin, not I. Neither the words nor the visions are mine. I am merely the conduit for whatever has chosen to speak through me."

"And what might that be, Vistana? What power speaks through you? Others of your ilk have claimed it is the gods."

The Vistana shrugged with a diffidence Azalin did not normally associate with Vistani. "Perhaps it is. They do not confide their nature to me, nor their purpose."

"Nor even their meaning?"

"Nor even their meaning."

"And yet you claim to be certain that, when your visions have all come to pass, Darkon and Barovia and all the lands of the mist will be destroyed."

"That destruction is the one certainty. That and our own desire—both yours and mine—for it to come about."

Azalin was silent a moment. "You wish these lands destroyed?"

"It is the Vistani's only salvation, as it may well be yours."

"Your salvation? How so?"

"Like you, Lord Azalin, we Vistani are strangers to this land. If—"

"What do you know of my origins?" Azalin demanded, uneasily remembering the Vistani crone who had greeted him only hours after his emergence into Darkon from the mists, when his own origins, even his identity, had been a mystery even to himself. She, too, had professed to knowledge she could not have come upon by natural means.

The Vistana shrugged his black-clad shoulders. "In Barovia, your arrival is still spoken of, as are the efforts undertaken by yourself and Count Von Zarovich to find a way to leave this place and return to your native land. My own desire, and that of all Vistani, is the same: to return to the land that is our true home."

"And the destruction of this land will accomplish that end?" Azalin asked sharply. "What is the logic in that?"

"More hope than logic, I fear," the Vistana said, "but there is some sense to it. All the lands now here within the mists were once elsewhere, perhaps in other planes of existence, as were those who lived in those lands. By means far beyond my understanding, those lands and their people were brought here from those other worlds. Even Count Von Zarovich was master of Barovia before Barovia was enveloped by the mists. But this is not true of the Vistani, nor, I am told, of you. Our ancestors were brought here independent of our land, as were you. The Vistani homeland must still exist somewhere beyond the mists, as must your own. And if these lands imprisoned within the mists themselves come to an end—or are returned to the world or plane from which they were stolen, as some say will happen—then who is to say that those who do not belong to any of these lands will not be returned to the lands to which they *do* belong?"

"Who indeed? Are you saying that is what *will* happen?"

The Vistana shrugged. "Only that it may. And that, for the Vistani, is chance enough. Is it not the same for you?"

"For me, the destruction of this land is my only goal," Azalin said grimly. "What happens to the Vistani, or to me, is immaterial. Now tell me of these visions."

*   *   *   *   *

To Azalin's great suspicion, the meaning of the final so-called prophecy came to him in a flash the moment the Vistana described his vision of the tiny figure plunging from the heights of Strahd's castle even as the castle and everything around it faded into nothingness.

The meaning could not, his suspicions told him, be both so simple and so closely linked to his own frustrated desires.

He had visited that time and that place a thousand times in his mind, for it was in that time and place, he had long ago convinced himself, that lay his only chance of escape from his mist-bound prison.

More than a century ago, he had admitted to himself that his efforts to kill or defeat Strahd in the here and now were doomed to failure. Had he undertaken the task wholeheartedly during the decades he shared Barovia with Strahd, he might conceivably have succeeded. But now, barred by the mists from ever again physically approaching his old enemy, he could only send his agents to make their feeble attempts. None had proven a match for Strahd in any way, and it was doubtful than any ever would. And even if one did, even if one managed somehow to destroy the undead lord, Azalin doubted greatly that the land itself, despite Strahd's oft-intoned claims of mystical unity with the land, would either vanish or set its other prisoners free.

But in the past, before Barovia had broken loose from the world of which it had once been a part, before Strahd had struck his bargain with the dark powers and become its immortal vampire lord . . . in that time and that place, if only it could be reached, anything was possible.

If only it could be reached . . .

Time and again Azalin had dreamt of finding a way, of penetrating the deepest secrets of the mists and finding the paths that led not through space alone but through time as well. That such paths existed, he had never doubted. His own unwilling travels through the mists proved as much. When his tormentors had thrust him into the mists surrounding Barovia, a part of him had emerged in Darkon, memoryless, a decade or more before the mists had swallowed him up.

Ever since that time, he had searched for the knowledge or the person who could spy out those paths through the mists and navigate them, one who could guide Azalin's agents back to the days of Strahd's mortality, when he was still vulnerable to sword and knife.

For if Strahd were to be slain before sealing his pact with the dark powers, the pact that had simultaneously given him ageless immortality and consigned to the mists both him and the land with which he proclaimed union, it was at least possible, perhaps even likely, that the lands of the mist would never be brought into existence.

Or so Azalin, in his desperation to be free of those lands, had long reasoned.

But for a hundred and fifty years, it had been only a dream, a wishful fantasy and nothing else.

Until now.

Once again he heard the words of the Vistana's final prophecy in his mind: "The bodiless shall journey to the time before, where happiness to hate makes land of lore."

The other prophecies, those supposedly fulfilled and those not, were so cryptic and vague as to be meaningless. The Vistana himself admitted that their fulfillment was more a matter of hindsight and wishful thinking than anything else.

But the last . . .

"I have always felt," the Vistana had said grimly, "that it is in reality the only one that truly matters, that its words are the only ones on that scroll that have any real meaning."

"Even though you know not what the meaning is?"

The Vistana had nodded. "Even though . . ."

But there *was* a meaning, Azalin now saw. And his interpretation of that meaning was such that he was willing to risk everything on it, even though he knew full well that it could be yet another trap orchestrated by Strahd or by his tormentors.

But if it was not . . .

 **THREE**

Darkon
740, Barovian Calendar (continued)

Oldar shivered and pulled his ragged woolen cloak closer about his broad shoulders as he looked down at the tombstone with his own name carved deep into the weathered surface. It was not his own grave but that of the great-great-great-grandfather for whom his half Vistani mother had, perhaps unknowingly, named him. Even so, it made him uneasy, though not as uneasy as the dreams that had brought him here on this dismal late-winter day.

"Is it truly you?" he asked of the weed-covered ground, hoping for he knew not what.

Certainly he was not hoping for a waking re-creation of his dreams, though the untended graveyard itself was almost indistinguishable from the one he had visited so often in his sleep.

In those dreams, the first Oldar—or something that laid claim to that identity—rose wisplike from the ground and spoke to him not in words but in bizarre images more vivid and real than the waking world around him: a rushing stream of water that glowed like a million fireflies as it rose out of the forest floor and vanished back into the darkness less than a hundred yards distant. An immense castle looming against a darkened sky, sounds of muffled laughter drifting through the night despite a disturbing feeling of impending disaster. A creature hideous beyond belief, who might once have been a man, advancing toward him across a rough stone landing in some castle tower.

Those and even more disturbing images had been burned into his mind night after night, but Oldar had told no one, least of all his father. He had not even told his mother, though she, if anyone, would be receptive to his story. For she, too, had her dreams, though she rarely spoke of them. The one time she had not only spoken of her dreams but also acted on them, his father said, was in the final days before Oldar himself had been born, and the dreams had told her what his name was to be. Even then she said nothing of their content—only that they had, in ways known only to her Vistani ancestors, placed the name irrevocably upon her unborn child.

But even with her, Oldar had remained silent, for the dreams were obviously sheerest foolishness. Or the beginnings of madness.

A dangerous madness.

In one of the most frightening and puzzling of the images, he was a killer. And not an ordinary killer, but an assassin, for the one he slew night after night was not an ordinary mortal but the lord and ruler of all Darkon, the sorcerer Azalin. The face was different every time, but still, in the dream, there was no doubt in his mind that it was Azalin, whose magic was said to be capable of peering into the minds and hearts of his every subject if he so desired. And to destroy those subjects without a touch if he came to suspect them of so much as entertaining the least thought of treachery.

And what could such dreams be considered but treachery? In Oldar's case, it would be a double treachery, for the Wahldrun family had, since the original Oldar had returned from Il Aluk a century and a half before, been under the special protection of Lord Azalin. More than once, according to family legend, that protection had been exercised. Oldar himself, when little more than a toddler, had been witness to its workings. Or so he was told when he had grown old enough to be able to understand such things.

But whether or not he understood at the time, the incident remained the most vivid memory of all of his childhood even now, almost fifteen years later.

It had been a warm summer day, dawning as clear and sunny as days ever did in Darkon. Oldar, his four-year-old eyes not yet familiar with the horrors that inhabited the night and often permeated the day, had slipped from the tiny farmhouse in midmorning, going in playful search of his father in the fields. He had been warned not to leave sight of the house when he was alone, but warnings as yet meant little to him.

The first he realized anything was different that day was when he heard a sudden burst of raucous laughter in the distance. At first he thought it must be his father, and he turned and made his way through the waist-high grasses toward the sound. When he reached the narrow creek that marked the boundary of the Wahldrun land, he realized he was wrong, for the sounds were coming from the shadows of the dark forest on the far side of the creek, an area Oldar had been even more firmly warned against.

When he was a hundred yards short of the creek, four men on horseback emerged into the sunlight and came to a stop at the water's edge. While the animals drank, the obvious leader—a fearsome-looking black-bearded man in heavy leather garments the like of which the boy had never seen before—surveyed the fields on the other side, perhaps spying the house and well-weathered out-buildings in the distance. But then his eyes fell on the boy, and his yellowing teeth were bared in a frighteningly malevolent grin.

Without hesitation, the man reined his mount's head up from the creek and sent the animal splashing through the shallow water. Suddenly frightened, Oldar turned to run, but after only a few lurching steps, a piercing whinny and a series of angry curses brought him to a stumbling halt.

Looking back, he saw that the bearded man's horse, its rear legs still not clear of the near side of the creek, was rearing violently while the man swore and tried to control the animal. The others were laughing at their leader's troubles and urging their own mounts into the water.

Their laughter was cut off an instant later as their mounts emerged from the creek. As one, the animals reared and whinnied, two so violently that they toppled backward into the water, their riders barely leaping clear and thudding to the ground just this side of the creek. The two horses, unencumbered now, thrashed and splashed themselves upright and bolted back across the creek before the two fallen riders could regain their feet and lunge after them.

The shouted curses of all four were cut off in quick suc-cession. The two still astride their mounts abruptly released the reins and grasped at the empty air around their necks, their faces contorting as their mouths gaped open. The moment their grip on the reins was relinquished, they were dislodged violently and thrown to the ground, where their companions were clawing at their own necks. The horses, still whinnying frantically, lurched backward through the water as if backing away from the devil himself, then turned and galloped into the trees where the first two animals had already disappeared.

The only sounds as the four dislodged riders writhed on the grassy bank of the creek were of their hands slapping and grasping at their own throats, the fingernails of some digging bloody grooves in the flesh. Their mouths worked desperately but silently, like fish that had been snatched from their watery home and held aloft in suffocating air. One, following the lead of his mount, managed to fling himself backward into the water and then scrabble to the other side, at which point his throat seemed to open once again. Without a backward glance or a word to his still-struggling comrades, he raced off into the woods.

The remaining three, who stood their ground through defiance or ignorance or the paralysis of fear, eventually died, their faces darkened and contorted.

For a long time after the last spasmodic twitch, the child stood silently, paralyzed himself. Finally, fearfully, he took a hesitant step toward the now-silent invaders.

Before he could take a second, a hand on his shoulder halted him.

"There is nothing that can be done for them," his father said quietly but with a sudden shiver of fear. "Nothing that *should* be done. The bodies will be gone before the next light of dawn."

"What—what happened to them?" the boy asked, his voice trembling.

"I don't know," his father said, "and I don't *want* to know. They meant us harm and they were stopped."

They meant us harm, and they were stopped.

And the bodies were indeed gone without a trace by morning, and the vultures that had begun their high, lazy circles shortly before nightfall were gone as well.

All was due to the magic of Lord Azalin, he was told later, when he was deemed old enough to understand. His father, however, seemed to have little more understanding of the situation than did the child. A century and a half before, it was said in family lore, the Lord of Darkon had placed a protective spell on that other Oldar, and it had since extended itself to his descendants, at least as long as they remained on the small farm the first Oldar had returned to after leaving Lord Azalin's service. No one knew what that Oldar had done to gain Lord Azalin's favor, nor why it would continue long after the original Oldar's death. A whim, some said. Lord Azalin had been known to destroy a man—or a family, even a city—on what seemed a whim, so why should he not do the opposite on occasion? No one knew, and it was unlikely anyone ever would, for Lord Azalin rarely spoke to anyone, least of all to lowly peasants.

No Wahldrun had ever tried to ask, certainly, for fear that the spell—if spell it was—was simply something that had been brought about accidentally or that had been long since forgotten about. Lie low and accept the gift quietly, it was said; don't call attention to yourself and risk having it taken away.

There were even some, Oldar's father among them, who feared that the protective spell was not in return for a service the original Oldar had performed but for a service yet to be performed by one of his descendants.

When the dreams began, Oldar had wondered if the latter were indeed the case—if, after five generations, the time for payment had finally come. The fact that his half-Vistani mother's dream had caused him to be named for the ancestor supposedly responsible for the gift had not lessened his wondering.

But he would learn nothing here. It was clear that his namesake, dead nearly a century, would not speak from his grave, not here in the waking world.

Both disappointed and relieved, Oldar turned and picked his way through the tangle of weeds and brush and fallen headstones to the rutted road—a path, really—that crept through the woods and past the remnants of the graveyard, and he began the long trudge home. Protection or no protection—and there had never been any indication that it extended beyond the bounds of Wahldrun land—he did not relish the thought of being abroad after dark.

He had gone barely a hundred yards when a bulky man in finely made cape and boots astride a sleekly groomed jet black stallion appeared at a turn in the path, ducking low to avoid an errant branch. Behind the stranger was a second horse, gray and riderless but obviously not a pack animal. In addition to a fine leather saddle, a pair of saddlebags were its only burden.

Apprehensive, Oldar lowered his eyes and continued walking, moving well off the narrow path. The man's clothes alone, a far cry from the rough and often ragged wool favored, of necessity, by the locals, were reason for concern. Nobles and other highborn folk rarely ventured into the hinterlands, and when they did it was even more rare that they came for anyone's benefit but their own.

When the sound of the horses' hooves halted, Oldar looked up surreptitiously and saw that the rider had reined the animal in and was staring directly at Oldar, frowning intently. The second horse stopped as well, as if it were invisibly bound to the first.

Oldar quickened his pace, lowering his eyes even further.

"Your name is Oldar, is it not?" The man's voice was rough and gravelly.

Oldar halted, his eyes on the toes of his own cracked and mud-stained boots. "It is," he admitted.

The man let out a whispered sigh. "I would have known you anywhere, lad," he said softly, and then went on, more loudly, more formally. "My name is Balitor, and I come representing Lord Azalin."

A chill even more profound than that which had gripped him as he stood over his ancestor's grave stabbed through to Oldar's very soul and set his knees to trembling as he wondered, Has the time for payment finally arrived?

 **FOUR**

Darkon
740, Barovian Calendar (continued)

It had been ages since last he had thought of himself as simply Balitor. It was the name his father had given him, but that had been nearly two centuries ago.

For a time, then, he had been called "Baron"—Baron of Il Aluk. But he had never, even on the best of days, been comfortable with that title. He had accepted it, and the riches and duties that accompanied it, because Lord Azalin had offered it, and Balitor knew well that no one who valued his life refused what the Lord of Darkon offered, be it gift or punishment. He had even thought, for the first few hours of his unexpected ascendancy, that his fortunes could not have been better. Riches were suddenly his, as well as a palace full of servants and a word that would be obeyed without question—except by those who themselves wished to be the next baron, of course, and he had little doubt that he could outwit any such schemers. After all, he had survived alone for more than a decade in the streets and back alleys of Il Aluk. Most often he had been penniless and possessed precious little property beyond what was on his back. There had been few who could even be counted on to acknowledge his existence, much less obey an order or carry out an errand. And yet he had survived, had even had moments of triumph and of comparative joy.

And then, in less than a single night, he had become—had been *made*—the most powerful man in the largest city in Darkon. What more, after all, he had wondered, could a lowly peasant hope for?

But even before that first night was over, reality had set in, bringing with it a renewed uneasiness, a sure knowledge that, no matter what his mortal power, he was merely a helpless pawn in whatever schemes Lord Azalin might be perpetrating. What Lord Azalin had bestowed upon him, Lord Azalin could just as easily take away—and more. That had already been amply demonstrated earlier that same night when Lord Azalin had executed the previous baron in a grisly public display. And it was demonstrated even more plainly only hours later. Balitor had barely had time to move into the baronial mansion, bringing his young friend Oldar with him to at least stay the night and share briefly in his newfound luxury, when the resurrected body of the previous baron—doubtless revived by Lord Azalin for his own dark purposes—had shambled mindlessly through the mansion to pull young Oldar from his bed and return him to Avernus. There could not have been a more vivid reminder to Balitor of the transitory nature of his power or of the fate that awaited him if his actions ever brought Lord Azalin's displeasure down upon him.

But that displeasure apparently was never aroused. Just the opposite, it seemed, for after a dozen years, it began to dawn on Balitor that he was not aging as other men did. It was another dozen years, however, by which time others had begun to notice it as well, before he learned the truth.

At the annual ball that brought barons from all corners of Darkon to feast and mingle fearfully in Avernus for one night, an overabundance of wine and an underabundance of common sense led one newly anointed baron, even before the body of the one whose place he was taking could be fully disposed of, to inquire if the boon of seeming agelessness that had been granted to the Baron of Il Aluk was one of the perquisites of his new office or if it was something that must be earned.

Silence had fallen as others less drunken seemed to lose the power of speech. Balitor himself cringed inwardly but let no sign of his distress reach his features. Azalin, observing and directing the festivities from the balcony that overlooked the great ballroom, smiled with the ageless face of Firan Zal'honan that he had adopted in those early years.

"It is something you would desire, then, Baron Anders?" he asked. "No doubt so that you could serve me longer than you could with a natural span of years?"

"Of course, my lord," the fool said.

"And from whom should I take the years that you would have me give you? From one who is less wholeheartedly devoted to me, perhaps?"

The new baron smirked drunkenly while most others gasped or held themselves in rigid silence. "It would seem only fair, my lord."

"And how am I to determine one's level of devotion, Baron? Is there some test you can propose?"

The sarcasm in Azalin's tone finally began to penetrate even Baron Anders's drunken haze. "Surely you can look into their hearts and determine such things," he said, uneasiness edging into his slurred words.

"Indeed. Indeed I can—and sometimes do, when nothing more diverting occurs to me. Would you have me demonstrate, Baron Anders?"

The new and rapidly sobering baron shook his head vigorously. "I'm sorry, my lord," he said, the seriousness of his situation beginning to truly dawn on him. "There is no need. Indeed, I was foolish to ask for such a boon, my lord. Your—your delightful and generously given wine had muddled my thoughts and loosened my tongue."

"I quite understand, Baron," Azalin said, looking around at the sumptuously dressed crowd of barons and their families and guests. "But perhaps there are others who have had similar questions come to mind. Perhaps for their enlightenment, I should demonstrate."

"No, my lord," Anders stammered, his voice now trembling. "I would not trouble you to—"

"You would deny your peers such enlightenment, Baron Anders?"

"No, of course not, I only—"

"Then I shall demonstrate. Pay heed, all who have interest in such matters."

Azalin gestured then, little more than a slow rippling of his fingers, and a path opened in the crowd between Baron Anders and Balitor, a dozen feet away. Continuing to widen, the path became a raggedly circular clearing with Anders and Balitor standing alone in its midst.

Another gesture, and a murmured word set the air between the two men to shimmering. After a moment it coalesced into a foot-thick translucence that linked them like a massive silvery umbilical cord. Balitor, not certain if the tingling that enveloped his entire body was a result of his own nerves or Azalin's sorcery, stood silent and stoic while Anders shivered and looked down in horror at where his brocaded jacket front seemed to melt and swirl beneath the translucence.

And then the translucence darkened, as if a pall of gray smoke were emerging from Anders's chest, and the darkness flowed along the connection toward Balitor, who clamped his eyes tightly closed and clenched his fists until he felt the nails biting into his palms.

A dozen gasps broke the silence as lines appeared in Anders's face, and his hair, previously black as night, became gray, first at the temples and then where it fell in loose curls over his forehead. And Balitor's face smoothed, the few lines it had once had vanishing while his hair thickened and darkened to the shade it had displayed when first he had come to Il Aluk, a dozen years before his first meeting with Azalin.

The translucence vanished. Anders lurched backward, almost falling.

"So, Baron Anders," Azalin's voice filled the silence, "your heart is perhaps not as loyal and pure as you thought. Else you would have been the gainer and Balitor the loser in this little demonstration." He paused to look about the crowd. "Are there others who would like to learn the true nature of their own hearts?"

There of course were not, nor were there ever again.

Only once in all the years that followed, more than a hundred of them now, did Azalin broach the subject, and that was the day that word reached Avernus that Balitor's one-time companion, Oldar, had died on the small farm he had returned to tend rather than share in Balitor's ruling of Il Aluk. By then Balitor had been allowed to step down from the rule of Il Aluk and was summoned to Avernus only occasionally, whenever Lord Azalin had some mission for which he would trust no other.

Azalin had summoned Balitor to tell him the news, and the sorcerer had seemed in a peculiarly melancholy mood. "It has always been one of my regrets," he said, "that the boy would accept virtually nothing in return for his service to me."

To Balitor's surprise, the sorcerer had gone on to speak of the "minor magic" that enabled him to extend the life of virtually anyone, and how the boy had refused it, as the sorcerer's own teacher, a wizard he called Quantarius, had also long ago refused it. "To take life from one who is unworthy and give it to one who is worthy—is that wrong?" the sorcerer asked then, but before Balitor was forced to reply, Azalin seemed to throw off his odd mood and, as if irritated that he had ever succumbed to it, dismissed Balitor with a stern warning to "Forget the foolishness I have burdened you with today. A friend of your youth is dead, and that is enough."

Now he had been sent on another mission, this time to fetch another young man named Oldar to Il Aluk. And as he reined in his horse and obtained his first clear look at the object of his mission, tears sprang to his eyes.

Hastily wiping them away, he waited until the boy finally, hesitantly looked up.

"I would have known you anywhere, lad," he said when the boy admitted nervously to being named Oldar. Swallowing the lump that had formed in his throat, he sat up more straight in his saddle and continued, "My name is Balitor, and I come representing Lord Azalin."

* * * * *

Trembling, Oldar said nothing. For a moment it had come to him that payment had finally come due for generations of protection, but then a second, even more terrifying thought had occurred to him as the man waited for a reply: the traitorous dreams!

"I have spoken with your family," the man said finally. "They directed me here. Your namesake is buried nearby, I believe."

Oldar nodded, the man's words only increasing his fears. Obviously this man, Lord Azalin's representative, knew of the dreams! Why else would he have come? "He is, my lord," Oldar managed to say.

The man smiled but his eyes seemed sad. "With your permission, young Oldar, I would pay my respects."

"Of course, my lord."

In a single fluid movement, the man dismounted, letting the reins fall loose. "Our animals will wait here," he said.

Lowering his eyes again, Oldar turned and led the way back to the graveyard and then through the weeds and fallen headstones to his ancestor's grave. The man's cape caught now and then in brambles, but he seemed neither to notice nor to care. When they reached the grave, the man stood in perfect silence, head bowed as he looked down at it for what seemed to Oldar to be a frighteningly long time.

"I'm sorry for its condition, my lord," Oldar said finally, "but it is a long journey, and—"

"No need to apologize, young Oldar," the man said, straightening abruptly and turning from the grave. "What matters is not the condition of his resting place but that he is at rest. There are many in Darkon not so fortunate. Now come. Lord Azalin is doubtless impatient for our return."

Oldar froze where he stood. "I don't understand, my lord," he said, though he desperately feared that he understood all too well. "Are you here to take me to—to Lord Azalin?"

The man shrugged beneath the cape, but there seemed a note of apology in his coarse features. "I would explain if I could, but I know little myself . . . only that he urgently wishes to speak with you."

"But why? Is—is it true what some say? Has my family's debt finally come due?"

The man frowned now, puzzled. "Debt? What debt?"

"Lord Azalin, it is said, has kept our family safe since the time my namesake returned from Il Aluk. I myself have seen the spells at work, turning back those who would come onto our land to do us harm. But no one knows why this is so. In gratitude of a service my namesake performed for Lord Azalin, some say, but others fear it is in payment for a service yet to be rendered."

The man smiled and shook his head. "Lord Azalin may well have some service he wishes you to perform, but it is not in payment for your family's safety. That was doubtless granted of Lord Azalin's own free will, when your namesake would not accept a more substantial recompense. Now come."

The man turned and strode through the overgrown graveyard toward the waiting horses. Bracing himself, Oldar followed.

The man was already mounted when Oldar caught up to him. He gestured at the saddlebags on the second horse. "Everything you need is in there. Now let us be on our way. You need not worry about your mount," he added when Oldar hesitated. "He is most gentle and will follow where I lead."

Clumsily, his only experience with horses having been from behind a plow, Oldar climbed into the saddle.

"Grip the pommel rather than the reins if it makes you feel more secure," the man said with a smile. "As I said, it is not necessary that you guide him."

And so it was not. After a few minutes, however, so smoothly did the animal move that Oldar released the pommel and took up the reins loosely. For nearly an hour, they rode in silence, through a small village, past another overgrown graveyard and a dozen farmhouses no grander than his own.

All the while, Oldar's heart pounded. If it was not the long-delayed payment for a century and a half of Lord Azalin's protection for his family, then it *must* be the dreams. Lord Azalin was indeed able to look into men's souls, and there, in Oldar's, he had seen the traitorous dreams.

But they were *only* dreams!

"You spoke, young Oldar?" the man asked over his shoulder. "What dreams?"

Had he spoken aloud? He must have, so accustomed had he become to being alone in the fields, where there was no one to hear when his thoughts turned to murmured words.

But it was for the best, he realized abruptly. If Lord Azalin already knew of the dreams, it was better that he speak now and try to explain rather than withhold the truth and add lying to his sins. And if Lord Azalin did *not* know . . .

Then it was possible that some other power was attempting to act through him, and Lord Azalin might be in danger, though Oldar could himself conceive of no way in which he could pose a threat to a sorcerer as powerful as Lord Azalin.

"For several weeks now," Oldar said, the words spilling out in a torrent as he rushed to explain before either he came to his senses or that other power, whatever it might be, cut him off, "I have been having dreams . . . nightmares. That is why I was at my namesake's grave, for he seemed to speak to me in those dreams. But there were other dreams, dreams of madness in which I—in which I slew your master! That is why I was at the grave, hoping I could learn the truth of it, learn if I was going mad or—or if he was actually speaking to me, perhaps warning me! And then when you appeared, coming from Lord Azalin himself, I feared that—that he had seen into my dreams, and that was why he had sent you!"

He fell silent, out of breath, waiting for the other's derisive laughter or explosion of anger.

But neither came. Instead, the man who called himself Balitor reined his mount to a standstill while Oldar's horse obediently followed suit. The man turned slowly in his saddle to look at the boy. His face was sober but neither amused nor angered.

"You say that in your dreams you slay Lord Azalin. How do you know it is he that you dream of slaying? Are you familiar with his features?"

"No! I have never seen his likeness. But I *know*—"

"And *how* do you slay him? Of my own knowledge, that would not easily be done. Many who are far more powerful than either of us, warriors and sorcerers alike, have tried and have failed miserably."

"A sword! A sword that is given to me by another!"

The man shook his head solemnly. "Only the most magical of weapons could touch Lord Azalin. Was this weapon enchanted?"

"I don't know! I only know that it is given to me and I use it to strike him down!"

"Given to you by whom? Does this benefactor have a name? A face?"

"In my dreams, there is a face, but it is never the same. And when I wake, it is forgotten."

"Well, then, there's nothing to be done about it, is there? In any event, I am more interested in other aspects of your dreams. You say your namesake spoke to you. What did he say?"

"I can't remember the words. They vanish when I awake, leaving only the visions."

"And the visions? What are these visions? Do they involve your namesake?"

"I don't know, but they must! Most often I am in a forest, deeper and darker and more silent than any I have ever encountered. But there is a clearing, and a light coming not from the sky but—"

"— but from a glowing torrent of water rushing out of the very earth!" the man finished for Oldar, his voice hushed.

Oldar's heart seemed to freeze in his chest for one terrified moment. "Lord Azalin *does* know my dreams, then!"

The man was motionless for several seconds before shaking his head. "That was from my own knowledge, not Lord Azalin's."

"Yours? But—"

"Tell me, young Oldar, does this glowing torrent of water in your dreams return to the underground without ever seeing the light of day?"

Oldar blinked. "It was night in my dreams—but, yes, it flowed back into the earth after only several dozen yards. And the forest was so thick that even in day, it is doubtful that the sun would ever reach its floor. But how can you— Are you a sorcerer like Lord Azalin?"

"Not a bit. Do undead things rise up from the grasses in your dreams?"

"Yes! They are hideous, and my companion and I barely—" Oldar broke off with a gasp. The man's face . . .

"It is *your* face I see! My companion in that forest—" He broke off again, his mind spinning.

The other man nudged his horse closer and laid a hand on Oldar's shoulder. "It has been a long time, old friend," he said, the words only adding to Oldar's puzzlement and confusion. "That part of your dream is not a dream. It is a memory. A memory you and I now share."

 **FIVE**

Darkon
740, Barovian Calendar (continued)

Azalin knew he had chosen well the moment the boy
entered the room. Not only did the boy bear his ancestor's
name but his features as well. There was even the possibility, if Balitor's reports of the boy's "dreams" were true, that
the original Oldar's soul resided in this young body. For a
moment he considered probing the boy's mind for confirmation, but rejected the possibility almost immediately.
Whatever confirmation he found would itself be suspect,
perhaps placed there by his tormentors. And if it were, they
would doubtless become aware of his probing and therefore of his suspicions, which could only make them more
careful as he proceeded. If this were indeed a scheme by
his tormentors, it would serve him better for them to be
unaware of his own suspicions. There was a remote chance
that this might lull them into a state of overconfidence in
which they were more likely to make a mistake.

If such mundane terms had meaning to such seemingly transcendent beings.

In any event, regardless of what a probe might reveal,
it could only further traumatize the boy, who would

doubtless be subjected to terror enough later on. Not that that was of any intrinsic concern, he told himself, but anything that frightened or alienated the boy in these early stages could only make it more difficult to gain the boy's trust and willing cooperation.

Under normal circumstances, such considerations would be meaningless to Azalin. Ordinarily any resistance offered could be crushed as easily as an errant insect, but the present circumstances were far from normal. He would soon be relinquishing most of his powers and putting his very existence into this boy's hands. Therefore it behooved him not to needlessly terrify the boy, certainly not to let any hint of his true nature show through the facade he presented. No mortal could be expected not to recoil in horror and to instinctively and violently resist all efforts at contact from such a creature.

And Azalin, under the conditions to which he would be subjecting himself, would be incapable of overcoming any but the most minimal resistance the boy might put up.

As part of his efforts, Azalin had chosen to greet his guest not in Avernus, where the very air reeked of darkness and horror, but in the sitting room of the modest mansion that Balitor had inhabited since he had moved from the baron's palace well over a hundred years ago. Located in the Desolatus Highlands overlooking Il Aluk, it was the first building that Firan had entered when he had emerged from the mists and found himself in Darkon. Then it had been the home of Lord and Lady Karawinn, whose treachery had earned them a painful death and a subsequent servitude that had yet to end. That death, however, had taken place in Avernus, and its aura did not cloud these rooms. Instead, Balitor's benign presence of more than a century overlay everything.

Holding tight rein on the illusory image he presented to

the world—to this boy before him—Azalin rose and smiled as he waved the men to a pair of plush over-stuffed chairs a few feet from where he now stood.

*   *   *   *   *

Oldar couldn't decide what to think, or even which explanation he would prefer for his seeming madness. Were his dreams the result of his long-dead namesake speaking to him? Or did the very soul of that namesake reside within him, as Balitor suggested? Was he in fact his namesake reborn, the bulk of the dreams merely memories of that earlier life? Either possibility, considering the nature of those dreams, was unsettling, and his heartfelt wish was that he could have them all wiped from his memory.

But that was unlikely. "Do not be surprised," Balitor had warned, "if Lord Azalin wishes to discuss them at length."

To Oldar's relief, however, the sorcerer-king seemed to have no such inclination. Instead, he merely nodded as Balitor performed the formal introductions. If anything, Lord Azalin struck Oldar as being somehow uneasy, although he could not imagine what could so affect a man who commanded virtually unlimited magical powers. Oldar was less relieved when, almost as soon as the introductions were completed, Azalin waved Balitor from the room.

Resisting an impulse to follow Balitor, Oldar remained standing, his eyes lowered, waiting. At least the sorcerer-king did not approach more closely but stayed at the far side of the room, standing near the sofa he had been seated on when they had entered.

Finally he spoke. "There is no easy way to begin, young Oldar," he said. "There is a task I would have you perform for me."

Oldar blinked but still did not look up directly at the other. "Surely there are many in your service more capable than I, my lord."

"I fear there are not. I cannot say I understand all the reasons myself, but you are uniquely fitted for this task."

"Is this in payment for the protection my family has enjoyed all these years?" Because the thought had been in his mind from the moment Balitor approached him, the words had been ready on his tongue, but he was still startled now that they were actually given voice.

But the sorcerer did not seem offended. If anything, his tone was apologetic as he said, "That protection was freely given and will not be withdrawn if you refuse."

"Is it possible, then, for me to refuse, my lord?" Oldar asked, surprising himself yet again.

"It is your right, of course. Your namesake had little hesitation in so doing, and he was hardly the worse for it."

Oldar blinked, raising his eyes to look directly at the sorcerer for the first time. "My ancestor refused you? But the protection—"

"As I said, it was freely given and will not be revoked."

Surprising himself again, Oldar asked, "What service did my namesake refuse you, my lord?"

Azalin was expressionlessly silent a moment, and Oldar swallowed nervously, wondering again why such words continued to emerge, wondering if his loose tongue had caused him to finally overstep the bounds. "I'm sorry," Oldar began, "I did not mean to offend—"

"You did not, young Oldar," the sorcerer said, his voice remarkably soothing. "I will say only that in refusing me, your namesake carried out instead the wishes of my son, for which, once I reflected upon it, I was grateful."

"As my family is grateful for several generations of safety on our land," Oldar said, the words heartfelt. An image of the small farmhouse and the faces of his parents flashed unbidden before his eyes, and a feeling of comfortable warmth enveloped him. For a long moment he savored it, his true surroundings almost banished from his consciousness.

But then those surroundings returned to the forefront of his mind, along with the reason he was here. "How may I serve you, my lord?" he asked.

"You are familiar with the mists that surround this land, young Oldar?"

"I have heard tales, but I have never ventured near them."

"A wise course to follow," Azalin said, nodding his agreement. "Any tales you may have heard are likely only pale reflections of reality, but even so, I can only hope that you will, at my request, relinquish that wise course."

A chill like the one that had accompanied his dreams flowed over Oldar. "You wish me to enter the mists, my lord? But why? Can you not more easily enter them yourself?"

"Sadly, no. I am barred from them, by powers even I do not understand."

"But you are the most powerful sorcerer in all of Darkon! Surely there are none who can keep you from going where you wish!"

"No mortal, certainly; perhaps no sorcerer. But there are others, possibly dwellers in the mists themselves, with far greater powers than mine, and they have barred my entrance."

"But what would you have me do there? I am neither sorcerer nor warrior. I would be utterly lost."

"While I am barred from entering, I can nonetheless observe your actions from afar and direct you—and protect you—as best I can."

"But surely one who is a warrior or sorcerer could serve you better."

"That is perhaps true in some ways, young Oldar, but you possess one thing that is possessed by no other that I have been able to find: You are honest and, like your namesake, have no grandiose ambitions. Like your namesake, therefore, you are a man I can trust, and that is of the utmost importance to me in this matter."

"But your sorcery . . . surely you can impose your will on whomever you desire."

"In this land of Darkon, yes, but not in the mists. There, I can merely exert influence, not control. In the mists, my only hope lies in the ability to trust the one I send. My only hope lies in you, young Oldar."

Oldar's thoughts were spinning, almost out of control. His mental image of the world was being turned upside down. Ever since that long-ago summer when he had seen Azalin's protective spell fall with deadly force upon the men and horses as they tried to cross the stream onto his father's land, he had known that Lord Azalin was all-powerful, irresistible in all ways. And yet now the sorcerer was saying that he needed help—Oldar's help. And he was asking, not demanding, as he had every right to do, nor threatening.

But Oldar could not refuse. Whatever he could do, he would. He owed the sorcerer that much and more, he and his father and his father before him, back five generations to his namesake.

"I will do whatever I can," Oldar said finally, "though I cannot imagine what that might be."

The sorcerer smiled warmly. "I will be forever grateful," he said. "I must warn you, however, that there may be danger for you. I will do what I can to keep you safe, but you will need to protect yourself as well." He paused, lifting his right hand out in front of him as if gripping something.

The air shimmered briefly, and a silvery sword appeared in the sorcerer's outstretched hand. A moment later, the weapon was enclosed in a jet black scabbard.

Oldar gasped but said nothing as he recognized the weapon from his dreams, the weapon with which he had again and again slain Lord Azalin himself!

The sorcerer reversed the weapon and held it out as he took a step toward Oldar. "This weapon bears my strongest enchantments," he said. "Carry it with you at all times, and even the mists will be hard put to harm you."

"These hands have held nothing but plow and pitchfork," Oldar began to protest, but then the hilt of the weapon was in his hand.

And he knew the meaning of enchantment, as he had when he had seen the invaders felled by Azalin's spells. As his fingers closed about the hilt, it suddenly seemed as if he had handled it a thousand times before, as if he had trained and fought with it from the moment he had been old enough to hold it. It was as if the weapon were a part of him, an extension of his arm that he could control as easily and deftly as his own fingers.

Both frightened and comforted by the phenomenon, he gingerly buckled the scabbard about his waist.

"You will spend the night here, with your friend Balitor," Azalin said, "and tomorrow he will escort you to Avernus, where you will enter the mists."

* * * * *

That evening, while Balitor watched sympathetically, Oldar sat at an ornate mahogany desk in an uncomfortably luxurious room of indeterminate purpose and wrote his parents a note, which Balitor solemnly promised to deliver. There was, of course, nothing in the note that concerned the mists or the sword or the implied dangers. Instead, he wrote only that Lord Azalin required his services for a time, as his namesake's had been required five generations before, and that he would return to his home as soon as possible.

When he showed Balitor the sword and explained that it was seemingly identical to the one in his dreams, the older man wanted to explore those dreams further. The boy resisted, however, for fear that such talk would only encourage the dreams to return, which prospect was even more frightening now that he knew there was some basis in reality for them. He had even begun to fear they might be visions of an inevitable future. The fact that the one he slew in his dreams was now nearby only increased his fears, but worst of all was the worry that the sword, because of the enchantments Lord Azalin himself had placed on it, might even be capable of slaying the sorcerer-king himself as no ordinary weapon ever could.

Oldar resisted sleep as well when Balitor finally delivered him to a velvet-draperied bedroom nearly as large as the entire house his family dwelt in. The room itself, so alien to what he was accustomed to, aided in his resistance, as did the opulent softness and comfort of the bed. Instead of lulling him to sleep, the silken sheets only reminded him with every touch that he didn't belong in this place, which in turn reminded him of the utter unknown that lay waiting for him when morning came.

Even so, after half an hour of nervous tossing and turning, sleep approached him with surprising suddenness. One moment his mind was spinning from one disconcerting thought to another, from what awaited him in the mists to what his parents must be thinking. The next moment, it was as if a muffling blanket had settled over his mind. The thoughts were still there, but somehow they were not nearly as disturbing. It was as if suddenly they were someone else's thoughts. He was only hearing them secondhand, and they were no real concern of his.

For a few moments, the sudden change itself sent a nervous tingle through him, making him twitch half upright in the bedcovers, but that, too, quickly lost its seeming importance to him.

His head was swimming. The whole room, still dimly lit by a pair of candles on a bureau that seemed more distant with every passing moment, began to waver, as if seen through a rippling sheet of water.

And then nothing. Oblivion.

Until, minutes or hours later, the dreams began. But not the dreams he had been expecting and fearing. There was no silvery sword, no faceless sorcerer dying beneath its blade, no glowing rush of water in a starless night.

Instead, he lay in the same bed he had fallen asleep in, the candles still burning across the room. But it was a dream—it *had* to be a dream—for floating in the air above him was the golden skull of a dragon, the candle-light glinting off it in a dozen spots, its curving, dagger-like horns nearly a foot long.

But then, even as he watched, it warped and twisted, as if seen in a distorted mirror, and seemed to shrink even as it plunged toward him . . .

And vanished as he forcibly, fearfully closed his eyes.

Suddenly his chest was afire, as if raked by hot coals, his heart not pounding but seeming to lunge wildly from side to side like a wild animal trying to escape its captors.

Then silence.

The fire in his chest was gone, replaced by a frightening numbness, as if the flesh no longer existed. Terrified at what he might see, he tried to raise his head from the pillows and throw back the covers, but his head seemed weighted down, his arms leaden, barely able to move. And his eyelids were becoming equally heavy, inexorably dragging themselves down.

As the final traces of the dim candlelight were shut out, he felt the world whirling about him, as it had when, as a child at play, he had spun around until dizziness threw him to the ground.

Unable to resist, he felt sleep—or unconsciousness—closing in on him once again.

And then it was morning.

He came awake with a start, feeling as if he had been dropped on the bed from a height. But he was still beneath the covers, tangled though they were, and light was streaming through parted drapes he had barely noticed the night before.

Blinking, he was relieved to discover that his eyes felt as they always did in the morning, slightly sandy behind lids that sprang lightly open. Gone were the leaden weights that had dragged them down the night before, as was the near-paralysis that had gripped him in the last moments of the dream.

The dream . . .

More vivid than any of the others, its images filled his mind, the golden skull of the dragon seeming to hover in the air before him.

And his chest . . .

Throwing the covers back, he tore open the nightshirt Balitor had forced upon him, and let out a huge whoosh of relief as his chest, unchanged and unharmed, was uncovered.

Only a dream—a nightmare. What else could it have been?

Bringing his feet to the plushly carpeted floor, he sat

on the edge of the bed for a moment, then stood. And froze, his heart suddenly pounding.

His hands darted to his chest as he looked down sharply. He had felt something, he was certain, but what? There was nothing there, not the slightest mark.

But still . . .

He could feel a pressure, as if some force were pushing against his chest—but from the inside!

A result of the sumptuous feast Balitor and his servants had provided him with the evening before, he told himself quickly. He was not accustomed to such fare, nor such attention. The very idea of men and women serving him in such a manner was itself upsetting. Add to that the richness and the unfamiliarity of the food, little of which he had even known existed prior to its being set on the table before him, and it was no wonder there was discomfort.

And it was becoming less noticeable, he realized after a moment. It was becoming less distinct now than the thumping of his heart, which itself was slowing and growing less intense with each passing second. So perhaps he would survive this ordeal after all, he thought, if only he could keep control of his own vivid imagination.

Pulling in a deep breath, he began to look for his rough woolen clothes, the only things in this place that gave him any sense of familiarity or comfort.

 **SIX**

Breakfast was as rich as the meal of the evening before, served once again by servants who smiled graciously yet never met Oldar's eyes directly, nor those of Balitor. This time, however, Oldar trod lightly through the courses, sampling rather than wolfing down, as was his custom at home where a single course meal, most often porridge, was not something to be dwelt over lovingly. The sense of a pressure in his chest remained, however, though it continued to lessen as the meal slowly progressed and Balitor kept up a steady stream of remembrances of the Oldar he had known. Somewhat to Oldar's relief, none of Balitor's stories appeared to have any relationship to the dreams, and he began to have hope that his being the reincarnation of his namesake, which had seemed almost certain the evening before, was after all a baseless fancy and nothing more.

When finally the meal was finished, Oldar self-consciously fastened the belted scabbard about his waist, covering it as much as possible by his rough woolen cloak. By the time Balitor led the way to the stables, where horses were saddled and waiting, the sun, so bright in the early morning, was invisible above darkening layers of clouds. A dampness was coming into the air as well, and a cold mist rose from the Vuchar as they crossed a worn and slippery stone bridge. There were few people about, but most of those who were nodded respectfully, lowering their eyes as the pair rode by. At one point, Balitor indicated a mansion, virtually a castle, half hidden from the street by a veritable forest of trees of all kinds.

"The present baron's residence" was all he said, and Oldar was glad he had at least been spared that. Being guest in Balitor's relatively modest mansion had been discomfiting enough.

Finally, as they left the city behind and crossed the South Canal, Balitor eyed the sword a moment and asked quietly, "What task does Lord Azalin have for you? You volunteered little last night."

Oldar shook his head. "I do not know. He said only that he required me to enter the mists in his stead. He said not the purpose, only that he would attempt to guide me in some way."

"The mists? But the nearest are many miles distant. Are the two of you to journey there, then?"

"He did not say. I know little more than I did when you first approached me at my namesake's grave. I can only assume I will be further instructed in some way."

"His journeying out would be most unusual. His leaving Avernus to greet you was itself remarkable. He did not say why he did this?"

"He did not."

Balitor fell silent then as they continued past the fields and the outer canals, the city lost in the thickening fog behind them. Soon they were passing through a forest, the trees leaning close to the road. Balitor pulled his fine cloak closer about his shoulders as they rode.

"If I were you," Balitor finally said, "I would turn myself around and return to my home."

Oldar looked at him questioningly. "You suggest I refuse Lord Azalin's request of me?"

"If you are able, yes."

"But it was you yourself who brought me here."

"I was ordered to do so."

"As you were ordered to escort me to Avernus?"

"I was not ordered to bring you there against your will. Nor, I imagine, were you yourself *ordered* to do this service for Lord Azalin."

"Indeed, he said I could refuse him without consequence."

Balitor nodded, smiling faintly. "As did your namesake."

"Lord Azalin said as much, but not what it was that he refused to do. You were there, you say. Do you know what it was?"

"Not entirely," Balitor said with a sigh. "I witnessed his refusal not of a task but of a magnificent gift—a gift of the very building you slept in last night, and all the treasures it held. He was even offered sovereignty over not only the land occupied by his father's small farm but all lands and towns ruled over by the local baron—Cauldry, I believe was his name. All this your namesake refused, and yet when he left, he was under Lord Azalin's personal protection—the same protection, I imagine, that you say continues to this very day."

"Lord Azalin implied as much when we spoke. He also said that, whatever task my namesake refused, it had to do with Azalin's son. 'He carried out the wishes of my son rather than my own,' he said, but would not explain further."

Balitor nodded, seeming to repress a shudder. "The son whose spirit your namesake encountered—or so he said—during his wanderings in Avernus that evening. I saw nothing of that, but later that night, when your namesake and I thought we were safely abed miles from Avernus, Lord Azalin sent two of his ghastly creations to fetch your namesake back. Whatever happened must have happened then, for at first light he was on the road to his home and family. He never returned and we never spoke after that night. Nor did Lord Azalin ever choose to confide in me."

Oldar sighed faintly. He wished Balitor had not urged him to refuse Lord Azalin, wished even that he had not learned the little he had of his ancestor's actions. He could all too easily understand refusing the offer to become baron of even a small domain. He would do the same himself, he suspected—hoped—even if loss of Azalin's protection were the cost. It was not his way, nor, he suspected, was it Balitor's. Even though the other man had appeared superficially at ease in his mansion, there had still been a sense of unease in his eyes whenever a servant, eyes averted, slid a plate in front of him or bowed and withdrew.

He had obviously adapted but had never developed a taste for such things. And he had successfully ruled Il Aluk for decades, finally stepping down not at the instigation of his subjects or of Lord Azalin but of his own volition.

Or so Balitor had said. And what reason would the man have to lie? Certainly he—

Oldar's fruitless speculations ended abruptly as he realized that the fog was thickening with alarming speed. They were passing through the deepest part of the forest, and the trees on either side of the road were little more osts. Their tops were totally obscured. And

Looking down with a start, he saw that a thicker blanket of fog seemed to be billowing up from the roadway, a silent, shallow river that already obscured the horses' hooves. And their previously staccato clacking was muffled, he realized, as if his ears had become stuffed with cotton.

"Balitor!"

Even his own voice seemed muffled, and when Balitor's came back to him, it sounded not only muffled but faint and distant. Dropping the reins and gripping the pommel of his saddle with one hand, he reached out to grasp at Balitor's arm, barely visible through the still-thickening fog. He felt his fingers dig into his companion's flesh, and yet the arm seemed to be slipping from his hold.

And still the fog thickened, blotting Balitor out entirely, and then Balitor's arm was torn from his grip as Oldar's horse whinnied and reared violently. A second later, he lost his grip on the pommel, and he was literally flying through the blinding whiteness, no idea of which way was up and which was down.

For what seemed an eternity, there was only the impenetrable whiteness of the fog, the fading whinny of his horse and the ever more muffled and distant sound of Balitor's voice calling his name.

Suddenly the breath was knocked out of him as he thudded to the ground flat on his back. But not on the rough, hard surface of the road. Instead, he had landed on at least a partial cushion of grass and weeds, and he realized he must have been thrown clear of the road.

Lurching to his feet, the sword and scabbard banging painfully against his leg, he shouted Balitor's name, but his own voice was so muffled it sounded as faint and distant as Balitor's had moments before. For an instant, he stood perfectly still, stiff with fright, then dropped to his hands and knees in an effort to see at least the ground beneath him.

But even that was impossible. And as he felt the grass and weeds beneath his fingers, he realized they were not damp and clammy, as such impossibly thick fog would surely suggest, but fresh and dry. His heart pounding, he lurched again to his feet, this time dizzily, for he had the feeling that the whiteness and silence that cloaked him so completely were also spinning madly.

Suddenly there was a sound. The shuffling of footsteps.

"Balitor?"

No voice answered . . . only the footsteps.

The sword! a voice hissed in his mind. At the same time, the nausea-inducing spinning sensation faded.

And the ground became visible beneath his feet.

The sword! the voice repeated urgently. *Take up the sword!*

More terrified than even in his dreams, Oldar grasped the hilt and pulled the sword smoothly from the scabbard. Once again it was as if the weapon had become a part of him, as if it were an extension of his own arm. But the feeling did not comfort him. Instead, it only increased his terror as the footsteps drew closer.

Swirling as if in a sudden wind, the fog withdrew a yard, then two, then ten. There was no road. There were no horses.

But emerging from the wall of whiteness was a horror beyond imagining. Except that he *had* imagined it, in his nightmares, on the banks of the rushing stream of glowing water! Clad in a rotting burial shroud, a skeleton with pieces of decaying flesh clinging to the bone, stiff clumps of hair sprouting unevenly from its skull, moved toward him. From the empty eye sockets, a dull red glow shone forth.

It must be slain! the voice hissed in his mind.

Then it was virtually upon him, reaching out with skeletal hands, the eye sockets glowing embers.

He swung the sword around, batting the arms away with the flat. Backing away, he brought the weapon back up. A greenish glow, almost like that of the water in his nightmare, was a blotch on the silvery surface of the sword where it had touched the creature.

Quickly! the voice hissed like a thousand snakes. *Quickly, or you are lost!*

Still backing away as the creature continued to shuffle toward him, its outstretched fingers only inches from his throat, Oldar brought the sword back even with his shoulders, gripping it with both hands now. In a bright, sweeping arc, he brought it back around. The blade erupted in a cascade of green phosphorescence, and its edge struck the bones in the creature's neck—and continued on.

For an instant the embers in the eye sockets burned more brightly, and the skeletal fingers were propelled forward to scrape at Oldar's throat.

But then, instead of collapsing to the ground, both skull and rotting body dissolved into an even greater shower of greenish phosphorescence. For a moment it hovered in the air, swirling chaotically, and then the fog closed in. The mists, Oldar finally realized, not a normal fog.

The mists closed in, and a tendril of greenish white struck at his chest like a serpent and vanished. His chest felt as if someone had deluged it with a pan of boiling water, but the burning pain lasted only a moment.

Then he was standing alone in the mists, so thick he could barely see his hand held inches from his eyes.

*   *   *   *   *

Azalin's "death" was far easier than had been Firan
Zal'honan's two centuries earlier. That first death had
been an eternity of torture compressed into what could
have been minutes or hours as he forced the vile, nause-
ating poison down his own throat and held it in while it
began its work, while he waited for the unconsciousness
that seemed as if it would never come.

This time it was over in a single sword stroke, a stroke
that his long-dead and half-decayed body didn't even
feel. It had experienced neither pain nor pleasure in two
hundred years, and it experienced neither now. There
was only a sudden feeling of lightness, of release, not
unlike the sensation that had once swept over his mortal
body whenever he had loosed his Sight to fly free.

But this flight was short and totally out of his control.
All he could see was the haven to which he was being
drawn by forces set in place before his first death: his
phylactery. The massive golden dragon skull that had
been guarded for over a century by the stones and spells
of Avernus had been transformed. Shrunken and folded
through unimaginable dimensions by a dozen spells, it
was now held within the young man's body, concealed
even from him by a dozen more.

And then, in less than a moment, Azalin—his surviving
essence—was safe within his sanctuary.

Safe, but until he could gain access to another body,
virtually powerless.

But first he must learn whether his interpretations of
the Vistana's words were valid or if he had set off on a
fool's errand of wishful thinking.

Wiping all other thoughts from his mind, he reached
out in an effort to touch the young man named Oldar. He

could neither see nor hear nor taste nor smell. He could only feel the young man's presence all about him, the way his mortal body had once felt the invisible air when the faintest of breezes brushed at its skin.

He visualized the young man's features, so like the original Oldar's, so like those of his own son. And he concentrated on those features and on the mind behind them, willing himself to become one with that mind. It was as if he were once again an inexperienced young sorcerer who had to focus all his thoughts on the objects of spells as he cast them, visualizing the desired results even as he spoke the magical words. But here in the mists, his body discarded, there were no words, no incantations. There was only the power of his own will. Forcing all other thoughts from his mind, he soon saw the boy's face as vividly as he had ever seen any object in the real world. And he drew closer, the features expanding until there were only the eyes, blue and frightened, and, through them, he seemed to flow into the boy's mind.

With startling abruptness, he found himself looking out through the boy's eyes at the swirling whiteness of the mists. And feeling the boy's terror. For a long moment he savored that terror, the first true emotion he had experienced in a century and a half, even though he knew that what he felt, filtered through the still-imperfect connection between the two of them, was a pale imitation of what the boy must be feeling.

Finally, cautiously, experimentally, he began trying to impose his own bodiless calm on the boy.

And when the terror was reduced to fear, when the boy's heart merely raced rather than pounded as if trying to escape his chest, Azalin spoke:

Oldar, do not be afraid. I am here and I will protect you.

"Lord Azalin?" The boy's shouted words were muffled even heard through his own ears, but the thoughts that generated them were sharp and distinct in Azalin's mind.

This was not the beginning I had hoped for, young Oldar, he lied, carefully shielding his true thoughts from the boy, *but you have already begun your journey into the mists.*

"But the creature that attacked—"

Was one of the dangers I warned you of. Your weapon disposed of it easily, as it will any others you may encounter.

The fear remained strong in the boy, as it would in any sane mortal, but he was controlling it himself now, needing no further help from Azalin. "What am I to do? I can see nothing! I can *do* nothing."

Do not be afraid, Azalin repeated. *I am with you and I will guide you. We will proceed together through the mists to our destination.*

Even as he formed the thought, he began to visualize that destination, for that was the only way to navigate the mists, the Vistana had said: "See clearly where you would go, and if you are truly fortunate, that is where the mists will transport you."

And the image formed, not just in his own mind but in Oldar's. In Oldar's mind, it was the castle from his nightmares.

In Azalin's mind, it was Castle Ravenloft, Strahd's home for the last four centuries. But not the castle as it existed now, empty of life, inhabited only by the undead Strahd von Zarovich. Instead, it was full of life and impending celebration, as it had been in the last days and hours before the mists had closed in and taken not only the castle but all of Barovia from its natural place and sealed it—and its soon-to-be vampire lord—in its eternal prison.

Holding the image in his mind, concentrating on it with
an intensity he had not achieved since his mortal days,
Azalin waited, the Vistana's words—"The bodiless shall
journey to the time before"—only deepening his concentration as they seemed to echo through the mists that
enveloped him and the boy.

*   *   *   *   *

The voice—Lord Azalin's voice—had barely faded
from Oldar's mind when the castle from his nightmares
leapt into his mind, its image more real and vivid than
any memory. Twin towers guarded the approach to a
drawbridge across a chasm whose lower reaches were
lost in a sea of fog. At the far end of the drawbridge, a
gate made for giants stood open. Beyond lay a courtyard
so large it was only dimly lighted by a dozen lamps and
torches, and beyond that loomed towers nearly as high
as the chasm was deep, many of their windows alight.
The distant murmur of voices he couldn't possibly hear
from this distance seemed to touch his ears, punctuated
now and again by a muffled peal of laughter. And along
the parapets atop the courtyard walls, torchlight glinted
off the chain mail of those who stood guard.

Without warning, the vision began to shift. Or he
began to move—to be moved—within it, floating like a
wraith between the twin towers, then across the drawbridge with its dizzying drop on either side and into the
courtyard, until he was so close to the buttressed walls of
the castle itself he felt he could reach out and touch
them.

This is our goal, the voice said in his mind, *and our
guide. See it and nothing else; reach for it with your
mind and we will succeed.*

Vertigo gripped Oldar as the mists that still enclosed him thickened even more, and he could no longer feel the ground beneath his feet, but even as he felt himself swaying and then floating free and tumbling helplessly, he held his grip on the image—the vision. Time and again, other images from his nightmares tried to intrude, but he managed to blot them out, or at least to keep them from becoming more than phantoms that played at the edges of his vision.

And the tumbling continued. Until . . .

Once again he felt solid ground beneath his feet, and he was struggling, flailing his arms to keep from falling.

And the mists were gone.

But the vision was not.

The vision was suddenly become reality, as solid as the ground beneath his unsteady feet, as cold and hard as the rough stone wall he crashed against as he struggled to keep his balance.

And the inner voice, filled with exultation, said, *We are here!*

 **SEVEN**

Barovia
351, Barovian Calendar

Despite his stunted senses, Azalin knew immediately that he had succeeded. He had successfully navigated the mists and emerged in the one place and time that could free him forever!

For this was unmistakably Castle Ravenloft, and it was equally unmistakably *not* the dark, uninhabited pile of stone and spells that he had seen and experienced countless times during his years in Barovia with Strahd. More than a dozen windows showed light, and he could sense the life that made use of it. Lamps and flickering torches lighted the courtyard, though dimly. And the guards who stood watch on the parapets of the outer wall were living humans, not Strahd's undead creations.

"Lord Azalin!"

The boy's whispered call seemed thunderously loud to his own ears, and Azalin hastened to reassure him.

Do not worry, young Oldar, I am with you. I will guide you as I promised. Azalin was relieved to sense that, while frightened, the boy seemed fully in control of himself. For he was dependent on the boy as he had never been dependent on another being in more than three centuries.

"What is this place, Lord Azalin?" the boy hissed. "Is this your home, Castle Avernus?"

You are far from Avernus, young Oldar. Indeed, the mists have transported you far from Darkon itself, but they will also transport you back once my business here—the business you must carry out for me—is complete, he added, carefully shielding his true thoughts.

"But where—"

I had planned to explain all to you before you entered the mists on my behalf, Azalin lied, *but circumstances, and that creature that attacked you from the mists, prevented that. Now time is of the essence, and there is none to spare for lengthy explanations. Nor can I allow my thoughts and energies to be distracted in any way lest this tenuous link through which I speak be lost beyond recall. You, too, would then be lost beyond recall, unable ever to leave this place to which the mists have taken you. Be satisfied in knowing that the first step in your task has been successfully completed and that when all is done, all will be explained.*

The boy swallowed nervously, obviously still frightened, still wanting to know far more, but in the end he said only, "What must I do, my lord?"

I know this place well, young Oldar. What your eyes see, mine do as well. Now give yourself over to me, and I will take you where you must go.

Cautiously, detesting the weakness his bodiless state imposed upon him, Azalin tightened his tenuous grip on the boy's mind, trying for the first time not to simply absorb secondhand what the boy saw and heard and felt but to control his movements.

*   *   *   *   *

Count Strahd von Zarovich was relieved when the
evening meal in the great dining hall at last dragged to
an end, and the need to maintain a public face of civility,
if not pleasure, was also ended. The dozens of guests
seemed ready to linger indefinitely, nibbling at the
remains of rich desserts and offering ever more repetitive
toasts of joy and happiness to the soon-to-be bride and
groom, but most took their cue to retire to their individual
rooms when Strahd rose abruptly from the head of the
banquet table and wished them all a pleasant evening
and strode from the hall.

As he made his way through the spacious entry hall
and up the broad steps toward his private quarters two
floors above, his features hardened into a grim mask. In
less than a day, Tatyana would be wed to another—to
Sergei, his own brother!—and all meaning would be gone
from his life. And he must stand by helplessly and wish
them well!

At first there had been hope—hope that Tatyana would
come to see in him the same qualities that had drawn her
to Sergei, only strengthened and matured by Strahd's tri-
als and his years. That she would come to see in him a
husband and lover more suitable than the callow youth
who was his brother.

But she had not. She had seen only the years that had
settled on his features. "Old One," she had called him,
stabbing him to the heart, though she meant it only as a
term of admiration and respect.

And now . . .

And now the wedding was less than a day away, to be
held under his own roof, before his own tortured eyes.
Unless . . .

He shook his head violently as he entered his bedchamber and crossed to the tall open windows that

looked out on the west courtyard and the drawbridge beyond. There was no time. For six moons he had studied the magical volumes his closest friend and second-in-command, Alek Gwilym, had brought back from his ambassadorial travels, but to no avail. Surely what he had not been able to find in half a year, he would not find in a single night!

But it was not in his nature to surrender or simply stand by while events unfolded around him! If it were, he would not be here now, lord of this castle and this land! Barovia would still be ruled by that pig Dorian, or some other who had the courage to—

For no reason he could fathom, a tingle raced up his spine, raising his back hairs.

He spun about, his eyes searching the shadows, his hand on the hilt of the dagger he always kept close. Such feelings, sudden directionless premonitions, had saved his life more than once, bringing him about to face an enemy too cowardly to approach openly. And with the threat of a Ba'al Verzi assassin never far from his mind even now, there was never a time to ignore such things.

But there was nothing, not the slightest movement, not the faintest sound anywhere in the room.

Still tense, his back still atingle, he turned again to the window and cautiously stepped through it onto the courtyard overlook. He frowned as a wisp of fog drifted up from below. The air was still enough, but there was no dampness that he could feel. There was constant mist in the depths of the chasm beneath the drawbridge and often in the forests at the base of the cliffs on which the castle was built, but never had he seen it within the courtyard.

But already it was gone.

Leaning over the parapet into the dimly lit courtyard,

he saw a roughly dressed peasant at the base of the
castle wall, not far from the main entrance. Doubtless
one of the servants accompanying the wedding guests,
he told himself, studying the man. But what was he doing
there? Lying in wait for someone to come out? Could that
possibly be a scabbard dangling from his waist? In the
dim light it was difficult to tell, but surely no servant . . .

No, there was no secrecy about the man, and even as
Strahd watched, the man pushed away from the wall and
walked unsteadily—drunkenly?—around the south tower
toward the rear courtyard.

Strahd smiled grimly, thinking that surrendering one's
senses to drink might not be the worst way to occupy
such a night.

* * * * *

Oldar could not repress a shudder as he felt his limbs
begin to move of their own volition, nor could he force his
body to immediately and completely surrender all efforts
at control. His reflexes, always swift, reacted against each
movement, resisting until he could consciously quash
them. The result was a lurching drunkard's walk for the
first dozen yards, the scabbard still fastened about his
waist smacking solidly against his leg with each step. But
also with each step, his movements—Lord Azalin's movements, he could not help but think—grew less uneven
until, by the time he reached the door at the base of the
wall that stretched across the entire side courtyard, his
legs them were moving in seeming unison.

The door opened at his touch, and Oldar found himself
in another courtyard, this one ending yards distant in the
rear curtain wall. No chain-mailed guards patrolled the
parapets here, he saw. And he knew, without knowing

how he knew, the reason: Beyond these walls, starting at their very bases, were drops of hundreds of feet down sheer rock faces. Any enemy who could reach those walls could not be stopped by mortal weapons.

But those walls were not his destination. Instead, his feet turned to the left, and he angled across the courtyard toward another gate, this one not in a hundred-foot-high wall but in what looked to be a small, roofed corridor that ran from the castle to the rear wall. At that point, the castle itself was little more than fifty feet high, making the entire section look as if it had been built as an afterthought. As if to add to that impression, a domed roof was dimly visible in the near darkness, in stark contrast to the peaks and towers of the rest.

A dozen yards short of the gate, the scent of flowers touched his nostrils. A garden? Here?

The chapel garden, Lord Azalin's silent voice said, and then he was through the gate and wending his way through artfully irregular rows of rosebushes, interspersed with varieties of flowers he had never seen. To his right, an opening in the curtain wall led to a broad, balconylike overlook that must project out beyond the edge of the cliff on which the castle was built. To his left, stained-glass windows looked out between sturdy buttresses, but there was no entrance, and he continued through a second gate. From the decidedly different odor here, he guessed that stables were nearby, logically close to the garden.

Another turn to the left past more stained glass and he came to a small featureless door that creaked loudly as he forced it open. He began to hurry now, each new sight a surprise to Oldar but apparently not to his guide, until all was darkness and he found himself going down a long flight of rough stone steps, then down another invisible flight, this one spiraling sharply around a central column, until . . .

The steps ended, and he continued another dozen yards on a slippery level floor. Finally he halted, still in total darkness.

And knew that he had reached his destination.

But not yet what that destination was.

Rustling sounds came from all around him, and the sound of wings, countless wings. He jerked spasmodically as something brushed against him, light as a feather but not a feather. Fur, the softest of fur.

And the odor—not that of the stables but equally unpleasant.

"What is this place?" The voice was his own, but high-pitched with fear, and it echoed back as if in a huge cavern.

My destination, the silent voice acknowledged. *Be patient, young Oldar. Your task will soon be complete.*

He felt the fire in his chest once again, but more briefly this time, more intensely, bringing a sharp cry to his lips.

And he was alone.

"Lord Azalin!"

There was no answer, no sound, no inner voice.

Again he called the name, almost a scream now, the echoes seeming to persist far longer than possible. The sound of wings grew louder as more and more seemed to join them until the air was filled with the sound.

"*Do not leave me!*" A full scream now, the echoes only adding to his terror.

The sound of stone scraping on stone came from only feet away, and he spun around to face the sound. In the sudden move, his foot slipped and he lurched backward helplessly, but instead of falling, he crashed against— something.

Cold stone, but not a wall, for there was a top to it, his fingers told him. And an end.

He froze as the scraping sound came again, more

loudly. Then abruptly the deafening sound of something as solid and massive as a boulder crashing to the floor.

And then different sounds, not the scraping of stone on stone but a rustling, a scratching, so faint as to be almost lost in the constant background of featherless wings.

And finally footsteps—footsteps that began by shuffling, then striding, seemingly directly toward him. For a moment he could see two faint dots of reddish light almost at eye level moving toward him like a pair of dimly glowing embers, but then they were gone. An instant later, he felt a sudden tugging at the scabbard still fastened about his waist, and an unseen hand jerked the sword free before he could react. He grasped at the blackness but caught nothing. A stench of decay added to the foul odors already assaulting his nostrils.

Then the footsteps were receding into silence, and he was truly alone except for the sound of wings that filled the dank, foul-smelling air.

 **EIGHT**

Barovia
351, Barovian Calendar (continued)

No sooner had the essence that was Azalin emerged from the phylactery and flowed into the decayed remains in the nearest crypt than he began to realize that all was not well, that there might still be great obstacles to overcome.

He had assumed that all would be well once he guided the terrified Oldar through the maze of Castle Ravenloft to these subterranean catacombs where centuries of the castle's former masters rested. He had assumed the strength and abilities that had been his for centuries would return as soon as he had departed the phylactery and was once again ensconced in a suitable body. However, even the simple task of entering the body and giving it a semblance of life struck him as extraordinarily difficult. But he had no experience with which to compare it, he told himself. Since the reanimation and reoccupation of his own decomposed body two and a half centuries ago, he had had no need to enter a new one. His sorcery had made that body virtually indestructible by any physical means, and he had been able to maintain an illusion of humanity whenever he desired.

So perhaps . . . perhaps the resistance was normal.

But that resistance, he realized moments later, was only the beginning of his troubles. Only with the most intense effort could he muster strength enough to force aside the heavy stone cover of the crypt and send it crashing to the floor. To climb over the five-foot side of the crypt and reach the rough stone floor, slippery with the guano of the hundreds of bats that made the catacombs their home, was almost equally difficult, as if all of his strength was being consumed simply to keep the body from disintegrating into dust.

Even his vision, normally as sharp in total darkness as a mortal's would be in full sunlight, was faded and indistinct. The familiar lines of the crypts were mere shadows in the massive chamber, and the hundreds of bats that fluttered and swooped about the disturbance that was himself and Oldar were not even shadows but a constantly shifting amorphous cloud.

But Oldar, though a shadow, was at least a well-defined one, and Azalin made directly for him, gaining enough control of his newly acquired body after a few steps to walk almost normally. Snatching the sword from its scabbard, he retreated before the boy could react.

For a moment he felt a twinge of pity for Oldar, trapped in a darkness his eyes could not penetrate, but Azalin had no choice. If this was truly the night he believed it was, there was no time to spare. He had a few short hours at most to find and kill his old enemy before that enemy struck his deal with the dark powers and became unkillable. Before dozens of lands, beginning with Barovia itself, were consigned to a misty prison.

Summoning all his strength, he bypassed the broad stone steps down which he had guided Oldar and made his way to a second, smaller enclosed spiral of worn stone steps, these leading, he knew, directly to Strahd's quarters and beyond. During the first labored steps, he briefly considered abandoning the body and attempting to occupy another of the dozens that waited in their crypts, but he discarded the thought almost immediately. It would take time he feared he did not have, and there was no guarantee that any of the other bodies in these centuries-old catacombs would be superior to the one he had chosen.

And perhaps his strength would improve as he continued, as he grew more accustomed to this newly acquired husk. If it did not . . .

*   *   *   *   *

Alek Gwilym was in the chapel, having paused briefly on his never-ending rounds of the castle, when a distant sound where there should have been none pricked his ears. The guard assigned to the chapel, stationed in front of the altar where he had a clear view of all three entrances in the back wall, gave no indication of having heard anything. Standing perfectly still, Alek listened for it to be repeated, but there was nothing.

His hyperactive imagination? No, it had been real.

Even so, at any other time, he would have dismissed it as just another sound of the ancient castle settling in on itself. Strahd had done wonders in the four years since he had taken possession of Castle Ravenloft, but all the artisans and craftsmen in Barovia could not completely remove the effects of age. Rooms could be cleared, walls and buttresses repaired, even rebuilt, ceilings and floors reinforced, doors replaced, but still occasional sounds would remind one of things undone, of things undoable.

But now, with dozens of guests strewn about the castle,

few of whom Alek would trust with his purse, let alone his life or Strahd's, he was not about to dismiss anything out of hand. On an earlier pass through the chapel, he had sensed rather than seen a motion through the stained-glass windows that looked out onto the chapel garden. Sure enough, when he shaded his eyes and put his nose to the glass and peered through, he had been able to make out a shadowy figure wending its way among the roses. By the time he had made his way through a half dozen passages and reached the garden himself, lantern in hand, there was no one.

Only a guest, he had told himself, not altogether sincerely. More than one, during daylight tours of the forbidding castle and its grounds, had remarked on the beauty of the garden. It had been a muddy morass when he and Strahd had first laid eyes on it, but now, thanks to Strahd's efforts, it was a tranquil oasis of sweet scents and colors. Many guests had also remarked on the difficulty of sleeping in strange quarters and might, despite the cautions of their hosts, have thought to find in the nighttime garden a remedy, although finding it without so much as a candle to light the way seemed both unwise and unlikely.

And where this latest sound—if it was not indeed his imagination—had come from was not a place where any guest would, with or without a lamp, seek nighttime solace.

His hand on the hilt of his sword, less to be ready for an encounter with a foe than to keep the scabbard silent as he walked, Alek gestured for the guard to be silent as well and approached the shadowy alcove to the left of the doors that led to the rest of the main floor of the castle. Pausing at the entrance to the alcove, he listened again.

A distant voice? Or his imagination still?

Slowly he continued into the unlighted alcove. The huge statues, fully eight feet tall, their muscular arms holding not prayer scrolls but massive blades, were little more than looming shadows. Beyond, broad stone steps spiraled downward into even deeper shadows.

Could it have been from below that the sounds had come? Servants' quarters as well as the wine cellar were one level down, though normally they would not be approached by this route, through the chapel. There were other less grand stairs for such mundane matters.

At the opening to the steps themselves, he paused again. The sound could have come from above or below, he supposed. The stairs themselves spiraled up from the subterranean catacombs all the way to the peak of the castle's highest tower, as did the enclosed air shaft around which the stairs wound.

After a moment, Alek returned to the chapel for the lantern that accompanied him on these nighttime rounds and, after a brief word with the guard, began his cautious descent.

* * * * *

Jarath, at his post by the main-floor entrance to the guards' stair, did his best to stifle yet another yawn but in the end was forced to once again surrender, the sound breaking the stillness in the long, narrow corridor. Luckily he had not suffered such an attack any of the times Captain Gwilym had come by checking . . . always checking. Did the man never sleep? Did he trust *no* one?

For five nights now, it had been thus, ever since the wedding guests had begun to arrive. In all the years before, no night had required more than a lone pair of chain-mailed sentries to patrol the parapets overlooking the drawbridge, the only possible approach to Castle Ravenloft for anything not equipped with feathers and wings. All others, soldiers and servants alike, would have no duties but to get enough rest so as to be ready and able to resume their duties with the return of the sun.

But now servants spent half the night cleaning up after the elaborate evening meal served to dozens of guests and then preparing to start all over again well before dawn the next day. And Jarath and the other soldiers took turns patrolling not just the parapets but virtually every hall and stair in the castle. Jarath himself was particularly vulnerable to drowsiness, not even having the luxury of movement to keep him awake. His assignment, standing guard at the main-floor entrance to the guards' stairs, kept him rooted to a single spot for half the night. Though who Captain Gwilym expected to try to enter those stairs or what any intruder might expect to accomplish was beyond him. True, the stairs led eventually to Lord Strahd's chambers, as did a number of other routes, but Lord Strahd himself and the sorcery he was reputed to command were surely far more effective deterrents than any single guard with mere mortal weapons.

But orders were orders, and Captain Gwilym was as good a man to serve under as any Jarath had known— fair and just, never requiring another to do what he would not do himself, and never above sharing a tankard and a joke with his men.

Still, he thought, surrendering to another yawn, he would be glad when whoever was to relieve him arrived and his watch was finished for this night. But that was still hours away, and his eyelids were growing heavier by the minute.

Shaking his head vigorously helped for a few seconds, as did stamping his feet now and then, but even so . . .

Abruptly he stiffened, sleep driven at least momentarily from his eyes by the sound of footsteps. Captain Gwilym again? Surely not already. And the sound was not coming from around the corner at the far end of the corridor, Captain Gwilym's normal route, but from somewhere in the claustrophobically enclosed spiral stair whose entrance he was supposedly guarding.

Surely Lord Strahd would not choose this back-stair route to descend from his chambers, even if he had a reason to be abroad at such an hour.

Turning, Jarath poked his head in through the open door and listened. Yes, there it was, but it was coming not from above but from below, echoing up out of the near darkness that led down to his own and the other guards' quarters and other subterranean areas. But he was not due for relief for hours yet, nor were any of the other guards.

Unless, unable to sleep, one was coming up early to relieve him? He could only hope.

But the steps, he realized as they moved still closer, were not brisk and firm, as any of Captain Gwilym's men would produce, even at this dismal time of night, but uneven and labored, as if pausing at every step to gain the strength for the next.

Suddenly his heart was pounding. The man was wounded! What had happened in the quarters below? Had Captain Gwilym's fears been justified? Had some traitor gained entrance despite all his precautions?

Jarath's sword was in his hand in an instant. Another instant and he was hurrying down the rough stone steps, the torchlight from the single sconce above the door casting a wildly wavering and jerking shadow on the curving stone wall.

He slowed as he descended into the deep shadow beyond the torch's direct reach, a chill aura of terror

beginning to pull at him. A dozen treacherous steps farther down, he would emerge into the flickering light from
the next sconce, a full flight below. All the while, the
laboring footsteps continued to approach, until . . .

A man, middle-aged and hawk-nosed, dressed all in
black, appeared in the shadows. He was not one of Lord
Strahd's guests, all of whose faces Captain Gwilym had
insisted his men learn and remember, but he could be—
must be—one of their servants. To learn the faces of the
nobles and their ladies was hard enough, but to learn
those of their retinues as well was impossible.

But whoever he was, the man didn't appear wounded,
as Jarath had suspected. And whoever he was, he certainly didn't belong here.

"Who is your master?" Jarath snapped. "And what is
your business here?" The man appeared unarmed but
Jarath held his own blade at the ready.

"I serve Baron Dilisnya," the man said after a moment
of blank hesitation, "though rather poorly at the moment,
I fear. For he sent me on an errand and I appear to have
lost my way."

"What errand?" If Dilisnya's current visit was anything
like previous ones, any errand run on his behalf after a
meal, particularly one the likes of which the guests had
been served this evening, would have to do with remedies
for an aching gut. His poor digestion had been a recurring
topic among the kitchen staff even before he had arrived.

"To the wine cellar," the man said, and then added, as
if confirming Jarath's thoughts, "As most know, my
master often suffers from indigestion, as he does this
very night, and Lord Strahd has graciously offered—"

"If Lord Strahd made an offer of wine to sooth your
master's stomach," Jarath said suspiciously, "he would
doubtless have sent one of his own servants, who know

where the wine cellar is, to fetch it."

The man was silent a moment, the shadows seeming to darken about his face. "If you doubt my word, sir, I suggest you accompany me and speak to Lord Strahd himself."

"A word with Baron Dilisnya would be sufficient."

The man fell silent again, this time staying utterly motionless, as if suddenly stricken by some form of paralysis.

"There seems to be more to your trouble than losing your way," Jarath said finally.

Still the man didn't respond, and Jarath began to wonder if he were truly ill.

"What—" Jarath began, but even as he opened his mouth to speak, the man's form seemed to waver like a torch-cast shadow. Frowning, Jarath backed up a step, his sword once more at the ready, pointed directly at the man's chest. Again the man's entire form wavered and . . .

Jarath gasped and lurched backward, almost falling as every hair on his head and body seemed to stand upright. In an instant, the man had vanished, and in his stead . . .

Once, Jarath had seen such a thing, on a ravaged battlefield more than a moon after the killing had stopped. A pack of wild dogs had found a too-shallow grave and had dragged the rotting contents into the light of day but then had left it untouched, too far into decay even for their empty stomachs to take in.

But *this* thing was upright—and once again it was walking. Shreds and tatters of what might once have been a burial shroud clung to what was left of its body. Hands that were little more than bare bones clutched a sword more in the manner of a cane than a weapon. Reddish pits glowed where eyes once had been.

And as Jarath stood, frozen, those glowing eye sockets seemed to fix on him.

As if suddenly granted new strength, the hideous apparition raised the sword and lunged toward him up the steps, its nearly fleshless mouth opening in a silent scream.

In purely visceral response, Jarath gripped his own sword in both hands and swung the blade wildly, all training in swordsmanship forgotten in his terror. And yet the blades met with a clang that echoed up and down the stairs.

Again the blades clashed, and yet again as Jarath fell back, retreating up the steps.

But then whatever had given the creature its sudden burst of energy seemed to fade, and its movements again became sluggish. And when the swords next met, the creature's was knocked free of its skeletal hand and clanged to the step at Jarath's feet.

But instead of turning and retreating or giving a sign of surrender, the creature reached down toward the fallen sword, its movements still sluggish. Without thinking, Jarath slashed at the creature's outstretched arm.

His blade, sharp enough to pass unhesitatingly through normal flesh and bone, was brought to an arm-wrenching halt as it struck and penetrated the creature's arm. And stuck, like an axe driven deep into a stubborn block of wood.

Suppressing a scream, Jarath pulled violently at the blade, but to no avail.

In desperation, he released his own sword and grasped the fallen one from beneath the creature's reaching fingers. And struck, not at the body but directly at the skeletal neck. The blade passed through it as if through smoke.

But the skull-like head did not fall.

Instead, at the point where the blade had passed

through, a greenish glow appeared and began to spread rapidly in all directions—including up the blade of the sword toward Jarath's hands.

Spasmodically he jerked backward, at the same time throwing the weapon from him, sending it clattering down the stairs and out of sight. As he scrabbled backward up the steps, the creature remained motionless, still half bent over in the act of reaching for the fallen sword, the greenish glow spreading farther and farther over the hideous body until . . .

In an instant, the glow seemed to solidify and, like a spirit leaving a body, disentangled itself from the creature and flowed down into the darkness the sword had disappeared into. A moment later, the creature itself collapsed into a pile of bones and tatters of burial shroud. Jarath's own sword, released from whatever held it, clanged to the steps at his feet.

As Jarath ceased his awkward retreat and once again got to his feet and stood, trembling, unable to take his eyes from the sight, the creature's remains shrank and shifted until there was only dust and a few ragged strips of filthy white cloth. Only then, when there was little more left than an untidy chambermaid might sweep beneath the rug, did he cautiously move close enough to pick up his own fallen sword.

For a full minute he stood silently, hoping that his heartbeat would someday return to normal, wondering if there was any way this could all have been a nightmare.

And wondering if there was any way Captain Gwilym could think otherwise, if Jarath were ever fool enough to tell him.

Pulling in a deep breath that did little to lessen the chill that still gripped him, he turned and made his way back up the stairs to his station.

 **NINE**

Barovia
351, Barovian Calendar (continued)

Despair gripped Azalin as he found himself—his essence—being dragged blindly back to his spell-bound refuge.

He had failed.

He had not even been able to defeat a lowly mortal sentry. How could he expect, even had he been able to slip past this and other sentries to Strahd's chambers, to defeat and kill Strahd, who, though not yet the immortal vampire he would become, had sorcery as well as physical strength at his disposal?

He couldn't. The struggle to keep control of the body had only grown worse the farther Azalin moved toward his goal, the farther he moved from the phylactery. For those last few steps before encountering the sentry, it had been as if he were moving through an ever-thickening liquid that threatened to congeal at any moment. The attempt to generate an illusion of humanity to trick the sentry had been the final straw. In Darkon, even on Oerth, maintaining such an illusion had been second nature, requiring little more effort than a mortal would require to continue breathing. And yet here . . .

He had known his powers would be drastically curtailed while he was confined to the phylactery, without the services of a body, but once he *had* a body, even that collection of dust and bones he had pulled from the crypt, most of his powers should have returned, enabling him to easily kill Strahd.

But his powers had not returned. It had taken all his effort and concentration simply to keep the body moving, even at the snail's pace he had been forced to adopt. Maintaining the illusion of humanity and trying to pick vital information from the guard's mind simultaneously had been too much. He had not even been able to retain his own sword in the confrontation that followed.

And then, when the blade of that sword, its enchantments still intact, had slashed through him, what little power he had retained had drained away in an instant, and the remnants of the body had been consumed by those enchantments, just as his original body had been consumed by them when struck by Oldar in the mists.

But why was he so weak, so helpless? Was it simply another obstacle thrown in his path by his tormentors? Did they know, after all, that he was here? But how could they? His journey through the mists had taken him to a time more than a century before his tormentors had even become aware of his existence. Decades, even, before his own *birth!*

The thought suddenly sobered him: Unless the mists have played an even greater trick on me than I supposed, I do not yet exist on my own world, wherever that world is.

I don't exist. . . .

And he wondered: Could that very paradox be the reason for his weakness? The mists had, at his own behest, carried him back to a time before his own birth. To a time and a place, perhaps, where the magical powers he had accumulated and mastered did not yet exist, at least not for him. Was it possible?

He thought he had known the rules of sorcery, but obviously he did not, any more than the arrogant fifteen-year-old Firan Zal'honan had known them more than three centuries ago when he had made his disastrous attempt at a Grand Summoning and lost the life of his beloved brother as a consequence.

Three centuries ago . . . yet half a century in the future.

His mind spinning, he felt himself absorbed once more into the spellbound phylactery.

*   *   *   *   *

Oldar had no way of knowing how long he had been standing motionless and alone in the foul-smelling darkness when the faintest flicker of light caught his eye. It was, he realized with a sudden burst of hope, coming from somewhere far up the stairs he had descended minutes—or hours—before. Now that he could see to find the base of the stairs, his immediate thought was to make his way there across the filthy floor quickly, before the light vanished. But before he could urge his reluctant limbs into motion, it occurred to him that he hadn't the faintest idea who or what was carrying the light. And that he himself was an intruder, whom the castle's master might welcome not with open arms but with open dungeon. Cautiously, keeping his back pressed against the solid carven rock of the object he had been leaning against, he edged away from the stairs and around the corner of the huge object. Turning then, he crouched low and, heart pounding, peeked ever so carefully around the corner of the object toward the stairs.

And waited.

And wondered. What had happened to Lord Azalin? Why was the sorcerer's voice no longer in his mind, guiding him as it had when it had brought him to this place?

After a minute, he heard the faint sound of footsteps accompanying the still-distant light.

But now both grew quickly closer, and soon the direct rays of the light were emerging from the stair, giving him his first look at his surroundings: The shadowy forms flapping in the air all about him were, as he had feared, bats of a dozen different sizes. Row after row of the same type of structure that he crouched behind stretched from one end of the cavernous room to the other. And on the floor, a dozen feet away, lay the massive stone slab he had heard crash to the floor.

Crypts, he realized, but that realization—and the realization that *something* had most likely just climbed out of the one whose cover adorned the floor—couldn't make him any more fearful than he already was.

Finally, a tall, handsome man, perhaps about forty with a dark stripe of a mustache, emerged from the stairs, holding a lantern in one hand, a drawn sword in the other. The man scowled when he saw the fallen slab of stone, but the scowl was accompanied by a touch of fear as his eyes darted in all directions and his hand tightened on the sword.

An instant later, Oldar gasped as an invisible flame seemed to scorch his chest.

*   *   *   *   *

Alek Gwilym gripped his sword and lantern with equal strength as he tried to probe the shadows of the catacombs. It was obvious from the crypt's displaced cover that someone was here—or had been here only minutes ago. Someone strong enough—or versed well enough in sorcery—to move a slab of solid stone weighing hundreds of pounds. There were, of course, other ways out of the catacombs than these stairs, though he had never used them himself. Nor had he used these he now stood on all that often, he thought uncomfortably. He had never liked these subterranean depths, least of all the catacombs and its forest of crypts, where lay the dust that was all that remained of a millennium of Barovia's rulers. Even worse for one of his fastidious nature was the filthy floor, covered with decades of droppings from the bats that infested the place like the vermin they were.

A sound—a gasp?—audible over the faint fluttering of the bats snapped his attention toward the nearest crypt on the left. Nothing moved in the dim light from his lantern, but even as he scowled into the shadows, another sound, faint and rustling, came from the direction of the crypt.

"Come out where I can see you!" Alek said loudly, his voice reverberating throughout the cavernous room.

But there was only silence, except for the continued sounds of the bats.

For a time, he stood on the bottom step, holding the lantern high, waiting. Twice he repeated his demand, listening for the slightest sound in response, but still there was nothing.

Abruptly he smiled, realizing what must have happened. A guest who had overindulged himself in Strahd's excellent vintages had wandered too far from dining hall and bedchamber. Perhaps even the same one he had glimpsed in the chapel garden earlier. And once here, the drunken wanderer had succumbed to morbid curiosity and tried to get a look at the remains of a previous

master of Castle Ravenloft, possibly even to make off
with some small memento of the occasion.

Alek chuckled silently, thinking of the din the stone
slab must have made as it crashed to the floor. Probably
it had frightened the drunkenness out of the fool, and
now he was crouching behind the nearest crypt, terrified
that Strahd's reputation for punishment of even minor
transgressions would prove justified. In all likelihood, he
had dropped his lantern, and now he was stranded here
in the dark, amid the dead, his boots and possibly much
more coated with the filth that littered the catacombs
floor.

Punishment enough, Alek thought, lowering the
lantern and turning to move back up the stairs. Particularly if the fool had indeed lost his lantern and would
have to find his way out of here in the dark. There would
be time enough when the wedding festivities were con-
cluded on the morrow to bring some strong backs down
to replace the crypt's cover.

* * * * *

The sudden pain in Oldar's chest lasted only an
instant, but that instant was enough to pull a gasp from
his throat, enough to make him involuntarily reveal himself to the man who stood at the bottom of the stairs.

After only a moment's hesitation, the man shouted for
him to step out of hiding!

Trembling, Oldar hesitated, but with Lord Azalin no
longer there to guide him out of this place, he knew he
had no choice. Even a dungeon would be preferable to
this.

Pulling in another breath, he straightened, still hidden
behind the crypt, and stood for a moment, working up

the courage to step out into the dim light as the man called to him a second time, then a third.

Stay where you are, young Oldar! Azalin's voice thundered in his mind, turning the boy into a shivering statue. *And be silent! I will take care of this interloper!*

Relief flooded through Oldar. It was all he could do to keep from shouting a glad reply.

But he managed to hold his silence. There were no more shouts for him to show himself. And after a minute, there was the sound of footsteps, not approaching his hiding place but retreating up the stairs. The light faded into total darkness.

Finally Lord Azalin's voice returned, but with far less strength than it had possessed only moments before: *Give yourself over to me once again*, it said. *I will guide you to where we must go.*

*   *   *   *   *

Alek Gwilym had climbed the steps almost to the chapel when it belatedly occurred to him that the guest—if guest it was—he had seen in the chapel garden earlier couldn't have been the one who had been lurking in the catacombs. The one in the garden had not been carrying a lantern.

It was foolish enough to wander unfamiliar grounds with only starlight to guide you, but surely no one in his right mind would descend a hundred feet or more into total darkness. And if the fool were drunk enough to consider such an idea, he probably wouldn't have been able to force the massive stone cover, unmoved for decades if not centuries, off the crypt. How many hundreds of pounds must it weigh?

And yet, when he had been standing at the entrance to the catacombs, it had seemed perfectly reasonable. . . .

A chill rippled up his spine as he turned to look back down the steps into the shadows. What *had* happened in that godforsaken place? And what had possessed him—perhaps literally?—to dismiss it as the minor depredations of a drunken fool of a guest?

Gripped with a sudden urgency, he took the remaining dozen steps two at a time and raced through the alcove to the chapel. "Janos," he called to the guard, still at his station in front of the altar and its flickering candles, "stand guard here, in the alcove. Listen for any sound coming from below. I will rouse the rest of the troops and send someone here to stand with you."

Before Janos could reply, Alek was through the chapel doors.

*   *   *   *   *

It took all of Azalin's willpower not to simply give up or, at the very least, to take a few minutes in a desperate attempt to restore his strength. He felt utterly drained by the massive effort it had taken to prod Alek Gwilym's thoughts along the path that had sent Strahd's chief of security up the stairs and away from the catacombs. It had been as difficult, in its own way, as it had been to control that useless body from the crypt.

Worse, Azalin knew that the effects on the man would be far from permanent. Alek Gwilym was an intelligent man; that, if anything, he had learned from Strahd's recollections during the decades Azalin had spent with Strahd, trapped in Barovia. Gwilym was also, if not devoted to Strahd, certainly intensely loyal and as close to a friend as someone like Strahd could ever have. It would take Gwilym very few minutes to begin wondering about the odd chain of thoughts that had led him to leave the catacombs, dismissing the open crypt as drunken vandalism. And once he had begun to wonder, the lingering effects of Azalin's mental proddings would crumble under any kind of logical attack. Gwilym would know that someone or something had been tampering with his mind, and he would doubtless be returning to the catacombs in short order, most likely with more of his men and weapons, almost certainly by way of these same stairs.

And Gwilym's likely return was not the only reason for haste and desperation. If this were indeed the night Azalin thought it was—and almost certainly it was—he had hours at most, perhaps only minutes, to accomplish what he had come for: to find and slay Strahd Von Zarovich before he became unkillable. And his only chance to accomplish that, now that his first effort had failed so miserably before it had even been properly begun, lay entirely in the hands of the boy in whose body he had been transported here. And in his own ability to manipulate that boy.

Manipulate, not control.

For he could not, he now knew, control the boy's body against his will. To make use of the boy's body, he needed the lad's full cooperation, and even that, he was discovering as he tried to hurry through the catacombs toward a different exit, was no guarantee of success. Despite Azalin's repeated assurances, the boy was terrified, and justifiably so. To the boy's eyes, it was utter darkness that Azalin was trying to make him race through. Only Azalin's memories of this place—memories from two centuries in the future—and the pathetic remnants of his Sight enabled him to guide the boy's feet without crashing into wall or crypt. And he could share neither the memories nor the indistinct visions of his Sight with the boy, to whom the darkness remained truly impenetrable.

As a result, his movements were almost as erratic as when, in the castle courtyard less than an hour earlier, Azalin had first tried to govern the boy's movements.

"I'm sorry," the boy said again and again each time he lurched to a stop, his instincts fighting Azalin's efforts at control.

Slowly, though, the boy's ability to clamp down on those instincts grew greater, and their progress became less spasmodic fits and starts until, by the time they came to a stop before a rusting iron door at the far end of the catacombs, he had been covering the last few yards almost at a trot. Giving the boy a brief respite then, Azalin sent his Sight through the as yet unopened door and down the dank, narrow tunnel beyond, a tunnel he had last seen nearly two hundred years in the future.

But it was almost precisely as he remembered it, narrow and confining, the uneven stone walls slippery with moisture. And the only hazard, now as then, was a trapdoor that could easily be cleared as long as the boy didn't balk at the wrong moment. And at the far end, almost at the limit of his stunted Sight, was the first of many sets of stairs that would, after a brief descent even farther into the subterranean depths, give him access to every part of the castle.

Explaining to the boy as best he could what lay ahead—but not his ultimate goal—Azalin guided the boy's hands to the rusted bolt that held the door. With all the boy's strength, he forced the bolt back and then the door itself, which opened with screeching reluctance that echoed through the catacombs more loudly than the stone slab when it had fallen.

The tunnel came as a relief, its floor merely gritty and slippery, not covered with the filth of the catacombs, and even the anticipated leap across the trapdoor resulted in nothing worse than a slip and tumble on the far side.

When they came to the end of the tunnel, still in total darkness, Azalin paused long enough to warn the boy that they would be descending several steps before actually beginning the ascent. Even so, progress again slowed until they reached the bottom, made a dizzying turn, and headed back up a second set of steps, going up much farther than they had just descended.

Finally the steps ended at a door, this one wooden and not nearly as noisy as the last. Stepping through, they were still in darkness, with only Azalin's Sight and his memories to guide them through one subterranean room after another until . . .

Pushing cautiously through a final door, they entered a hall, a dim glow visible at the far end, an open archway halfway down on the right. In Azalin's time, when Strahd had no need of living servants, this area had long been deserted and mold-encrusted. Now, as Azalin had discovered on his earlier foray, a half dozen of Gwilym's men slept on cots in alcoves beyond the archway.

But one, he realized, did not sleep.

Bringing Oldar to a halt just inside the door, he calmed the boy as best he could and reached out to the one waking mind. In Darkon, a single gesture would have brought sleep or death, but here, unfortunately, such powers were far beyond him. Here he could do nothing but direct his thoughts at the man and hope that, like Gwilym, he would at least briefly accept them as his own.

And he did, thinking drowsily, irritably, that the castle's rat population was getting altogether too bold as some of its members scuttled about in the hall only yards from his cot.

Then Azalin was past the archway to the end of the hall and the lower end of the guards' stairs. And there, a half dozen steps up, glinting in the light from the single sconce above the entrance to the stairs, was his immediate goal: the sword he had lost while struggling to control that other body.

Ignoring the boy's sudden uneasiness at the reappearance of the weapon, he snatched it up and slid it into the scabbard, still at the boy's waist. In the same moment, voices drifted down the spiral stair, and Azalin recognized the loudest as that of Alek Gwilym.

Hastily Azalin retreated the way he had come, back past the still-sleeping guards and into the large room beyond. He had hoped to take the guards' stairs all the way to their end, at the courtyard overlook just outside the windows of Strahd's private quarters, but that was obviously impossible now. One guard he might be able to divert, but not two or more, particularly when one of them was Gwilym, who would doubtless recognize almost instantly any further attempts to influence him. Recognize and resist.

But there were other stairs, other routes through this mazelike structure, and Gwilym could personally block no more than one.

*   *   *   *   *

Jarath, still wide awake and uneasy from his earlier inexplicable encounter, looked around sharply as he heard footsteps approaching rapidly. An instant later, Captain Gwilym rounded the corner at the far end of the corridor and came toward him almost at a run.

"Do you have anything to report?" Alek snapped as he came to a stop less than a yard in front of Jarath.

Jarath opened his mouth, the words "Nothing, Captain Gwilym" forming in his mind, but the captain's urgent tone and demeanor brought him up short.

"Well, Jarath?" the captain prompted impatiently. "Have you seen or heard anything at all out of the ordinary?"

Suddenly, despite his determination to keep the nightmarish encounter safely to himself, Jarath found the words pouring out of him in a torrent, as if Captain Gwilym's question had broken through the dam of his reluctance. Even so, he could not help but watch the captain's eyes, dreading the disbelief he knew would fill them as soon as the utter insanity of his story became clear.

But the disbelief never came. Instead, the captain's eyes narrowed as he listened intently, seeming to take in every word without the slightest trace of doubt. When Jarath stumbled into silence, the captain nodded with a frown.

"Come. Show me where this strange duel took place."

Still fearful that the captain was toying with him, giving him an extra allowance of rope for his self-constructed gallows, Jarath led the way quickly down the steps. "There are the remains," he said, pointing.

The captain knelt down, still frowning as he looked closely at the collection of dust and ragged strips of filthy, once-white cloth. Burial shroud, he thought with a shiver as he touched the cloth, his mind going back to the open crypt. A small piece of the cloth disintegrated even as he tried to lift it up for a closer look.

Abruptly he stood. "And the sword?"

"Down there somewhere," Jarath said, looking down into the shadows.

"And you didn't retrieve it?"

"I—I thought it best not to stray any farther from my post."

For the first time, a glint of anger appeared in the

captain's eyes, but then it was gone. "Then we will retrieve it now," he said, striding down into the shadows.

But there was no sword on the steps, nor in the hall at the bottom that led quickly to the barracks, where the rest of the troops still slept.

"Return to your post," the captain said, and Jarath hurried back to the stairs. As he made his way up the steps, he heard the faint sounds of the captain rousing the sleeping guards.

* * * * *

Alek Gwilym, lamp in hand, grimaced as he led the way into the catacombs. Behind him, three of the guards he had roused only minutes before followed nervously. Few bats remained fluttering in the air, most having flown up the air shaft into the outside darkness a hundred yards above. Those that remained scattered before the interlopers.

Keeping his eyes on the floor, Alek could easily see the tracks that appeared first a few feet from the bottom of the stairs, where the bat droppings began in earnest. Only one set moved away from the steps and toward the crypt where Alek had earlier heard the sounds.

But then he saw a second set, these approaching the steps but coming from someplace off to the right.

From the opened crypt, he realized a moment later. Though the realization sent a new chill racing up his spine, it did not surprise him. He had been half expecting something of the sort since he had seen the disintegrating pieces of a burial shroud on the stairs. And both were, he reluctantly admitted to himself, possible confirmation of the suspicions he had for months now tried not to consider seriously.

As such, it deepened the feeling, not of fear but of . . . ominous foreboding that had long been pawing at the edges of his mind. Not that he was ever completely free of such feelings. When one is both friend and protector of one such as Strahd, the lord of the land and, as such, the object of envy and potential plots too numerous to even catalog, such uneasy feelings are everyday companions.

But in recent months, Alek's feelings had taken on a new and even darker dimension, and he had reluctantly begun to look at Strahd as their possible source. And to blame himself to some extent.

Six moons ago, he had, contrary to his own better judgment, presented Strahd with a saddlebag filled with cracked, leather-bound volumes supposedly discovered in the ruins of an ancient monastery in one of the lands whose ruler wished to curry favor with Strahd. "The magic they contain," the royal-robed toady had said, "is far beyond my comprehension, but it is known throughout the land that Lord Strahd is well versed in such things and is always interested in adding to his store of knowledge."

The very presence of the volumes in the saddlebag had seemed to cast a pall over the return trip, with Alek's trusted lieutenants more than once almost coming to blows. If Strahd had not already received word of the existence of the volumes via the toady's own messenger, Alek would have been sorely tempted to drop them into the deepest, swiftest river he crossed. Since then, he had come to wish that he had done so anyway and taken his chances with Strahd's resulting wrath.

For Strahd had become obsessed. Not that he neglected matters of state or any of his other duties. Certainly he had taken a large role in the elaborate preparations for his brother Sergei's wedding, now less than a day away. But still . . .

Strahd's mood had grown darker by the day, and virtually every time Alek had entered Strahd's study, regardless of the hour, he had found him poring over one or more of the volumes, trying to make sense of words in a language neither of them understood. And yet Strahd continued, his frustration growing with each failure to comprehend.

Nor had he responded kindly when Alek asked even the most basic of questions regarding the ancient volumes: "What do you hope to learn from them?" Instead, Strahd had grown angry, angrier even than when a bad decision had been made on a battlefield, costing both time and lives.

And now this.

Alek was torn between two opposing hopes. For the safety of Strahd's physical being, he hoped that whatever had happened here was indeed Strahd's doing, that he had finally penetrated some small secret of the volumes and had plucked that horror the guard had encountered out of its tomb and sent it on its short-lived jaunt. For the safety of Strahd's soul, he hoped that it was the work of another, that it was something he and Strahd could combat together, standing side by side, as they had stood so many times in the past.

But whatever was happening, there was no time to waste. Holding his lantern high, he motioned for the others to follow as he began to trace the other set of footprints, the ones that had entered the catacombs but had not left.

 **TEN**

Barovia
351, Barovian Calendar (continued)

Though mentally exhausted, Azalin was beginning to have real hopes that he would succeed. On his circuitous route up from the nether reaches of the castle, he had encountered, and successfully diverted, no fewer than three guards. And now he was emerging from the last of the stairs into a narrow hallway lined on both sides by alcoves containing more statues of long-dead warriors, supposedly heroes, though the deeds that had earned them such credit were as long-dead as the warriors themselves. At the near end of the hall, a series of secret doors—did Strahd already know of them in this distant past?—led directly to Strahd's bedchamber.

But that was not where Strahd would be, not if Strahd's accounts of this night were true. He would be in the study, poring for one last time over the ancient volumes that Gwilym had procured for him several months earlier.

At the far end of the statue-lined hall, Azalin turned right into the cross corridor that led from the north tower stairs to Strahd's study. The study door, not surprisingly, was closed, and Azalin sent his Sight skimming ahead into the darkened room. And recoiled in sudden terror and despair!

For Strahd was not alone in the pitch-black study.

Time and again, while he and Strahd had searched for a way to escape the mists, while they had struggled to understand how and when and why the mists had first enveloped Strahd and the land he ruled, Strahd had told him of this night.

Death, Strahd said, had come to him in the darkness and offered him eternal life as reward for the thousands of lives he had given over to Death in all his battles and conquests. "*You have fed me well,*" Death had said. "*You are due your reward.*"

And Death—what Strahd had believed was Death—was in the room now, speaking the words that Strahd was hearing for the first time but that Azalin knew by heart.

But Azalin knew it was not the voice of Death that spoke to Strahd.

It was the voice of Azalin's tormentors, those unreachable, untouchable *things* that had, down through the centuries, tricked and betrayed him again and again and laughed at his defeats.

He should have known! Strahd had described them often enough: voices speaking out of the shadows, assuming the tones and cadences of mortal friends and family, promising and promising and never revealing, until too late, the payment that would be exacted.

Or perhaps he *had* known, but had been too cowardly to admit it, even to himself.

Or his tormentors had conspired to *keep* him from knowing! Doubtless they had been listening and laughing as he and Strahd had gone over this night again and again, searching for a reason that didn't exist, for an escape that could never be.

But even they were not omnipotent. There were forces that opposed them, forces that had pointed the way, however obliquely, to this time and place.

And his tormentors had not here given any indication, even now, that they were aware of his presence. How *could* they suspect he was here? He would not be born for another three decades, and they would not even become aware of his existence until nearly a century after that.

No, there was no way they could know who and what he was, not here in this world, in this time.

Which meant that there was still a chance, no matter how slim. For, though Strahd had been offered eternal life, he had not accepted it, *would* not accept it for at least several minutes yet.

There was still a chance, if he could overpower the boy's inevitable resistance for a few short seconds. . . .

My goal is beyond that door, he spoke to the boy's mind. *This is the reason you are here. If you are to suc-ceed, if you ever hope to return to your family, you must surrender your body to me even more fully than you have until now. Do not speak aloud, but indicate that you understand.*

The boy nodded wordlessly, and Azalin could feel the acquiescence.

Whatever happens, you must not resist. Even a moment's resistance by you could mean total failure and eternal damnation for us both.

The boy nodded again. He would, of course, Azalin knew, resist. He could not help it. He had even resisted striking down the horror that had been Azalin's true body when it had feigned to attack the boy in the mists. Azalin's only hope was to grip the boy's mind and body as tightly as possible and accomplish the deed as swiftly as possible, before that inevitable resistance gave Strahd a chance to escape or strike back.

Very well. It is time.

Husbanding his limited strength, Azalin let his hold on the boy purposely loosen as he approached the door. Just outside, he stopped and sent his Sight tentatively into the room once again. Strahd lay sprawled on the floor in total darkness, just as he had described so often. The voices he thought of as Death had made their offer and left him to contemplate—and come to accept—it. Soon someone would approach, someone whose name Strahd had never revealed during any of their long, searching discussions. "It makes no difference," he had said when Azalin asked about it repeatedly. "It matters only that to accept Death's reward, I was required to take yet another life."

For another moment, Azalin stood outside the door, letting the images his Sight was providing burn themselves into his memory. In the darkness, this would give him an advantage, both over Strahd, whose vision was still that of a mortal, and over the boy, who would not be able to see Strahd as the sword was brought down upon his neck.

Bracing himself, Azalin reached out his hand to the door, and . . .

A sound!

Not from Strahd's study but from the stairs that opened into the corridor barely a dozen feet behind him!

Gwilym! His Sight told him the tale an instant later, and he knew he had lost, for the boy had heard the sounds as well and was, despite his vows, turning toward the stairs and the approaching sounds.

Unless . . .

As he had in the catacombs below, Azalin concentrated all his thoughts on Alek Gwilym. . . .

*   *   *   *   *

The footprints led Alek through the filth of the catacombs past a half dozen untouched crypts to a rusting
iron door just short of the back wall. The door was closed
but the bolt was not thrown, and from the wedge of
scrapes on the floor, it was plain that it had been opened
recently.

Alek hesitated. Though he had never entered the tunnel that lay beyond the door, nor been able to fathom its
intended purpose, he knew where it led. He and Strahd,
when first exploring the nether reaches of the castle, had
studied the drawings left behind by Dorian, the previous
master of Castle Ravenloft. The tunnel was treacherous
at best, which under present circumstances was a stroke
of good fortune. A trapdoor in its middle could—if it were
still functional—drop any unwary trespasser into one of
the dungeons a level below the catacombs. With any
luck . . .

"Valmar," he said to one of the guards, "go directly to
the dungeons and see if Lord Strahd has a new prisoner.
If not, spread the word to all the guards that there is likely
an intruder somewhere in the castle. I will notify Lord
Strahd myself."

The guard nodded as he turned and, at a cautious run,
headed back through the catacombs toward the main
stairs. At the same time, Alek sheathed his sword,
grasped the door's rusting bolt, and forced it home, cutting off this avenue to whoever or whatever had passed
through it. He grimaced as he recalled what he and
Strahd had found at the far end of the tunnel: rooms, now
barren and empty, that gave access to what had looked
to Alek very much like a torture chamber. From these
same rooms, one set of stairs led up to a secret door on

the same subterranean level where servants and armsmen were quartered, though again neither Alek nor
Strahd had been able to determine the reason for the
existence of such an arrangement.

A second set of stairs had a more easily discernible
reason for its existence. These stairs, enclosed for their
entire length, led directly from the area of the torture
chamber to what had been Dorian's private quarters,
now Strahd's. And Dorian's reputation was such that
Alek could well believe that the man Strahd had defeated
and killed in the last days of the war would have made
ample use of those stairs and the subterranean rooms to
which they led.

Leading the remaining guards back through the catacombs at only a slightly slower pace than Valmar had
taken moments before, Alek left one of the guards stationed at the bottom of the stairs at the entrance to the
catacombs. With the two remaining guards, Alek hurried
to the next level up, then through the servants' and
guards' halls to the deserted room that concealed the
secret door.

But the room, not having its own colony of bats and
being kept reasonably clean, showed no telltale tracks,
nor any obvious indication that either of the room's doors
had been opened in the recent past. Nor was there any
proof that they had not.

Leaving another guard at the room's outer door, Alek
hurried toward the stairs that led down to the dungeon,
only to be met by Valmar, breathing heavily from his
errand. "The dungeons are still empty, Captain."

Alek had expected—feared—as much. That left the
one other route, the enclosed stair that led directly to
Strahd's study. He thought of racing through the laby-
rinth that led down to the base of those stairs and then

up, but he dismissed it quickly. He had no way of knowing if that was indeed the route that had been taken, and even if it were, whoever or whatever had taken it would have had more than enough time to reach Strahd's quarters.

And Alek still could not know for certain if it was a creature come to harm Strahd or to do his bidding. Either way, there was no time to waste.

Sending Valmar and the other two armsmen down to stand ready at the base of the stairs, Alek raced to the north tower stairs, the most direct route that he knew of to Strahd's quarters. Pausing only long enough at each entrance to the stairs to be recognized by the guards and to warn them of a possible intruder of unknown nature, Alek hurried up the broad stone steps two and three at a time, his hand on his sword hilt to keep the scabbard from slamming repeatedly against his leg.

Within minutes, he was racing up the last flight before Strahd's quarters. The stairs opened on a short corridor that led directly to his goal, Strahd's study.

But as he neared the open archway to the corridor, he slowed, realizing that he was more afraid of finding Strahd in control than of finding him in danger. If he burst in without warning, he could well be adding to Strahd's danger rather than lessening it.

No, he needed to get at least some small idea of what, if anything, was happening before he shoved the study door open and leapt in, waving his sword about.

The overlook . . .

Of course. A few feet beyond the arched opening to the corridor was a second opening, this one leading directly to the courtyard overlook, a walkway with a waist-high parapet that stretched around three sides of Strahd's quarters. Windows would allow him to see into at least three of the rooms, including Strahd's bedchamber. Which was, Alek told himself, where Strahd most likely would be.

And the moonless night, Alek thought, would certainly not betray his spying presence.

If there proved to be nothing to see, if Strahd were simply asleep in his bed, gathering his strength for tomorrow's festivities, Alek would return to the stairs and then enter, as he normally would, through the study door. No one, least of all Strahd, would have to be the wiser about his fears and suspicions.

Almost tiptoeing now, Alek made his way to the archway and stepped out onto the overlook. The mixed aromas of the chapel garden and the stables hung lightly in the moist night air, but moments later they were sent flying by a sudden gust of wind. Looking up, he saw that storm clouds had already enveloped the peaks of Mount Ghakis to the west and would soon be upon the castle.

Hurrying again, Alek reached the corner tower and turned to move toward the series of tall, narrow windows that marked Strahd's bedchamber.

Relief flooded him as he saw only total darkness. Not even a candle flickered within. Strahd was, as Alek had very much hoped, asleep.

But then there was a sound, a muffled cry of anguish, and it came not from Strahd's great bed, almost within reach of the open window before him, but from beyond, from the study, where Strahd had spent the bulk of his life the last six months, ever since Alek had returned with those damnable volumes!

Memories of a lifetime of friendship stabbed at Alek, urging him to take his sword from its scabbard and leap unhesitatingly through the windows, charge through to the study to stand side by side with his longtime master—

his friend—and join him in battling whatever threat might present itself.

But years of battle-bred caution and the vivid memory of what he had just seen in the subterranean reaches of the castle held him back.

And a feeling, unlike anything he had ever felt and yet eerily familiar. More than once he had survived a battle not alone because of his skill or his strength but as well because of a sudden prickling of his skin that caused him to turn in time to fend off a blow already descending. He had seen Strahd do the same, and he had often thought that such feelings were simply the mark of a good arms-man, an instinct possessed by all but heeded by few.

But this was different. It was not a prickling of his skin but a chill that seemed to permeate his entire body, orig-inating within, in his very core. And it inspired in him not a sudden urge to turn and face an unseen attacker but a directionless sense of foreboding, as if the entire sky were turning to darkness and descending upon him.

And then he heard Strahd's voice, barely a whisper, yet as clear as if his lips had been within an inch of Alek's ear.

"What must I do?" it asked, and never had Alek heard such desperation, such resignation, in anyone's voice, certainly not in Strahd's.

And yet he held fast in his concealment, listening, waiting for he knew not what, while all he could hear was Strahd's breathing, strangely loud in the silence.

For what seemed forever, Alek stood frozen outside the window, barely aware of the rising wind.

Until finally the scratch of flint against iron came, fol-lowed an instant later by a tiny flickering flame of a tinder in Strahd's hand, then a steadier one as a candle was lit, then another and another.

Alek had to suppress a gasp as Strahd, tiredly looking about the study, as if needing to confirm its very existence, turned briefly toward the windows where Alek stood hidden. In the bare hours since Strahd had risen from the dining table and retired for the evening to his quarters, his darkly handsome face had become more haggard and lined than Alek had ever seen it. Sweat beaded his brow despite the suddenly chill air that swept down Mount Ghakis and into Strahd's chambers.

And the face was filled with the same resignation Alek had heard in the whispered sound of his voice.

The pit of Alek's stomach was suddenly leaden, as it often had been on the battlefield when a valued comrade had fallen, but this time it was far worse. On the battlefield, there was a chance for vengeance, bringing new strength to the tiredest limbs, new purpose and determination to the most exhausted mind.

But not here, not now. For this there could be no vengeance. This, Alek knew with utter certainty, was not the doing of Strahd's enemies. Strahd would not show this face to any foe, be it swordsman or sorcerer. Even if he were forced to his knees before a headsman's axe, his features would be fixed in defiance, not resignation. He would either remain pridefully silent or burn his executioner's ears with his words. He would never plead with an enemy as he had pleaded here, with a whispered, "What must I do?"

Never.

This was Strahd's own doing, whatever it was. He had succumbed to some terrible temptation that no mortal could resist, and now . . .

I should have thrown those damnable volumes into the flames when I had the chance! Strahd's rage at such disobedience would have been less painful than this. Even death at his master's hands . . .

Unable to bear witness to the spectacle any longer, unable either to help his friend or to forgive himself, Alek pushed away from the windows toward the south tower stairs—and was almost deafened by the sudden scrape of metal against stone!

His scabbard! In his pain, he had added unforgivable carelessness to his sins, and now Strahd would . . .

Even as he turned back to face in the direction of the windows, he heard Strahd racing from the study, heard the snick of a sword, probably the one he kept within reach on the wall above the head of the bed, being drawn. As he drew his own and put it up in a purely defensive position, Strahd burst through the window.

Their eyes met in the starlit darkness. Alek braced himself as the winds of the coming storm gusted into the keep with sudden violence. Gone was the look of resignation that had dominated Strahd's features minutes before. Instead, there was slit-eyed suspicion, as there was wariness in his own. Was this still fully his friend who stood before him? Or had some horror discovered in those damnable volumes already begun to devour his soul?

"My lord?" Alek said, unable to keep the questioning tone from creeping into his voice. "Forgive me, but I came to tell you—"

He broke off as Strahd, his blade held ready, strode quickly forward, stopping barely a pace short of Alek. "What?" Strahd demanded.

Alek flinched at the tone, at the dark look of suspicion he saw in Strahd's eyes. It was not a look he had ever seen there before.

Without warning, Strahd whipped his blade up, slashing at Alek's head. Only the younger man's lightning reflexes saved him as his parry struck sparks from the blades, and he fell back a pace.

"No, Strahd! Do not—"

But the man—if man he still was—was deaf to Alek's shout, deaf to reason. Again the sword lashed out; again sparks flew as Alek parried and fell back.

"Strahd, I beg of you, there is no need for this!" Alek pleaded, but a balance-threatening gust of wind, as if summoned up by his adversary, seemed to rip the words from his lips and send them, fluttering and unheard, into the darkness of the gathering storm.

Darting a glance behind him, Alek saw that the corner turret was only a few feet behind him, the arch to its stairs open to a shout or a retreat. A guard, posted there by Alek bare hours earlier, was only a floor below.

But he had been placed there to protect Lord Strahd! If he was summoned and saw the battle under way . . .

Another flurry of thrusts and parries and feints, and Strahd had somehow maneuvered past Alek, cutting him off from the stairs.

"Don't do this, old friend," Alek implored. "You must resist this thing that is in you!"

But Strahd was not listening. Even if he heard the words over the rising wind and the clash of swords, they meant nothing to him—or to whatever it was that looked out through his eyes.

With Strahd's next attack, Alek, his heart breaking, abandoned his purely defensive stance and countered with full force. Countless times they had battled through practice matches with blunted blades, only to clap their arms about each other in boisterous laughter as one or the other failed to parry what would in true battle be a deadly thrust. But here there were no blunted blades, no thrusts intentionally halted inches from their intended mark. The only pause was not to exchange knowing or challenging smiles but to throw the other off-balance or to gather new strength.

Strahd's features, unlike Alek's, showed no trace of regret. As the lightning flashed above the heights of Mount Ghakis behind Alek, he could see Strahd's face take on the kind of berserker joy that sometimes came over him in the heat of battle.

Alek knew he had no choice but to abandon all thoughts that this thing before him had once been his friend and summon up that same furious energy and ruthlessness himself if he hoped to survive. With a practiced move, Alek drew his parrying dagger with his free hand. For a moment Strahd grow more wary, but then he redoubled his attack.

Then the rain struck, lightly, tentatively for a few brief seconds and, with a deafening clash of almost simultaneous lightning and thunder, became a deluge, blinding them both until they could blink the water from their eyes.

Thankful for the gloves that gave him a firmer grip on his weapons than Strahd's bare, rain-soaked hands, Alek struck and could almost feel Strahd's blade slip in his hand as he desperately parried. For a moment hope flashed through Alek, and he darted in with a lunge and twist, trying to break Strahd's grip completely. If only he could disarm him, perhaps then . . .

But Strahd kept his grip, though his arm was forced wide, and Alek instinctively lunged with the dagger.

And felt it penetrate, as if slicing into a ripe melon.

Instantly Alek pulled back, withdrawing the dagger. A lightning flash showed him a red stain already spreading out like death across his master's sodden white shirt, plastered to the skin beneath it by the pelting rain and now by his lifeblood.

But instead of the surge of triumph he would have felt on any battlefield at the sight of such a wound in an enemy, Alek felt only a sudden leaden weight in his stomach and heart.

For a moment that seemed to stretch into eternity as the rain pounded down on them both, Strahd did not seem aware of the injury. Then, in a flash of lightning that likewise took an eternity to build to its ultimate brilliance, his eyes went down and he saw the spreading crimson.

And he knew, just as Alek knew.

They had both seen such wounds a dozen times, and both knew the only possible outcome.

Pain appeared in Strahd's eyes, and then disbelief as they raised and met Alek's. His knees began to buckle.

Alek's soul was in turmoil. He had won. He had survived. But he had slain the man he was oath-bound to protect, the man who had been his truest friend for nearly two decades.

Until tonight.

Then, as Strahd began to fall, the pain and disbelief in his eyes turned to hate, and Alek knew it was not Strahd alone who was dying before him.

Impossibly, as if the creature within Strahd gave him a final moment of strength, the dying man thrust his blade out even as he fell.

Alek, his reflexes slowed by the conflict that raged within him, brought the dagger around to parry—but too late. He felt a blow to his stomach but knew it was more than a blow. A moment later, as his parrying dagger clashed against the embedded sword, the lead that had seemed to fill his stomach was replaced by jagged fire.

With a cruel twist, Strahd pulled the blade free and continued to fall, landing on his side, his knees pulling up almost to his chest as if to stanch the blood that still spilled out of his own wound to mix with the rain.

Alek grunted and fell with a thud to a sitting position, sword still in his hand. Still lucid, he felt a sudden urge to use every ounce of his remaining strength to raise his own sword and bring it down on Strahd's now defenseless neck.

But he did not. He *would* not. Strahd was dying—they were *both* dying, and dying quickly—and he would not compound his already grievous offense by one final act of anger and pointless vindictiveness.

Instead, he let go of his weapon and sank gently onto the rain-battered walk, as though settling for sleep in his own bed.

ELEVEN

Barovia
351, Barovian Calendar (continued)

As Azalin felt the last flickers of life draining from Alek Gwilym's body, he turned his concentrated thoughts from the dying man to Oldar. Gripping the boy's mind as tightly as he could, Azalin sent him racing through the study and bed-chamber and out through one of the tall, narrow windows onto the rainswept walk. The boy lurched to a halt, almost tripping over Strahd, who still breathed heavily but was barely able to move. Pulling the sword from its scabbard at the boy's waist, Azalin raised it above the boy's head, but when he was about to bring it down on Strahd's defenseless neck, the boy stiffened, and his body, caught in the struggle between two wills, lurched backward, slipping and falling on the rain-slick walk, the sword clattering down and skittering halfway to the corner tower a dozen yards away.

And still Strahd held on to an ember of life!

Desperately Azalin fled the boy's body, as he had in the catacombs, and flowed with his Sight into Alek Gwilym's. And felt the body around him, as firmly as he had felt his own before he had tricked the boy into destroying it.

Gwilym's sword was within inches of the hand that had dropped it. Surely even the massive limitations imposed on him in this time and this place would still allow him the strength to . . .

Too late, Azalin realized that Gwilym, like Strahd, still kept a stubborn grip on the remnants of life.

The body was not a freshly dead corpse, emptied of its lifelong inhabitant and ready now to be filled by another. It was still Alek Gwilym, and Azalin could no more control it now than he had been able to before. He could only concentrate as he had when he had gently nudged Gwilym ever deeper into his mistrust of Strahd, ever closer to the mortal duel that had finally come about. And now that he had directly invaded Gwilym's body and mind, even that influence was gone. For Gwilym was now aware of Azalin's presence, becoming more aware by the second of what Azalin had done and what he was still trying to do. And resisting even more strongly than Oldar had, despite, or perhaps because of, his rapidly approaching death.

For what seemed like forever, Azalin continued to struggle, feeling the agony of Gwilym's wound, feeling the rain pounding on his face and hands and body but unable to break the other's hold and set that body into motion.

Finally he surrendered, and Gwilym's body was suddenly a boneless sack of flesh as the two opposing wills ceased their tug-of-war.

And Azalin himself relaxed with a mental sigh as he realized there was, after all, no real reason to continue other than his own ego and his desire to personally destroy Strahd. He had already won. Strahd, though he still clung to life, could not do so for long, and that was all that mattered, not that he personally deliver the *coup de grace*.

As he relaxed, waiting for death to claim Strahd in its own good time, his mind drifted back across the centuries to the night the mists had first deposited him in Barovia. And he wondered: If I was right, if Hyskosa was right, if those lands now never come into existence, will I, too, cease to exist?

And even as he wondered, it seemed to him that the memories of those years—the memories of all the years and centuries in Barovia and Darkon—began to become less vivid, less real. Was this the way it was going to be? And if he survived in some form, in some place, would he remember any of this?

As his mind turned such thoughts over and over, he heard a faint whisper of a voice over the rain that still pelted down on Gwilym's barely living body. A voice that spoke, he realized with a jolt beside which the pain of Gwilym's wound was as nothing, directly into his mind, even as it spoke into Strahd's.

Don't you want to live, Strahd? it asked, and the voice was that of Alek Gwilym.

His tormentors! They were here!

Then another voice, this in the tones of a young woman he had never heard: Don't you want to live?

Live? A man's voice, young and gentle.

Live? A woman, older, sterner.

And then Strahd, weakly mouthing the words aloud: "Yes . . . damn you!"

Laughter then, not from one but from a multitude of voices, laughter that Azalin had grown to know—and hate!—over the centuries.

And then: You know what to do.

Azalin—and Gwilym—heard the wet rustling of clothes, the scrape of boots and fingers as Strahd stirred and tried vainly to raise himself and then began to cross the few feet between them the only way he could: on his belly, his blood doubtless mixing with the rain and dirt as the wound scraped on the walkway.

And still Gwilym clung to the last dregs of life. He forced his eyes open, rolled them toward the approaching sounds. Azalin could feel the blood filling Gwilym's mouth and spilling from the corner where his cheek lay pressed against the walkway.

"Didn't have to, my lord," Gwilym managed to force out.

Strahd, only inches away now, said nothing.

"I'd have helped you . . . no matter what," Gwilym said between shallow, painful breaths. "This . . . did not . . . have to be."

Strahd found the strength to grimace. "I'm afraid it did."

Then Gwilym was choking on his own blood, coughing, regaining the power of speech. But his mind, Azalin saw, was beginning to drift as death came ever closer. "Should have let me die on the mountain," Gwilym murmured weakly, "spared me from seeing this."

"Alek—"

Gwilym's hand spasmed up and clutched at Strahd's shirt but couldn't hold. His mouth filled again with blood, his mind with vivid flashes of memory but no sense of time or place. Azalin waited for death to take its final step.

"Traitor in . . . the camp . . ." A dying mind, wandering ever farther afield. "Ba'al Verzi . . ." Images of other places, other deaths danced through his fading mind.

The shallow breathing was done, the heart barely fluttering, and yet death was not complete.

And Strahd was fumbling weakly at Gwilym's belt. A moment later, his hand appeared before Gwilym's eyes, and Azalin saw in it the dagger he had pulled from the belt, though he doubted that Gwilym did.

In sudden terror, Azalin knew what it was the voices had meant when they had said to Strahd: *You know what to do.* He saw the meaning in Strahd's eyes, then in his mind.

Once again Azalin was fighting frantically to gain some control over Gwilym's body, anything to prevent Strahd from . . .

He felt the dagger slice effortlessly through Gwilym's throat, felt the blood gush out, saw Strahd's waiting mouth, saw him drink and gain new strength and a new form of life even as the old life drained away to nothing.

Behind Strahd, far down the rain-pelted walkway near the corner turret, Azalin saw the rain seem to gather and solidify, but it was the mists, he realized. Even as Strahd's eyes glowed ever brighter with renewed vitality, the mists gathered around Oldar, still standing as if paralyzed.

And the boy was gone, swallowed up by the mists. The phylactery, enfolded within his chest, was gone. Only tendrils of mist remained, tendrils that swirled and stretched out toward Azalin as the voices of his tormentors united in a chorus of laughter that he knew both he and Strahd could hear.

He had failed.

No, he realized with an overwhelming rush of despair even greater than when his son had risen from his sarcophagus to reveal the grotesque parody of life his doting father had conferred upon the boy. He had done far worse than simply fail. He had brought about the very thing he had come to this time and place to prevent. Without his misguided attempt to use the ancient body from the catacombs, Gwilym would never have become so suspicious and would never have come racing to Strahd's quarters just as Strahd was learning of the depths to which he must sink if he truly desired to live forever. Without Azalin's mental urging, Gwilym would never have drawn his sword against his friend and master, would not have died under Strahd's blade only to provide the very thing that Strahd required to gain both eternal life and eternal damnation: the lifeblood of his most loyal comrade and friend.

And the mists were upon him, billowing in from the edges of his vision to meet the wavering tendrils that danced before him. In seconds, he was enveloped in blinding whiteness, and he felt himself being pulled free of Gwilym's body, could see it receding through the mists. Desperately he tried to keep his grip, still hoping that, miraculously, the body would suddenly respond to his exhortations.

But then it was gone, and with it Strahd and the rain and the walkway and all of Castle Ravenloft.

And his hopes.

All that remained as he floated helplessly through the mists was the endless laughter of his tormentors.

*   *   *   *   *

With neither heart nor breath to mark the passage of time, Azalin could only wonder whether seconds or days or centuries were passing, or whether time had any meaning here in the mists. The only evidence that time was indeed passing was the gradually increasing control he gained over the rage and despair that had at first made chaos of his thoughts.

But when he finally began to set those thoughts in order, he also began to fear what would happen when—

if—the mists cleared and deposited him—somewhere. The body he had been clinging to—the body his mind still reached out to—was most likely still in Strahd's castle, which was, along with Strahd himself and all of Barovia, sliding through the mists toward—what? And his phylactery, the only refuge where he could exist independent of a body, was—where? Oldar, in whose body it was enfolded, had vanished into the mists, possibly to be transported back to Darkon or to some other, deeper hell. Or simply snuffed out of existence.

And if Azalin emerged from the mist with neither body nor phylactery within reach . . .

Would he emerge? Or was he trapped here forever?

No!

The very thought was unacceptable! To think in such a way was to give up all hope, and that he would never do as long as he was capable of thought.

As if in answer, he felt a faint tug, as if something were calling for his attention.

But there was nothing around him but the mists, seen not through his nonexistent eyes but through something that, he abruptly realized, felt very much like his Sight.

Had that been true before? He didn't know.

The tugging returned, strengthened, and he realized it did indeed feel much like when his Sight was being drawn back to his body. There was even a sense of motion, despite the total featurelessness of the mists.

Then, in an instant, he was not in the impenetrable whiteness of the mists but in darkness.

But only for a moment.

He was once again in a body, a body over which he had full control. A room sprang into shadowy view around him. He was lying on a floor, his head pressed hard against a wall, his neck twisted at an unnatural angle.

Clothes of every description filled the space above him.

Bringing his right hand up to his throat, he felt the parted flesh and knew with sudden elation that it was Alek Gwilym's body. His grip on it had been so strong that even the mists had not been able to tear it loose!

And now he had been rejoined to it!

How much time had passed? Was Strahd's transformation complete? Was there still a chance that the transformation and everything that followed could be aborted? The fact that Strahd had apparently hidden Gwilym's body in what must be Strahd's closet must mean that he was still not all-powerful. And Strahd himself had more than once said that the transformation took several hours to complete.

Lurching to his feet, Azalin saw a pair of windows in the wall his head had been pressed against. Still dark, but with the faint sparkle of starlight. The storm had passed but dawn had not yet come.

Sweeping aside a heavy curtain, he found himself in Strahd's dressing room. As dark as the closet, but still he could see that it was empty.

Silently crossing the room, he eased open the double doors that nearly filled the opposite wall.

Strahd's bedchamber, candles all snuffed out, lay before him. And in the huge canopied bed . . .

Strahd!

Sprawled beneath the covers, the Lord of Barovia lay as if dead. He made not the slightest movement in response to the sound of the doors or of Azalin's footsteps as he crossed the floor. But still he breathed, still his heart beat faintly in his chest. Obviously the transformation was not complete, else Strahd would be fully awake, his senses preternaturally sharp, his heart and breath both stilled.

A sword—the sword with which Strahd had slain his friend?—hung on the wall next to the bed. Azalin reached for the weapon, hardly able to believe this sudden turn in his fortunes. A single stroke, severing head from shoulders, would suffice, no matter how far the transformation had progressed.

But even as his fingers closed around the hilt, a flicker of white brushed at the sides of his vision, and he darted a look toward the windows, hoping it was a distant lightning stroke, the lingering remnant of a dying storm.

In the same moment, something tugged at him, just as it had moments before in the mists, but this time . . .

Yanking the sword from the wall, he raised it high as he turned toward the bed.

And the flicker of white came again, but this time it was not a single flicker but was followed by a rush, as if floodgates had been opened, and even as he began a frantically hurried downward stroke with the blade, the mists enveloped him, and the fingers that had been gripping the hilt of the sword suddenly closed on nothingness.

As if from a great distance, he heard the muffled sound of the sword clattering to the floor.

Then nothing, no sound, no sight but the endless, smothering whiteness of the mists.

Not even the laughter of his tormentors, though he knew they could not be far away as they added this final twist of the knife in his soul.

INTERLUDE

Barovia
735, Barovian Calendar

When the mists cleared, the lone Vistana found himself in a place he had never been, yet a place that he instantly recognized. Looming high on a mountainside nearly a mile distant stood Castle Ravenloft, home to Count Strahd von Zarovich, Lord of Barovia. Though the Vistana had never seen the castle itself, had never even been in Barovia, the massive structure was unmistakable.

He had heard it described a hundred times around the campfires when the story of the exodus from Barovia was told, and he had seen it in his dreams, dreams he had always suspected were visions given him by his many-times-great grandfather, whose brief imprisonment in the castle's deepest, most spell-guarded dungeon had sparked the Vistani exodus.

But why? Why was he now here, of all places?

He had entered the mists, as had countless Vistani before him, in search of a vision, a vision that all hoped would point the way for all Vistani to return to the Home Forge, to the land their ancestors had left and lost centuries ago.

But he had failed. No visions had come.

Or had they? For an instant, a chaos of images flickered at the edges of his mind like distant lightning just below the horizon, but then they were gone, and no amount of struggle or concentration could bring them back.

Wishful thinking, he told himself sternly. He so desperately *wanted* a vision that his own traitorous mind was not above trying to provide at least a hint of one.

Or perhaps he *had* been given one, but now it was forgotten.

Or it had been taken from him. . . .

No! he told himself sharply, shaking his head as if to clear it of such foolishness. I will make no feeble excuses. I will return to my people, and I will confess my failure.

Abruptly he turned his back on the distant castle and began picking his way through the trees toward, he hoped, the nearest road that led back to his people.

PART II

THE FINAL SEARCH

 **TWELVE**

Darkon
740, Barovian Calendar

Oldar blinked and shook his head as he looked up
from the tombstone with his own name carved deep into
the weathered surface. How long had he been standing
there, lost in the memories of the dreams that had
brought him here?

With a shiver, he realized he didn't know.

He also realized he had been a fool to come here hoping for answers. Dreams were just dreams. It didn't matter what his half-Vistani mother might sometimes say.
Nor did it matter what Oldar himself might think for a few
brief moments each time he awakened from ludicrous
but frightening dreams of death on a rain-swept castle
parapet, or of a rushing stream of water that glowed like
a million fireflies as it rose out of the forest floor, or of an
all-encompassing fog that flowed out of nowhere to
envelop him.

Nor even did it matter that his long-dead namesake
had in those dreams risen like an insubstantial mist from
his grave, calling to Oldar across more than a century.

Dreams were just dreams, but if he tarried any longer,

the trip back to his home might become not a dream but a nightmare, most likely his last. The protection his family enjoyed, supposedly because of some unspecified service his namesake had performed for Lord Azalin a century and a half ago, did not extend beyond the boundaries of their small farm, and being abroad after sundown anywhere in Darkon was considered foolhardy at best.

Pulling his ragged woolen cloak closer about his shoulders, Oldar turned from the unkempt grave and picked his way through the tangle of weeds and brush and fallen headstones to the rutted road that crept through the woods and past the remnants of the graveyard toward home.

A hundred yards along the road, he paused, frowning as he looked around. For an instant he thought he had heard the sound of hooves coming from somewhere ahead, beyond where the narrow road curved around an oak with low-hanging branches.

But there was nothing, just a fading memory of something that had never been, except perhaps in his dreams.

Shrugging his shoulders to rid them of a sudden tingling chill that penetrated his cloak as if it didn't exist, Oldar lowered his eyes to the ground and began the long trudge home.

* * * * *

Balitor awoke in a cold sweat, his heart pounding, the fading image of his long-dead friend Oldar hanging in the darkness of the bedroom. For a long time he forced himself to lie still while his heart slowed and he tried to think what could have prompted such a nightmare. It had been nearly a century since he had last consciously thought of the boy, much less of the man he had become. Occasionally, with a twinge of envy, he had thought of Oldar's peaceful death, but never for long. It only reminded him—as if he needed reminding—that two hundred years is a very long time and that each year seemed longer than the last.

And this nightmare was unlike any he had experienced before. For years, he had been plagued by grisly images of the deaths—the sadistic executions—he had been forced to witness in the Great Hall of Avernus and by the fear that, if he displeased Lord Azalin in some way, such a death would be only a prelude to his real punishment.

But this one . . .

In this one he was once again with Oldar, the boy seemingly no older than he had been a century and a half ago. They were on the road from Il Aluk to Avernus when the mists rose up and enveloped them and . . .

He shivered as he felt their cold, clammy touch and wondered how something that had never happened could seem so frighteningly real.

*   *   *   *   *

This time it seemed to the furiously resisting Azalin that the mists had barely closed about him when they turned to tatters and began to swirl away from him. For just an instant, before they vanished utterly, hope surged through him. Earlier this night he had clung to Gwilym's body with such intensity and determination that even the mists had not been able to tear him free. He had returned to that body, but before he had a chance to act . . .

Was it possible that his grip on that time and place was such that he could not be torn free of that, either? Had his willpower broken the grip of the mists themselves, letting him return yet again?

In the instant the mists vanished, his hope turned to fury and despair. He was not in Strahd's bedchamber but once more in Darkon, where he almost certainly was once again a prisoner.

And, as if to give the knife in his soul yet another sadistic twist, the mists had returned him to the one place he least wanted to be: within the room that held his son's sarcophagus. The wraith that pretended to be his son hovered next to the sarcophagus, as fully formed as Azalin had ever seen it, its hands reaching out as if to pluck at his sleeves.

But at least, he realized grimly as he glanced down to where the phantom hands brushed at him, he was still in the body of Alek Gwilym, not the decaying horror that he had inhabited for more than two and a half centuries.

And he *had* gained one crucial insight into his condition, an insight that could eventually lead to his escape: It was the *body* that he inhabited that was held prisoner by the mists. The essence that was Azalin, unfettered by a body, could journey as freely through the mists as the Vistani. But until he found a way to be permanently free of a corporeal shell, with no need of a phylactery or any other physical refuge . . .

Abruptly an image of the rain-swept parapet where Gwilym had died filled his mind, and fear shot through him as he saw the boy Oldar swallowed up by the mists.

Turning from the wraith, Azalin raced from the room and up the tower stairs, past one landing, past a massive timbered door, past another landing and yet another until . . .

Abruptly he halted on the uppermost landing, just before the stair made one final loop and emerged onto the tower roof. For one quivering moment, he stared at the massive oaken door with its huge symbolic eye of beaten silver surrounding the blood-red luminous ruby that served as its pupil. Beyond that door . . .

In a single motion, he swung the door open and stepped inside onto the gritty stone floor.

Everything was the same as when he had last left this huge circular room—a day ago? a century ago?—except for one. The paintings, with their grim depictions of three and a half centuries of his past, still clung to the walls. A waist-high stone pedestal, round and smoothly polished, still stood in the very center of the room. And on that pedestal sat the massive golden skull of a horned dragon.

His phylactery.

A mixture of relief and angry puzzlement swept over him.

Relief because the phylactery was there as it had been for over a century and a half, available to him should he require it.

Puzzlement because it should *not* be there.

Stretching his sorcery to its limit, he had transformed the phylactery and folded it into a tiny object that barely existed in this plane and then embedded it in young Oldar's body. And Oldar had . . .

For a moment, the memory refused to come. Oldar? Oldar had died a century ago. He remembered notifying the boy's friend Balitor; he remembered regretting Oldar's decision a century and a half ago to forgo the bulk of the rewards he had been offered; he remembered . . .

No! That was not *this* Oldar. That was another Oldar, the ancestor of the one he was trying to remember now.

And then memory crept back into his mind: *This* Oldar was a boy in his late teens, living with his family on the same small farm his ancestor had returned to long ago. He had sent Balitor to fetch the boy. He had spoken with him in Balitor's home, had embedded the transformed phylactery in his chest, retreated into it when the boy had been tricked into destroying the decaying *thing* that had been Azalin for two and a half centuries, somehow traveled through the mists to Barovia and a time before his own birth in order to . . .

In order to *what?*

Fear gripped him as, for an interminable moment, he was unable to remember either how or why he had journeyed back in time through the mists.

But then the image of a black-clad Vistana flashed through his mind, and it all came flooding back: Hyskosa the Seer's obscure vision, everything!

His tormentors!

They were behind this! They were trying to make him forget it all, make him forget he had been able to escape through the mists, even momentarily!

But they would not succeed!

Clinging fast to his memories, he raced down through the maze of Avernus to the dungeon where Hyskosa was held.

But the dungeon was empty. There had been no one there to disturb the dust for months or even years.

But he was not beaten yet.

Concentrating, he reached out to the unburied dead throughout Darkon and peered out through their eyes. One, a child barely into his teens when he had been crushed beneath the wheels of a Rivalis noble's coach only days before, stirred on the banks of the Vuchar where a servant had tossed the body out of sight. Beyond the trees that lined the bank, a campfire glowed and flickered.

Good, Azalin thought as he focused all his attention on this one body and carefully freed it from the tangle of weeds and vines that had begun to ensnare it at the water's edge. The Vistani were just the ones he wanted to speak with. As he finally urged the boy's body to its feet, he thought for a moment of disguising the ravages the water and the insects had inflicted on its features, but he quickly discarded the idea of such a subterfuge. Most Vistani would recognize the body for what it was, and under the circumstances, that was best. It would serve as a convenient reminder of his power.

A half dozen pairs of eyes turned toward him, glittering in the campfire, as he walked the body through the line of trees and into the clearing. Two colorful, round-topped Vistani wagons faced away from the campfire, short sets of steps leading up to narrow doors in the backs of the wagons. Four horses stood untethered near the wagons, quietly grazing.

No one spoke as he approached the fire, the condition of the body becoming more obvious with each step. A young man, mustached and wearing a red and green bandanna wrapped tightly around his head, swallowed in obvious nervousness and lowered his eyes to the fire. A woman who might have been seventy or a hundred and seventy despite eyes that could have graced the face of her granddaughter flowed smoothly to her feet, her lower limbs hidden beneath a full black skirt.

"Tend to the horses, Carlito," she said to the bowed head of the young man. "They will need reassurance while our visitor remains."

Gratefully the man sprang to his feet and half ran to where the horses were beginning to shift nervously. Taking all four sets of reins in his hands, he led them slowly to the far side of the clearing, murmuring calming sounds as he went, seemingly speaking to himself as much as to the animals.

Azalin halted the body a dozen feet from the campfire,

its discolored, bloated features plainly visible in the flickering light. Experimentally he moved the lips and tongue
and found them still serviceable.

"I seek the whereabouts of the Seer Hyskosa," he said,
the voice deeper than the boy's had ever been in life.
One of the horses whinnied and flared its nostrils as the
young man tightened his grip on the reins with one hand
and gently stroked the horse's flank with the other.

"There is no Vistani seer of that name, Lord Azalin,"
the young-eyed woman said, "except occasionally in our
dreams."

"And what do your dreams say of him?"

"That he prophesied the Vistani would someday find
their way to the Home Forge, that these lands we exiles
now travel would come to an end. But obviously they are
only dreams, Lord Azalin."

Obviously . . . to everyone but him. Whatever had been
at work on his own memories had been more successful
with others. His tormentors? If they were capable of this,
of transforming the memories even of the Vistani . . .

Finally he nodded. "Only dreams," he said. He waited
another moment, peering into the memories of the boy
whose body he controlled. Somewhere a family still
awaited his return.

"Deliver this body to Lord Voros," he said, naming the
noble whose carriage had run the boy down. "Tell him to
live up to his responsibility to the boy's family if he does
not wish to deal with me."

A faint smile seemed to flicker across the young-eyed
woman's face. "It will be our pleasure, Lord Azalin."

Releasing the body to crumple to the ground, he let
himself be drawn back to Avernus and the unoccupied
dungeon cell.

"Only dreams . . ." he murmured again.

And he wondered: If I had succeeded, if I had slain Strahd and prevented this land from ever being formed . . . would I still exist? And if I did, would I remember what I had done? Or would it—would my entire existence— become a fading dream? As Hyskosa's existence had apparently become to the Vistani?

His mind began to spin. Were his *present* memories real? He remembered going back four centuries through the mists in order to kill Strahd, to prevent his transformation and the theft of his land by the mists, but he also remembered that in reality he had then become instrumental in *causing* that transformation. If he had *not* gone back . . .

For an instant he thought of finding Oldar again, of having *this* body destroyed and then reentering the mists and trying to repeat everything he had already tried, and then he thought of trying to go back not four centuries but four years or even four *days* and warning his earlier self *not* to return through the mists or to return to a still earlier time or to . . .

No! Such thoughts were sheer nonsense! First, there was no reason to believe that he *could* once again find his way through the mists to another time. In all likelihood, it was not he but his tormentors who had guided him this time. They were still playing with him, giving him hope and snatching it away and plunging him ever deeper into despair, tricking him into doing the very thing he most wanted to prevent!

And making a desperate, unthought-out attempt either to undo what he had just done or to do it a second time, differently, would only play into their hands. Doubtless they were waiting, ready to turn on its head whatever he tried to do, just as they had done for at least two and a half centuries.

But why? Why had he been selected for this attention? Surely they had a reason. There had been a reason for their dealings with Strahd, or so Strahd had believed.

"*I gave them my soul,*" the vampire lord had long ago confided to Azalin more than once, "*but they took not only that but the land to which it was bound.*"

None but Strahd, perhaps through his magic, perhaps through sheer force of his spirit and his blood, had been capable of forging such an unbreakable bond with the land.

"*I am Strahd. I am the land,*" he had intoned on the day of his conquest, blood drawn by his own dagger dripping onto the Barovian ground at his feet. "*I, Strahd, am the land.*"

And so it had been from that time on.

And that had been their reason: to draw Strahd and all of Barovia into the mists. And once that had been done, once a single land was imprisoned within the mists, once that seed had been sown, that foundation laid, other lands became easy to summon and imprison.

Or so Azalin reasoned, though he had yet to imagine what higher purpose there was to such imprisonments, unless they were simply the kinds of games the gods played, with whole lands and people taking the role of mere pawns, good only for the amusement of their manipulators.

But even so, why had his tormentors attached themselves to Azalin, to the human sorcerer Firan Zal'honan?

And what had they gotten from this last exercise in futility, if that is indeed what it was?

He didn't know and, as yet, could not imagine. But no one, not even the gods, did anything without a purpose.

He would, he vowed, discover that purpose. He would not again fall into their trap. He would not immediately strike out in an attempt to rectify his mistakes. He would take his time, for that was the one thing his tormentors had given him that worked to his advantage: time.

He would analyze his every decision, his every act that had the slightest connection to his tormentors, and he would, in the end, deduce the truth—if such truth existed—of what it was they wanted from him.

Then and only then would he act.

With a final look at the empty dungeon cell, he sent the door crashing shut, as if he were slamming the door on his past rashness, and began to contemplate his plans as he climbed the stairs.

But whatever shape those plans would eventually take, the first step was obvious and inevitable.

*   *   *   *   *

Bracing himself against the agony he knew was coming, Azalin pushed open the darkly glowing bronze door and stepped from the stair landing into the greenish yellow glow that permeated the room, seeping from the walls like a ghostly discharge from an infected wound. But the expected pain didn't come. Whenever he had entered this room previously, agony had gripped every square inch of his body like a blanket of fire. But this time there was nothing, except . . .

His hands went to his throat—to Alek Gwilym's throat—as he felt Strahd once again draw his blade through the unresisting flesh and lean close to drink the gushing blood. Then he doubled over, hands clutching his stomach as Strahd once more drove his sword home, twisting cruelly as he withdrew it.

But there was no Strahd here except in Azalin's mind, and there was no blood. And even as he straightened, he could feel the wounds closing, could feel the pain lessening, until . . .

Like an alien animal that had burrowed into his chest and had only now awakened, his heart pulsed once, then again.

And his lungs . . .

After one aching gasp, he felt for the first time in centuries the sensation of air rushing into his lungs.

And the pain of the wounds was gone with the wounds themselves. He—this body he now inhabited—was once again alive!

Exhilaration welled up inside him, the first genuine emotion, the first true physical sensation he had experienced in centuries.

But the joy was short-lived. Within seconds it turned to despair and anger as he realized what was happening to him. For what was happening now was undoubtedly the same thing that had happened to him those other times he had entered this room: The body he inhabited was being restored by whatever incomprehensible power saturated this room.

But those other times, beneath whatever illusion he had maintained, the body being restored had been that of Firan Zal'honan, a long-dead corpse half eaten away by decay. It was little wonder, then, that he had been engulfed in searing pain: a preternaturally conscious mind trapped in a body that was nothing but bone and shreds of rotting flesh as its senses, starting with that of touch, were restored. Second had come the overwhelming nausea, what he had thought of as the second stage in an escalating series of agonies, which meant only that the forces had been reaching deeper and beginning to restore his inner organs, originally destroyed by the impossibly revolting brew he had forced himself to drink to end his natural life and begin his endless living death.

But this time the body was that of Alek Gwilym, still
sound but for the wounds that had killed him. It had not
lain for days or months before being reclaimed. And now
those wounds had been closed, life restored.

But only as long as he remained in this room.

For a time he simply stood there, unable to keep from
luxuriating in the unalloyed pleasure of once again being
alive.

But then the anger and despair reasserted themselves.
I could have had this at any time in the last century and a
half, he thought grimly.

All he had had to do was eliminate his Firan body and
occupy a less ravaged one, one that had been dead not a
month or a year or a century but an hour.

Or, had he only had sufficient determination—sufficient *courage!*—he could have forced himself to with-
stand the escalating agony for another minute, even
another hour, and even *that* body would once again have
been made whole. The pain would have been at an end.

I could have restored my son to true life! The thought
hit him like an overwhelming physical blow. He would
have had to remain in this one room in order to maintain
that life, but with his Sight fully restored, with his other
powers enhanced, it would not have been an unendurable hardship. It would, in fact, almost certainly have
been a far richer existence than the one he had endured
for the last century and a half in that lifeless body, in this
mist-bound prison.

And his son . . .

But it was too late. His son's spirit was out of his reach
now. And even that was his own fault. He had had neither
the imagination to deduce the truth nor the courage to
endure the pain.

His own fault . . .

Though his tormentors were silent in reality, he could hear their laughter in his mind, and he thought grimly, Perhaps it *is* simply a game to them. Perhaps they have no purpose in their lives but to amuse themselves at my expense, at the expense of the hundreds of thousands they have imprisoned here over the centuries.

But now that he knew the truth about this room, now that he could wield whatever magic he could find . . .

Perhaps, finally, he would have a chance against these creatures, whatever and whoever they were. Even they could not be completely invulnerable.

But first he must find the answers to a few basic questions about the land to which the mists had returned him. First and most basic, was it indeed the same Darkon he had departed from only hours ago? And if it was, had time passed here at anything resembling the rate at which it had passed for him? His previous excursions through the mists, let alone his experiences with his tormentors, gave him no reason to take either of these assumptions for granted and every reason to doubt them.

Half afraid of what he would find, yet gripped by a sense of optimism he hadn't felt since his early days as a mortal sorcerer, he sent his Sight soaring out into the land.

 **THIRTEEN**

Darkon had indeed changed.

Whether it was a result of whatever he had or had not accomplished in his fatal encounter with Strahd or was just a whim of his tormentors, Azalin saw that the very geography of his mist-bound prison had been altered. In the east, the southern border of Darkon had shifted southward, bringing hundreds of square miles more of mountains and farms and wilderness that had been Arak within his reach. Closer, directly south of Il Aluk, at the border where G'Henna had slid into existence less than forty years ago, there was a sheer drop into nothing. Did this mean that G'Henna had been returned to wherever it had been stolen from? That in this version of the present, it had never been imprisoned by the mists in the first place? Or that it and its people were somewhere in that seemingly bottomless pit?

Or had the land simply been destroyed, as Hyskosa had predicted all the mist-bound lands would be destroyed?

Whatever had happened to it, people's memories of it did not appear to have been tampered with, as apparently had been done with memories involving Hyskosa and his so-called prophecy. Probing the mind of a Nartok merchant who had crossed the border from G'Henna only minutes before it vanished, he even found vivid images of the disappearance itself.

The merchant had spent the previous night in the river town of Dervich, barely a mile inside G'Henna. On horse-back, he had forded the river just downstream from Der-vich and passed through the mists that marked the border only a mile or so farther on. His horse, normally the most placid of animals, had been skittish from the moment the saddle had touched its back that morning, but it had not been bothered in the least by the river, even though its waters were moving with uncharacteristic speed and tur-bulence. Instead, the animal had seemed almost eager to dash into the river and make its way across. Though it reared and whinnied at even an inoffensive rabbit darting across its path, it needed no urging to plunge into the bor-der mists, and when it emerged, only a strong hand on the reins had kept it from breaking into a gallop.

Little more than a hundred yards along the barely dis-cernible path through the trees, a hissing sound like that of a massive serpent made the merchant turn in his saddle to look back. Moments before, the mists had been calm, little more than the thick fog they so much resembled, but now they were stirring, as if disturbed by a rising wind. At the same time, the horse whinnied and bolted, forcing the man to turn his full attention to staying in the saddle and trying to wrench the animal to a halt.

Even so, it took nearly a quarter mile before the horse, its mouth raw from the bit, finally stopped, allowing the merchant to turn once more toward the G'Henna border. The serpent's hiss had grown louder, but now it was drowned out by a rumble, and the border mists were churning as if stirred by some giant hand. And they were no longer the simple white of a fogbank, but shot through with flashes of light, alternately blood red and eye-piercing violet.

And then, for just an instant, the mists and all the turmoil in them vanished, as if a conjurer had whipped back his concealing cloak to reveal the result of his magic. In that instant, the merchant saw that, where solid earth had rested beneath his horse's hooves only minutes before, there was now a bottomless pit, its far wall a dozen—a *score* of miles distant.

Just as abruptly, the misty border returned, once again as placid as a morning fogbank, blotting out the impossible scene that lay beyond it.

And so the mists remained, Azalin's Sight told him. What lay beyond them, however, he could not tell, not directly, not any more than he could know for certain what lay beyond any of Darkon's borders. Even his enhanced powers, he found, could not propel his Sight beyond those borders.

Uneasily he withdrew, letting his Sight flow back toward Avernus. If such massive and obvious changes had been made to the physical structure of the land itself, how many other, more subtle, even invisible changes had been made? Could there even have been changes in what passed for laws of nature in Darkon?

If so . . .

*   *   *   *   *

Slowly Azalin crossed the threshold, emerging from the sickly yellow glow that tainted the air within the room, and stepped onto the gritty stone landing beyond the door.

For an interminable moment, nothing happened. He even began to hope against hope that the heartbeat and breath he had been given were permanent gifts, not a tantalizing reminder of what once had been.

But no. Within minutes, Alek Gwilym's body began to die—to be slain—a second time. The same brief stabs of pain gripped him as the wounds opened once again. The same blood spilled out and soaked the front of his shirt as the body's heart briefly raced and then slowed.

Delving into his memory, Azalin pulled forth a half dozen spells that would, in any other body, have sealed the wounds and restored at least a semblance of life. But for this body, as it had been for his old, it was as if he were once again a child reciting nothing more potent than a series of nursery rhymes. He could cloak it in whatever illusion he desired, but he could not alter its basic substance a jot.

Despite the changes to the land, despite the changes to himself, this had not changed. Whatever sorcery he performed within that tainting yellow glow, the results still vanished as if they had never been as soon as he stepped outside, and there was nothing he could do to alter that.

Without waiting for Gwilym's heart to fully stop, Azalin flowed down the steps. There was one more thing he needed to know, one more hope that needed to be dashed.

*   *   *   *   *

The spell he chose was one of the simplest in the ancient grimoire, the sort that any would-be sorcerer of even the most modest talent could master within minutes. As a child barely old enough to read, he himself had cast far more complicated ones. A lowly levitational spell, it had no advantage over any of a dozen similar spells of greater strength and effectiveness he had known and used for centuries. Its only value lay in the fact that this particular spell was one that he had not long ago mastered, had not even seen before the mists had snatched him away from Oerth.

It took only a few seconds to memorize the half dozen words and the single, uncomplicated gesture, but he continued to read and reread the pretentiously ornate text for nearly half an hour, until finally he closed the grimoire and placed it on the dusty table before him.

He raised his hands, palms outward toward the grimoire, and began.

Only a single syllable had passed his lips when the remainder began to slip away, to be obscured in a mental mist as thick as the border mists that held him prisoner in this land.

So, he thought, this has not changed either. Outside that room, I am still helpless to learn even the simplest of spells.

Even so, he tried a second time, then a third, all the time wondering, futilely, Why?

Was it simply another method of tormenting him? Part of the game?

Or could it be that his tormentors were *afraid* of the powers he might gain? Considering the kind of power they obviously wielded, the idea seemed absurd on its face, but even so . . .

During the next attempt, he concentrated not on the spell itself but on the manner in which it faded from his mind. Obviously his mind was being tampered with, but how? By the tormentors themselves? By a spell they had placed upon him when first they had propelled him through the mists? A spell so subtle that even he had not yet been able to detect it?

Abruptly his mind darted back to the time when Hyskosa had been brought to Avernus. Through his Sight, Azalin had sensed something that clung not to the Vistana seer's body but to the essence that was Hyskosa, something more subtle even than the magical spoor of another sorcerer.

"You sense the traces of those who spoke to me in the mists," the Vistana had said.

Azalin had not only realized the truth of the Vistana's words but had also subsequently been able to sense similar traces hovering about the wraith that pretended to be his son. Could he do the same now? With himself?

With a gesture, he sent the grimoire floating back to the dusty shelves, where it inserted itself among its hundreds of companions and flowed from the room. Within seconds, he found himself once more stepping across the threshold into the sickly yellow glow.

Impatiently he waited as the painful restoration of Gwilym's body repeated itself. When at last it was complete, he allowed himself the luxury of a single deeply drawn breath, held it for a moment, then let it out in a sigh that was a mixture of pleasure and nervous anticipation.

A moment later, his Sight hovered free in the room, as if it were the separate entity he often imagined it to be. He looked down at himself, at this new and still unfamiliar body, through "eyes" that responded not only to light but also to sound and scent and taste and countless other nameless forces both natural and supernatural.

And he saw a thousand things he had never seen—had never *bothered* to see—before.

There, like the remembered trail of a firefly, *something* floated loosely between his Sight and his body: the link he had always known must exist but which he had never seen, had never visualized.

And there, flickering in and out of existence, encasing the body like a ghastly cocoon, was a translucent image of what had been: not only the decayed flesh of Azalin— the blotches of exposed bone, the glowing red pits where eyes should have been—but an even more ghostly image of Firan as he had been in life.

And hovering about both his body and his Sight, a shadowy aura—the aura that, he knew, sent chills and feelings of dread through all living things that approached him, warning them of his presence.

But observing such blatantly obvious manifestations of *himself* was not his objective. He sought traces of other beings, other influences, other *touches*.

Slowly, cautiously, like a man trying to examine countless overlapping images formed of smoke that the least breath of air could dissipate, he searched and probed.

And found the scars, the ghostly imprints of . . .

His mentor Quantarius, three centuries dead but still strong enough to conjure up feelings of both gratitude and guilt.

Strahd and the countless skirmishes with his minions.

The spell that his wife Olessa had had cast upon him and upon herself in a futile attempt to deprive him of a son and heir.

The death of that son by Azalin's own hand.

His own "death" and the voices of his tormentors speaking to him out of the shadows.

His being swallowed up by the mists and imprisoned, first in Barovia and then in Darkon.

Through all these and a thousand more, each with its own feel, he searched for those times and places he had been touched by his tormentors. They were everywhere, but still not as omnipresent as he had long assumed. Their signature was strongest on events that had been accompanied by their voices and their laughter, but almost as strong on others at which they had been silent.

They had watched as he and Corsalus had summoned up the creature that had possessed his brother. They had watched as he gave the unappreciated gift of renewed youth and vitality to Quantarius. They had watched as he selected Olessa for his bride and as he looked into the obsidian mirror and discovered her treachery. They had watched as his son was born and again when he died.

And theirs was the mark upon his mind that stole from his memory each new spell he attempted to learn.

But their mark, he realized with surprise, was not upon the attempts to tamper with the memories of his journey through the mists to ancient Barovia. Nor was it imprinted on any aspect of that journey except those brief minutes when he was with Strahd, and even then it was so faint as to be almost undetectable.

As if, he thought abruptly, they had been focusing solely on Strahd and, as he had tried to convince himself at the time, had not even been aware of his presence!

But another's mark *was* upon that journey, he realized, and upon the efforts to tamper with his memory of that journey. The same mark that the Vistana seer had acknowledged as being made by those who had given him his vision, the vision that had led directly to the journey. The same mark he had found upon the wraith that pretended to be his son. The same mark, he realized with a start, that had been present, along with that of his tormentors, the night of the Grand Summoning and the death of his brother.

The mark perhaps—just perhaps—of a force that opposed his tormentors, a force that . . . what? Wanted these lands destroyed, as he did himself? Wished these lands had never come into being, as he did himself?

But if that were true, why should it attempt to erase his memory of its efforts? Why had it not acted that long-ago night when his brother had died? Why did it not simply reveal itself to him and offer its plan?

And the obvious answer came to him: It did not wish his tormentors to know of its existence, or at least of its involvement.

Which meant, he thought with a sinking feeling, it feared them. It was not as powerful, and therefore must do its work in secret.

Unless, as he had thought a thousand times about his tormentors, the whole affair was only a game. A game with not one but two players, neither of whom had the slightest regard for the pawns they ruthlessly manipulated in furtherance of whatever their dark, incomprehensible goals might be.

But then, as he allowed his Sight to merge once more with this still new and living body, he realized there was a difference between his tormentors and this other presence. The memory of both sent a chill, a prickling apprehension through this body, this body that was still capable of experiencing such feelings.

But the memory of his tormentors brought with it as well a feeling of pure dread.

And he recognized that feeling. Or rather, this body recognized the feeling—Alek Gwilym's body, which somehow retained certain visceral memories as if they were engraved in its very cells. And that feeling was, Azalin realized, virtually the same feeling that his own presence—the shadowy aura his Sight had noted hovering about him—had inspired in Gwilym.

As if fleeing from himself, Azalin bolted from the room.

*   *   *   *   *

When finally he reentered the room, Azalin was determined not to leave again until he had learned everything that room made it possible for him to learn. There was, he had convinced himself, no reason to leave and every reason to stay.

Inside, he was free to roam all of Darkon. No secret could be hidden from his Sight. If ever the people or the barons who ruled them in his name became too restive for even his Kargat secret police to handle, or if the Kargat themselves began to entertain thoughts of independence or rebellion, he would soon know of it and could rouse armies of the dead from their shallow graves all across Darkon to do his bidding.

The room was also, in effect, his oasis of life, the only place in all of his Darkonian prison where he could experience life rather than death. Whatever he desired—food and drink to be savored, silken sheets to sleep between—could be conjured up and conjured away. Outside, there would be no need of food or drink, no possibility of sleep. There would only be a continuation of what he had already endured for more than two and a half centuries.

The key to his quest, as he believed it was the key to all things, was knowledge, beginning with a thorough review and analysis of his own past, of all things done to him and by him that had led to his current situation. Thus it was with a shock of exhilaration that he found in one of the grimoires a simple spell that would eliminate the need for him to rely upon either his own imperfect memory or the ability of his Sight to sift through the insubstantial shadows that still clung to him. It would literally give him complete access to his entire past existence.

He leapt upon the spell hungrily but also suspiciously.

He could not, however, sense the slightest trace of either his tormentors or their seeming opposition, either on the spell itself or on the entire volume.

Learning and casting the spell was itself exhilarating and only increased his determination to remain where he was for as long as it took.

For days, then months, he literally relived great stretches of his life, most often from his days as a mortal sorcerer, particularly those when he was apprenticed to Quantarius. They had been the happiest—perhaps the only happy—years of his life. Every day he had been learning, every day he met a new challenge, every day Quantarius was there, a part of his life, sometimes approving his actions, sometimes scolding, but always there. . . .

Finally, though, he realized he was simply indulging himself, burying himself in pleasanter days the way a drunkard buries himself in imagined friends and pleasures.

Methodically, then, he began to search his life—and his death—for traces of both his tormentors and their opposition.

And found them.

He found unmistakable, indelible imprints of his tormentors, of course, at each of the times they had spoken to him: familiar voices mouthing alien words as they tempted and tricked and taunted him again and again. The strongest, however, was on a night when they had been silent, when he had not even been aware of their presence: the night his younger brother Irik had died, the night of the Grand Summoning that had gone so terribly wrong. His Sight had already detected their ghostly imprint on that night, so the discovery hardly came as a surprise. Now, though, he was almost overwhelmed by their loathsomely eager presence, could even almost *see*

them in the unnatural shadows that had hovered in the
rafters above the gateway to the nether regions that he
and Corsalus had prized open, and he marveled that he
had not sensed them at the time. His concentration on
the summoning itself, on the plight of his brother, must
have virtually blinded his senses to all else.

And he wondered, Was that when it began? Did I summon them up myself from their hellish darkness?

He shuddered, knowing it must be the truth. He and
Corsalus had created the Opening, and something even
worse than the horror that had possessed and transformed his brother had come silently through and
attached itself to *him* that night. Something more subtle
than the slavering creature they had summoned Quantarius to banish, more subtle and yet more powerful,
more dangerous, something that had not possessed him
outright but had put its mark upon him, like fastening a
bell around a cat's neck, so that ever after he could be
found whenever his tormentors so desired.

He shuddered again at the image but found it unnerv-
ingly apt.

But that night was not, he soon discovered, the true
beginning. The massive Opening had allowed his tormentors to flow through in all their dark strength, to
establish a link that could not be broken by the Closing
of the Way, a link that allowed them to come again and
again, whenever they pleased.

But it was not the first time they had *touched* him.

A year farther back, then five, then ten, he felt them.
Insubstantial, muffled, but unmistakable, as if it had
taken all their strength to force even that small part of
themselves through the barriers that kept them confined
to the nether regions, from which he and Corsalus had
later unwittingly released them.

Another year back, and nothing changed. Yet another year, and another, until finally he was present at his very birth!

And the unmistakable mark of his tormentors was faintly but firmly upon him even then!

And even earlier, he realized with a start!

Though the spell would not allow him to go back beyond his own birth, he *could* detect the spoor of his tormentors not only on the bawling infant but on both his father and his mother! *They* had both been touched by these things, not then and there but at some time past!

His mind reeled. How many generations back had these creatures marked his ancestors? And why?

But there were no answers to such questions. He could discern his tormentors' marks and where they had touched him, but he could not discern their reasons, if reasons they had.

Finally, still shaken, he turned to that other force. Evidence of its existence was far less ubiquitous, far less obvious. It had touched him the night of the botched Grand Summoning. It had touched him when he set out to follow Quantarius. It had touched him when he left Quantarius, to set out on his own. It had hovered most closely about the Vistani woman, she of the youthful eyes in the face of a crone, who had, he now realized, offered him wise counsel when he had encountered her in the mists between Barovia and Darkon and again in the forest on the road to Il Aluk his first hours in Darkon. It had somehow set free his son's spirit and put in its place the thing that now pretended to be his son—the thing that had brought Hyskosa's prophecy to his attention.

But the knowledge told him no more about this force's purpose than it told him about his tormentors', except that it opposed them.

Yet again came the thought that it was nothing more than a game to them both. But even for the gods, four centuries was a long time to devote to something that simply provided them occasional amusement.

No, there had to be a purpose, just as there had been with Strahd.

His tormentors had used Strahd and his mystical bond with the land to begin the creation of this mist-bound prison.

And Firan Zal'honan? What had they used *him* for? Like Strahd, he had been given eternal living death. Like Strahd, he was held prisoner in this land. Like Strahd, he would give anything to escape. As Strahd was obsessed with finding his lost Tatyana, he was obsessed with finding and redeeming his lost son.

But Strahd could learn new magic. Was that the only essential difference between them? And why was it so? Were his tormentors afraid that, without this handicap, he would someday be able to best them?

A flash of perverted pride shot through him at the thought. The very gods were fearful of him? So fearful they had created this entire land simply as a prison, where they could control him?

Was it possible? In a few short years, he had outstripped his mortal mentor Quantarius and become the most powerful sorcerer in a dozen lands, most likely in all of the Flanaess. And he had added to his powers for another century, until he had been stolen away by the mists and imprisoned here.

But to outstrip the gods?

Even he could not entirely believe it, but neither could he reject the idea out of hand. And if it *were* possible . . .

And if, here in this room, he *was* capable of learning new magic, of progressing to even higher levels . . .

 **FOURTEEN**

Darkon
741, Barovian Calendar

To any other sorcerer, the entrance to the long-gone
creature's lair was nothing more than an irregular granite
outcropping, one among the many that made the upper
reaches of Mount Nyid among the most treacherous and
inaccessible areas in all of Darkon. To Azalin's Sight, the
rock was tinged with the same dark aura that surrounded
him, and fissures invisible to any mortal skilled and foolhardy enough to venture here were plain and vulnerable.

Bracing himself against contact with the aura, he sent
his Sight cautiously drifting downward until he felt the
first of the barrier spells he had been virtually certain
would surround this place. But it was old and rigid, as
were the ones he sensed beyond it, dead things left
behind to guard this place, not living shields controlled
by an entity that still dwelt within. They could be shattered like a diamond struck at precisely the right point by
an expert cutter, but for the moment Azalin only studied
them. Hundreds of years after the creature's departure,
the spells remained as powerful as any a mortal sorcerer
could cast.

Still cautiously, he probed and analyzed and cast subtle and delicate counterspells, until finally he felt his Sight slithering through the resultant fissures in both spells and rock.

And his Sight, unhindered by darkness, was within the cavern, within Mount Nyid itself, and he knew instantly he had found what he had sought. Back in Avernus, his body gasped. Before him, on shelves carved effortlessly out of the rock walls themselves, lay a thousand grimoires and journals and magical paraphernalia of kinds that even he had never seen, all still protected by the creature's lingering spells from the dank air and eyeless crawling things that inhabited this eternal darkness.

In the center of the cavern stood a flat rock platform—a table, carved out of the rock itself, like the grimoire-laden shelves. Another of the creature's spells bathed it in a faint glow, discernible only to others like himself. On the platform—the table—two things lay: a grimoire open to an ornately lettered spell.

And a small, intricately carved silver box. The creature's phylactery.

But the phylactery was empty. The creature's aura still clung to it like an ominous shadow that billowed out to engulf the entire cavern, but it was empty.

And on the floor of the cavern, sprawled next to the platform, lay the final proof that Azalin needed: a body as decayed and hideous as the one he himself had been confined to for two and a half centuries.

He had known almost from the beginning of his imprisonment in Darkon that beings like this—beings like himself—had once infested the land and most likely still existed in its darker corners. They were the subject of countless fearful rumors but few verifiable reports. What little was written about them dated to the centuries before

Darkon had been taken prisoner by the mists, and all made casual mention of neighboring lands now long gone, presumably left behind in whatever world Darkon had been stolen from.

It was obvious, however, that the creatures were universally feared and loathed, and anyone who successfully hunted one down and destroyed it quickly became the stuff of legends. As a result, Azalin had kept his true nature to himself, maintaining at all times the illusion of the mortal sorcerer he had once been.

The similarities between himself and these creatures, however, were largely superficial, or so he told himself. They ruled no one and had no interest in ruling anyone. They spent their time almost exclusively in whatever lair they had fashioned for themselves, be it a ruined castle or the labyrinthine depths of a cavern or a rock- and spell-sealed aerie like this one. Despite their supposed intelligence, they were obsessed with one thing and one thing only: finding and mastering new and ever more powerful magic. It was, in fact, their hunger for new magical items that was most often their downfall. More than one had been lured out of their virtually impenetrable lairs, enticed to destruction by promises of newly discovered magical trinkets or spells of a kind they had never before encountered.

For Azalin himself, magic had never been an end in itself but a means to an end, never more so than now.

But it mattered not what this nameless creature's motives may have been, Azalin thought as his Sight probed every corner of the cavern for even more subtle protective spells. What mattered was that the creature had *not* been lured from its lair and destroyed. According to the fragmentary journals and distorted folktales that had brought it to Azalin's attention, it had simply vanished after more than a century of depredations in the lands south of Lake Korst. No lair had ever been found, nor any further trace of the creature itself. No one even falsely claimed credit for its extermination, perhaps for fear that the creature was not truly gone and that such a claim would attract its attention.

Azalin, his Sight free to roam all of Darkon, had spent weeks scouring an ever widening area around Lake Korst. Twice he sensed the chilling, shadowy aura that marked these creatures, but both times it led him not to abandoned lairs but to occupied ones, the occupants so absorbed in mastering their latest acquisitions or planning their next foray into the world of the living that they were never even aware of his brief approach.

But then, uneasily, he crossed over what had, until the change, been the southern border of Darkon. Half afraid that this was yet another of his tormentors' traps, he had probed gently at first, staying within meters of the one-time border. But the mists did not spring up, reestablishing the border and trapping his Sight—and himself?—in a foreign domain. This new territory, in fact, differed in no way from what had originally been Darkon, except that it almost certainly had originally been part of a different world, a different existence.

Finally, not satisfied but less uneasy, he continued his search.

Within days, he had found the lair, almost at the barren peak of Mount Nyid. And it held, he now saw, precisely what he had hoped for: evidence that the creature had abandoned his grotesque body, not to retreat to his phylactery or to possess another corpse but to begin a new and different existence totally free of the physical world.

And in the grimoire lying open upon the granite table was the spell that had made it possible.

He considered matters for a time. The barrier spells were still strong. While they had been relatively easy for his Sight to penetrate, it would doubtless be less easy for any physical being to enter or leave. Even reaching the mountain peak would be an extraordinary feat for any but winged creatures. And many were the lingering spells that hovered about the grimoire itself, spells with purposes that even he could not entirely divine. Some were familiar preservative spells, not unlike the ones that had maintained his own long-dead body, but others had a feel of destruction about them. It would not surprise him if at least some were precisely that—spells that would turn the grimoire and all its precious contents instantaneously into dust if they were interfered with or if the grimoire itself were moved or even touched by any but the creature itself. All such creatures were misers regarding their troves of magical treasures, and there was no reason to believe this one had been any different. If anything, it would have had even greater reason to want to keep this particular bit of magic out of the hands of others.

Wherever it had gone, whatever form it had taken, it doubtless did not want others to follow.

But no safeguards were perfect, no spells impenetrable. The very fact that his Sight was here in the creature's lair was testament to that.

Long ago, while still a mortal sorcerer, before his Sight had been half blinded by this mist-bound prison, he had mastered the art of looking out simultaneously through both his Sight and his mortal eyes, just as he was capable of seeing ten or a hundred dark vistas through the eyes of the unburied dead. And now, with his Sight restored and raised to even higher levels . . .

Back in the room that housed his body, he opened Gwilym's eyes. For a moment, the shifting double image of the distant cavern and the room bathed in its sickly yellow glow were too much for the living body and its visceral memories. But the dizziness and nausea were easily controlled, and Azalin began his preparations.

First a blank sheet of heavy parchment appeared before him and settled onto the oaken table he had conjured up many days past. What appeared to be a quill pen appeared as well, hovering above the parchment. Azalin moved to stand over the parchment as his Sight moved to hover directly above the open grimoire.

The parchment shifted minutely as he aligned it so that it precisely overlay the grimoire page in his Sight.

And he began. Slowly, painstakingly, more precisely than any physical hand could do, the quill traced every letter, every embellishment, every seeming flaw. He could feel the power draining from the grimoire, and he half feared that even this would trigger some treacherous safeguarding spell that would wipe out the grimoire before he could finish.

But finally the two images were literally one, and he could feel the power not only in his mind but also in this body as the hairs on its arms stood tinglingly erect, as if a lightning bolt were about to strike. Fearing that some form of self-destruction might have been woven into the spell itself, he sealed the parchment with the most powerful protective spell he knew and hoped it would be enough.

Cautiously he withdrew his Sight from the distant cavern, half expecting the grimoire to disintegrate as he eased back through the still-powerful barrier spells. But it remained intact, at least until it was beyond the reach of his Sight.

For a timeless moment he hovered there, high above the barren peak of Mount Nyid, then relaxed his grip on this area and let his Sight be drawn back to his distant body.

*   *   *   *   *

For several days Azalin studied the spell, dissecting and analyzing it as he had no other. It was, he eventually realized with a touch of awe, the work of a true master. It was not an individual spell but a composite of many. Its individual parts had been altered and woven together into an intricate tapestry that promised far more than the individual threads. Some, in their original forms, were familiar. One seemed to be an odd variation of the one he had once used to extend his own life and that of others, draining the life-force from one person and transferring it to another, but here both source and recipient were shrouded in ambiguity. Another thread appeared to be a form of summoning, or at least a reaching into other planes of existence, but again it was different from anything he had ever encountered. Yet another strand seemed to invoke protection, though not against creatures summoned up from the nether regions but against unknown but natural forces. Perhaps, he speculated, it was to noncorporeal forms what an ensorcelled suit of armor would be to a mortal, which led him to wonder again concerning the nature of the transformation this spell promised and the destination of any who underwent it.

Even without such worries, the dangers in making use of such a spell were many, foremost among them the fact that, even after days of intense study, he still did not fully understand the spell. As many a hedge wizard—and others far more advanced—had learned, a lack of understanding could be fatal.

Perhaps, he thought with a new quiver of unease, it had been fatal to the creature who had used it last, the creature whose discarded ruin of a body still lay in its lair. The creature itself was gone, but there was nothing to say where it had gone or what form it had taken. Or if it had simply ceased to exist, not only in this plane but in all others as well.

Finally, though, he decided that, regardless of the dangers, he had no choice but to make the attempt. Even if he failed utterly and simply ceased to exist, he would have achieved a form of freedom.

In the manner of a last meal, he sent word to the best chefs in Il Aluk and ordered them to prepare their finest delicacies, which, when completed, vanished from their ovens and stove tops and reappeared, no worse for the instantaneous trip, on a plain oaken table in the only room in Darkon where he could taste and savor and consume them.

When at last he was finished, he reveled in a feeling of satiety he had not experienced since his days in Rauxes when grateful clients had honored and thanked him with incomparable banquets and feasts. For a moment, the thought of staying where he was, of retaining and enjoying this living body for ages to come, darted through his mind.

But almost immediately he thrust the idea aside with disgust. He would be no better than those other creatures and their single-minded pursuit of magic. Worse, he would be—and the thought repulsed him so sharply that in a single gesture he scoured the room clean of every trace of the meal—no better than his loathsome brother Ranald, who had centuries ago eaten himself to death while neglecting the country and the people who depended on him for leadership and justice.

Ashamed that he had considered surrendering to such gluttony and cowardice for even a second, Azalin cleansed the room of everything but the central slab and the parchment that lay upon it.

Standing over the parchment, focusing on it and only
it, he began. The words came easily but with unnerving
uncertainty because he still could not fully visualize the
desired results of each strand of the magical tapestry.
Around him, the greenish yellow glow that permeated
the room seemed to take on a mistlike substance. Tiny
vortices appeared then, like miniature storms with flickering dots of firefly lightning, everywhere but directly
above the parchment and the slab on which it lay. There
shadows began to gather, forcing the glow to retreat.
Beyond the shadows, the stone ceiling seemed to waver,
as if seen through muddied and rippling water.

And still he could not visualize those things his words
were calling for! He should stop, he knew, should call
this to a halt and not begin again until he *did* completely understand the spell and all its parts. This way
lay disaster.

But he dared not stop. Like a rider on a mighty run-
away stallion, he had set the process in motion and was
being carried at deadly speed across uncharted ground.
The convoluted words and phrases inscribed on the
parchment were coming from his lips as if they had a life
of their own.

And then he realized: He was *not* in complete control
of what he uttered! He had begun in a monotone, but
after a half dozen lines, his voice had taken on a singsong
quality, single syllables modulated into two, then three
and more. And then, as if echoing back from a distant
mountain, he heard the first lines being repeated in a
faint reflection of his original monotone.

For a moment he tried to stop, tried to tear his eyes
from the parchment, but the words continued to roll out
of him, now in a thunderous chant he was certain he had
not consciously initiated.

But even as he wondered desperately what sort of trap he had fallen into, the objective of the spell came clear to him. The individual, incomprehensible strands became a meaningful whole, like multicolored threads woven into a fabric suddenly becoming a beautiful, complex image.

In his mind now, he saw himself—his essence—emerging slowly from this body, emerging and transforming into something that could exist on its own, with no need for either body or phylactery. Something invisible to mortal eyes, yet plainly visible to his senses.

The words of the spell continued to flow out of him, and now there was not one echo but more than he could count until, as the final word roared from his throat, it was accompanied by every other word he had spoken, all pouring out at once, as if the entire spell had somehow been captured and concentrated into that single moment.

For another moment, nothing happened, but then a tearing sensation gripped him, like a thousand embedded hooks being ripped from his flesh.

And he was free.

He watched with momentary regret as Gwilym's body collapsed, empty, to the floor.

The shadows, the turmoil in the greenish yellow air, quickly faded.

He saw in the distance the beckoning mists, and he knew that, in this form, he could travel them freely.

He was free not only of his body, of his phylactery, but of this land that had been his prison for two centuries. It felt not unlike the first time he had sent his Sight swooping through the sky, but there were tremendous differences. It was the difference between a kite guided—weighted down—by an earthbound hand and an eagle soaring free. It was the difference between a blind man feeling his way through the rooms of a prison and a man with all his senses intact exploring the forest and the meadows.

After a time, he directed his attention to the sarcophagus, where the thing that pretended to be his son still hovered.

And he saw now with crystal clarity what before had been the faintest of traces to his Sight, what had been even less to his stunted senses when he had emerged from this room. Those who had tampered with his son's spirit, breaking the spell that had bound it to this place, had left a trail as clear as a footprint.

And so had the spirit itself, the spirit of Irik, his son.

With a sudden burst of hope, Azalin—the bodiless thing that Azalin had become—swooped down to the sarcophagus. He could see and feel it all—the counterfeit spirit approaching, Irik starting to warn it away, not wanting any other spirit to take his place, then letting it pass as he saw that it was not a true spirit but an artificial creation.

Then leaving, flowing out through the walls of Avernus, only to be enveloped in the mists.

To the Azalin that had been, that trail had been invisible. But now, in this form, he could not only see the lingering trail but also follow it with ease.

And follow it he did. After a century and a half, the ghostly trail was plain to him, and as he moved along it, a pocket of mists rose up and enveloped him. Even in the mists, he could see the ancient trail, could sort it out from the thousands of others that crisscrossed again and again.

For the first time in a century and a half, he began to feel hope. If he could find the true spirit of his son, no matter where it had wandered . . .

But as he drifted through the mists, the trail still before him, his vision—all the senses that he was now capable of using—began to fade.

And he felt a tugging. Something was holding him back, keeping him from following the trail. And now he was being drawn backward no matter how hard he struggled, as if his body were being . . .

No!

In his exultation, he had virtually forgotten, had forced from his mind, the fact that this had been an experiment, performed in the one place in Darkon where he *could* perform it. And now that he—not his Sight but *himself!*—had left that place . . .

Even as the thoughts raced through his mind, the trail he had been following dissolved into the mists along with the thousands of others. The tugging increased, and he realized he didn't have the strength to resist.

Or the will.

The experiment had failed.

The mists boiled away and vanished, and he was hovering in the night outside the towers of Avernus. He could see the force that was pulling him back to the abandoned body. It wasn't the shimmering cord that he had seen linking his Sight to his body, but a tunnel of shadowy blackness he was being dragged through.

He couldn't hear his tormentors laughing, but he was certain that, somewhere, they were.

FIFTEEN

Darkon
741–748, Barovian Calendar

There *had* to be another way, Azalin told himself with far more certainty than he felt.

For another year, then two, then more, he continued the search so single-mindedly, kept his Sight in such nearly constant use that he had to remind himself to turn his attention now and then to the Gwilym body that he again inhabited, to tend to the needs that, here in this one room, it still retained. There were no more sybaritic trappings, no self-indulgences of any kind. All thought of such luxuries had been banished since the loathsome memory of the gluttonous Ranald had been resurrected. And it was good that the three-centuries-old memory had briefly returned to serve as a grim reminder of that time in his life and of the principles he had held to ever after, of the obligations he still had. The obligations he had, to his shame, forgotten for a few brief moments.

And as his Sight scoured Darkon, searching for the elusive signatures of ever more ancient, ever more thoroughly concealed troves of sorcery, the Kargat searched lands he could not reach: Falkovnia, Dementlieu, Tepest,

Valachan, even Barovia. For these lands, though they
now existed cheek by jowl in their misty prison, had once
been integral parts of other, greater lands, each with its
own unique approach to sorcery and to life. Their borders had been altered at the time of their imprisonment,
sometimes their landscapes as well, as rivers and valleys
and mountains shifted amorphously to match without
break their new neighbors, but their populations and their
histories were, more often than not, unaltered. And so,
instead of the heritage of a single world, he had in truth
the sorcery and the traditions of nearly twoscore to draw
upon in his quest for escape and freedom.

And hardly a day passed that another searcher did not
return to Darkon, saddlebags laden with odd devices and
records and fragments of parchment. For years the results
were nil, but still Azalin sent the searchers out, covering
the same ground again and again, until one day . . .

* * * * *

His name was Domran, and until his recruitment by
the Kargat he had been in the service of Baron Mahdli,
doing nothing more exciting than patrolling the back
alleys of Nartok. Like most people, he had heard tales of
the Kargat, a shadowy force that was rumored to be Lord
Azalin's eyes and ears throughout Darkon, meting out
punishment and reward or delivering malefactors to
Avernus, where they would be dealt with by Lord Azalin
personally. He was therefore startled when he and a
dozen other similarly raw recruits were sent on what
appeared to be an endless series of missions—aimless
searches, really—through other domains. Bring back
anything that so much as hints at new knowledge, he
had been told by Lord Azalin himself, be it mundane or

arcane, sorcerous or scientific. Better to return with a
thousand useless devices and journals and fragments of
parchment than to leave behind the single item that
might prove to be that which Lord Azalin sought.

It was on his twentieth, or perhaps his thirtieth, mission
that Domran, having just stuffed his saddlebags with
ancient but well-preserved volumes he had found in an
abandoned monastery near Morfenzi in eastern Falkovnia, was approached by a roaming band of soldiers.
Knowing the Falkovnian military's reputation for
overzealousness and their deep distrust of those from
other lands, he didn't attempt to reason with them but
left the road and plunged immediately into the dense,
black-trunked forests of what he assumed were the
foothills of the Balinoks.

The soldiers, apparently more interested in intimidat-
ing strangers than in arduous pursuits, gave up their
sport after a few noisy minutes, but Domran felt obliged
to avoid Falkovnian roads thereafter. For a few miles, he
threaded his way northwestward toward the border with
Darkon, roughly paralleling what had once been the border with G'Henna but which was now the rim of the bottomless pit that was the Shadow Rift. As night
approached, however, the forest—the entire landscape—
began to change. The smooth, black-trunked giants
unique to Falkovnia gave way to even more massive
trees, but these were gray and heavily corrugated and
infested with greenish brown vines that sometimes
seemed to be strangling the life from their hosts. At the
same time, the rolling foothills were replaced by a maze
of narrow valleys that seemed to grow ever more intricate and disorienting until, as the last of the dull, cloud-
filtered sunlight faded into darkness, he had lost all sense
of direction and could only hunker down and await the

dawn. He had hoped to eventually come upon the dried-out bed of the river that had once emerged from G'Henna and paralleled the Darkon border westward until it joined the Vuchar near the border with Lamordia, but now he was ready to count himself fortunate if he could find his way out of this bizarre region before being tumbled into the rift itself.

He tried briefly to start a small campfire to push the darkness back a few meters, but the fragments of vines and branches he managed to break free seemed no more flammable than a rock. In the end, he decided his failure was for the best, since a flame could only attract attention, and an encounter with anything that wandered these twisted valleys would most likely be even less desirable than an encounter with the soldiers he had fled here to avoid.

With no stars to gauge the passage of time, he drifted in and out of an uneasy sleep, his back pressed tightly against a rocky outcropping that jutted incongruously out of the forest floor. After half a dozen such cycles of dozing and wakefulness, his horse, which had been shifting its hooves uneasily ever since being tethered to one of the vines, whinnied loudly and jerked backward, brought up short by the sturdy tether.

Domran came awake instantly, every hair seemingly on end. A faint gray light, dimly visible through the trees, brought a momentary feeling of relief, but the feeling turned abruptly to spine-tingling uneasiness as he realized that the light did not herald the approach of dawn.

For the light was not coming from the sky but was radiating dimly *into* the sky from somewhere within the forest. He felt the ground shake beneath him, felt the rock shift against his back as if alive, sending him lurching to his feet. Half to comfort the animal, half to comfort

himself with the feel of another living being, he gripped
the horse's reins and stroked its quivering neck.

And then it was over. The light faded into total darkness, and the ground was once more steady beneath his
feet.

Domran slept no more that night, but when dawn
finally came, he took his courage and the reins firmly in
hand and began picking his way toward the spot in the
jungle where the light had come from. To his surprise,
the ground leveled off within a hundred yards, and within
another fifty, he found himself near the edge of a clearing, the only clearing he had seen since entering the forest nearly a full day before.

Beyond the clearing loomed the rift, and even here,
more than a hundred yards from its edge, he involuntarily leaned backward, as if to keep from being swept in,
from sliding uncontrollably toward the yawning abyss.

For a long time he stood silently at the edge of the
clearing, his hands tightly on the reins, both to keep the
horse from backing nervously into the forest and to keep
himself from lurching forward.

Finally able to take his eyes from the rift, the far wall of
which was easily visible a dozen or more miles distant,
he saw that the clearing was not empty. Barely visible in
the knee-high tangle of grass and weeds a dozen yards in
front of him were the crumbled remains of at least one
building. At first he thought it might be another
monastery, but the remnants of the walls, an odd mixture
of granite and marble, looked like no monastery he had
ever seen.

Obviously it had been a building of some importance,
he thought, his mind turning back to the reason he had
been sent to Falkovnia in the first place. And important
buildings, be they monasteries or palaces, had been the

source of virtually every item that had filled his saddle-bags. He would surely earn Azalin's wrath if he bypassed such a place without so much as a look.

Tethering his mount securely a few yards back, he returned to the edge of the clearing, a line so sharply demarcated that, like the precipice overlooking the rift, it seemed the meeting of two different worlds. For a time he hesitated, but he knew he had to step across, had to search the ruins now that he had found them, no matter how accidentally. If the tales of agents far more experienced than he could be relied upon, Azalin would be able to see in his eyes, perhaps in his very thoughts, what he had or had not done here. And Azalin's punishments for disobedience and cowardice were legendary.

Finally, taking his courage in hand, he stepped across the line. A wave of dizziness swept over him, blurring his vision. As he tried to steady himself, the air above the ruins shimmered and wavered, and suddenly the jagged remnants of walls were not level with the knee-high grass but looming above him, a double row of vacant windows on either side of a massive metal door hanging loose from a single hinge.

Finally the dizziness passed, and he took a tentative step closer, then another, half expecting the vision before him to vanish like a mirage or to metamorphose yet again. But it remained stable even though the air above it continued to shimmer and waver, almost in time with the grass swaying in the cool wind that now blew steadily in from the edge of the rift. As he came closer, he could see a rusting placard still fastened to the sagging door, the lettering ornate but indecipherable.

Cautiously he eased through the opening, afraid that even the slightest touch would loosen the last of the hinges and send the door crashing down.

Then he was inside, in the midst of silent, dust-covered chaos. What the room had once been, it was impossible to tell. There had been furniture, but now there were only random piles of sticks, as if a giant hammer had smashed everything to bits and flung the remains savagely about. Countless gouges in the walls, once covered with a rich wooden veneer, gave mute testimony to the violence that had erupted here. But whatever had happened had happened long ago and had almost certainly left nothing of value behind.

It was the same in the next room and the next and the next as Domran picked his way gingerly through the splinters and fragments of wood and shards of glass. It was a marvel that the walls themselves were still standing, so destructive had been the force that had swept through these rooms.

But then, in the center of the last room left to search, a small, windowless cubicle at the rear of the building, he saw something whole: a book, a sturdy, leather-bound volume held closed by a heavy brass clasp, half hidden in the midst of the now-familiar layers of wreckage.

Hardly believing his eyes, he leaned down and carefully picked away the detritus, an odd tingle brushing at his fingers as he worked. There was lettering on the cover, not embossed in gold as were the journals from the monastery but seeming to be burned into the leather as if by a hot iron. *Scientific Journal of K. Albemarl*, it said in plain, bold letters, surrounded by intricate swirling symbols burnt even more deeply into the leather.

Cautiously he gripped one corner, feeling the tingle intensify and envelop half his arm, and lifted. He half expected the volume to crumble into dust, but it did not. Swallowing nervously, he took it in both hands, picked it up, and stood holding it. Gradually the tingle faded rather than spread throughout his body.

With a shudder of relief, he hurried from the tiny room and out of the ruined building—and lurched to a stop.

Domran's eyes widened as a new chill gripped him like a vise. Between the ruins he had just exited and the edge of the rift more than a hundred yards distant, where before there had been only an expanse of knee-high grass, there now loomed another building, huge and imposing, thirty yards wide, three stories high, and of the finest marble. On either side, stretching all the way back to the edge of the rift, stood courtyard walls almost as high as the building itself. But the walls were incomplete, as if the portions that had extended out over the rift had been sliced cleanly off.

As perhaps they had, Domran thought with a renewed shiver.

But then his eyes moved down from the upper reaches of the building and the far ends of the walls and focused for the first time on the ground on which they stood, and his stomach lurched. What had seemed, in the periphery of his vision, to be the splintered and rotting ruins of other, less imposing outbuildings was instead a carpet of bones. A few still were covered with disintegrating remnants of clothing, some with rusting chain mail, but most—and in the area before the main door, they were stacked at least three deep—were bleached white, entangled in the weeds and vines that had replaced the grass while he had been exploring the ruins that had initially drawn him into this impossible place.

But there were no skulls, not a one.

Cautiously, reluctantly, he moved forward, the grass seeming to claw at his legs and feet. A dozen yards short of the nearest bones—the nearest *visible* bones—there was another line of demarcation like the one that marked

the edge of the clearing. Here it marked the division
between the grass and the tangle of weeds and vines.

For a time he stood just behind the line, wishing fer-
vently he had never seen this place, wishing that even now
he could wipe its memory from his mind so Lord Azalin
could never learn of its existence. He wanted desperately
to simply turn and run, but he knew he couldn't. If he
returned to Darkon and Lord Azalin without having even
attempted to investigate something like *this*, especially
after what he had already found in the smaller ruins . . .

Bracing himself for he knew not what, Domran pulled
in a breath and stepped forward.

For an instant he was gripped by worse dizziness than
when he had first stepped into the clearing. The entire
world seemed to spin crazily about him, and when it
stopped . . .

When it stopped, he was swaying precariously and
facing back the way he had come, as if the world had
indeed spun around beneath his feet.

But obviously it was he who had spun. Overcome by
the dizziness, he had reeled about and ended up turning
around.

Turning back toward the building, he stepped forward
once again.

And found himself once again swaying dizzily and facing back the way he had come.

Three more times he tried to cross the line, and three
more times he failed. Once he tried not simply stepping
across the line but running, and the resulting dizziness
and nausea sent him crashing to the ground several feet
back the way he had come.

Relief swept over him as the nausea faded. He *couldn't*
cross the line, *couldn't* reach that place of death. Surely
Lord Azalin would not blame him for *that*.

Clasping the volume tightly to his chest, he made his way through the heavy grass to the edge of the clearing. Pulling in his breath, he stepped across the line of demarcation. Dizziness struck him once again, but when it cleared, he was, to his everlasting relief, outside the clearing, not lurching back into it.

And when he looked back, the clearing was as it had been, the only ruins visible the stubs of walls almost hidden by the grass. The veil had been returned.

*   *   *   *   *

When Azalin's far-ranging Sight first touched the journal, packed tightly in the young Kargat's saddlebags with dozens of other items, the lettering on the cover—*Scientific Journal*—was enough to make him pass it by with no more than a token glance. He had long scoffed at the idea that science could achieve anything remotely as great as what could be done with sorcery, but this journal, even in the brief moment he let his Sight hover close, proved to have a remarkable aura, unlike any other. Despite the claim of the lettering, sorcery had touched this book often and with strength. Intrigued, he had almost had the agent pull the journal free so that, with his Sight, he could inspect it more closely without the dilution of the other volumes packed so closely with it. But, no, he had decided, it was fragile and was best not handled excessively by others, particularly in such close proximity to the border mists, particularly by a Kargat agent who, though of necessity loyal, was more accustomed to wielding a warrior's sword or an assassin's dagger than handling anything as delicate as centuries-old parchment.

Instead, Azalin placed a protective spell on the entire contents of the saddlebags, as strong as the distance would allow, and ordered the uneasy agent to make haste to Avernus.

When finally the volume came physically into his hands, he knew he had something both unusual and far more ancient than anything the searchers had previously brought him. The dates inscribed on individual pages matched no calendar of any of the imprisoned lands, nor of any land of his own native Oerth. His Sight, however, told him that these writings, whatever their nature and origin, had been made long before Falkovnia had become trapped by the mists, before even Barovia, the first of the lands, had been imprisoned. And the few place names—Mount Yaanek, Desidarata, Calumnatus—had no counterparts in Falkovnia or the world to which that land or any other known to him had once belonged.

Eagerly he devoured the pages, and when he had finished, a mixture of elation and dread gripped him.

The writer of the journal, a man who called himself only Albemarl, claimed to be both a sorcerer and a scientist in an unnamed land where such a combination apparently was not uncommon. "The disciplines complement each other in many ways," he wrote, "if one has talent in both and the patience to persevere."

Albemarl himself, like young Firan Zal'honan, had been precocious in his aptitude for magic, but he had been far less impatient and arrogant. He had studied with the foremost mages of this unnamed land, and with scientists as well. But rather than go out into the world in search of power, as Firan had done, Albemarl had become a teacher, one of very few who taught in both disciplines. Gathering other like-minded practitioners about himself, he had founded a school under the patronage of the land's sorcerer-king, Galron, who even allowed the school to be built on an out-of-the-way corner of the palace grounds. Albemarl had spent most of the rest of his life not only teaching but also constantly experimenting with new and more effective ways of combining the two disciplines.

For a time, Albemarl wrote, it had been an idyllic existence. Galron himself was often their student and always a deeply interested observer, particularly when their work involved the prolongation of life and the ability to store the life-force itself. But then, not long after Albemarl had perfected a particularly efficient method of storage, matters took a darker turn. Galron secretly brought the sorcerer-scientist to the palace itself and, after swearing Albemarl to silence, revealed his true nature. Like Azalin, he was one of the undead, creatures feared and loathed even more there than in Darkon. As Azalin had for centuries, Galron wanted nothing more than to be able to discard the hideous, decaying body he was trapped inside.

And he had known for more than a century how it could be done. However, his abilities as a sorcerer were insufficient to accomplish the transformation. For that, he needed the help of science, which was, in fact, the reason for his patronage of Albemarl's school and others in the past. Albemarl's institution, however, was the first to master the particular technique that was needed: the ability to store the life-force in highly concentrated form, which Galron could then take into himself in a matter of seconds. There was, Galron was convinced, a certain "critical mass" of life-force that would enable him to break free of his material body and continue to exist in a completely nonmaterial state. More powerful sorcerers than he had accomplished this transformation, this ascension, through pure sorcery, but Galron needed the help of Albemarl's science.

Reluctantly Albemarl consented to construct such a device in Galron's palace and was subsequently forced to watch in horror as his worst fears were borne out. Thousands of innocent citizens were drained dry, changed from robust twenty-year-olds to dying centenarians in a matter of seconds.

And Galron ascended, his body turning to incandescent dust as the device was activated. If any proof was needed that Galron survived in some form, it came before another day dawned. Albemarl, knowing that rumor had already turned the device into the holy grail of others like Galron and of half the sorcerers in the land, attempted to destroy the device before any of those seekers learned of its success and of Galron's apparent departure. But as he tried to make his way across the grounds toward the palace, Albemarl found it guarded by newly formed spells that were far beyond his own abilities and had, prior to this time, been equally as far beyond Galron's. Then, as he retreated to the now-deserted school, the entire palace faded from sight. An illusion, he could tell, but not one he could combat any more than he could combat Galron's other spells.

Knowing that his own hours were numbered, Albemarl tried to escape with the journal he had been keeping since he had been called to the palace and learned Galron's true nature.

But it was too late. Whatever Galron had become had sealed the entire grounds. When Albemarl tried to race out through the open gates in the slate gray walls, he instead found himself racing back toward the school. Climbing the walls was no better. No matter which side he leaped down, he landed on the inside of the grounds.

Returning to the school, he scribbled a final few lines in the journal and then—or so he intended, according to the last words he wrote—wrapped it in the most powerful spells he knew, burning their symbols into the journal itself, and waited for the destruction he was certain was coming, hoping that the journal would survive and provide a warning and a method by which the device could be destroyed by any sorcerer with the power and courage to do so.

Azalin grimaced as he closed the journal. The thought of destroying such a device was ludicrous. If this ancient scribe was to be believed, it was the solution he had been searching for for centuries. This Galron had obviously been another like himself, able to drain the life-force from others and manipulate it. And Azalin had found the means—been *provided* with the means—to use that life-force to escape his body. In all likelihood, that means still existed, hidden behind Galron's illusions and spells.

Azalin's Sight quickly found the Kargat agent on the road heading back to Falkovnia. A mile ahead, where the road passed close by a well-kept graveyard, the grass above the most recent grave rippled and then parted. By the time the agent approached, its occupant, a young woman who had died in childbirth, was waiting in the middle of the road, her burial shroud smudged and tattered in the moonlight.

"Lord Azalin would speak with you again," her voice said in siren-like tones as her hand was raised imperiously.

The horse reared violently, but Domran was able to keep his seat, and moments later was spurring it back toward Avernus, more than a little afraid of what he would find waiting for him.

 **SIXTEEN**

Darkon
748, Barovian Calendar

The dreams of his namesake never returned, but still Oldar found himself returning to his ancestor's grave each year at this time. He knew it was pointless, and each year he told himself firmly that the day it took to walk there and back could be better spent working on the farm, particularly now that his father was growing increasingly unwell. In just the last few weeks, his cheeks had become sallow, his kerchiefs ever more often stained with flecks of blood as he fought to stifle the coughs that had become more frequent and more wracking with each change of the seasons. But still Oldar came, this one day, to stand over the grave amid the brambles and the autumn trees.

And each time, as he finished clearing the year's growth of weeds and vines from the weathered headstone and began the long trudge home, he paused beneath a massive oak with low-hanging branches and imagined a voice calling his name.

But no one, of course, was there.

Until the eighth year.

"Young Oldar," an unexpectedly familiar voice spoke

from the shadows of the oak, "there is one who would speak with you."

*   *   *   *   *

For a time, Azalin's Sight hovered above the bed where Oldar, exhausted after his day-and-a-half journey, slept in Balitor's mansion. He was no longer a boy but a young man, but his troubled features still bore the look of innocence that had been the hallmark of his namesake centuries ago. As did his mind, and once again Azalin felt a twinge of envy. He had not experienced such feelings himself since earliest childhood, well over three centuries ago.

Gently he probed Oldar's memories and again found upon the tampered-with portions the mark not of his tormentors but of whoever or whatever it was that seemed to oppose them and who therefore, despite appearances, must be his allies. For a time he considered attempting to restore Oldar's memories but quickly decided against it. The present mission would be easier if the young man believed that this was indeed the first time he had been called upon to serve. It could only cause trouble if he were burdened with—frightened by—the horrors of that other, failed expedition. In fact, now that Azalin took the time to consider it, he realized that, had Oldar's memories not already been suppressed by another, he would likely have eliminated them himself.

And he wondered uneasily, Was that why it had been done? Had those powers, whatever they were, anticipated this development? Knowing that memories of long standing would be harder to erase, had they in effect swept them away before they could take firm root? Or could it have been done simply to put the young man's mind at ease, to make his everyday life easier these past eight years?

But, no, he thought abruptly, remembering. Both ideas were ludicrous. For it was not just Oldar's memories that had been tampered with. Everyone's had been tampered with, even the Vistani's, as if in an attempt to erase all traces not only of the journey into the Barovian past but of everything that was even remotely associated with that journey. There had even been an abortive attempt to alter his own memories.

All part of the game . . . whatever that game might be.

A game which, if his present plan proved successful, he might soon have the power to enter on a more even footing . . .

For a time, he returned to studying Oldar's memories, not for further signs of tampering but for their content, for the worries and fears they revealed. As before, he was about to trust Oldar with his very existence, and he wanted nothing that would raise a barrier between them, nothing that could cause that trust to be broken. It was even more important this time than last. Before, there had been a mutual dependence. While he had been dependent on the boy to transport the phylactery within his very body, the boy had been dependent on Azalin for guidance, both through the mists and during their time in the Barovian past. But now, when they would be traveling through the mists not to another time but simply to another land from which Azalin himself was physically barred, Oldar would be far from helpless. He could find his way home—or to any land within the mists, even Strahd's Barovia—on his own, and Azalin would likely have no choice but to follow or perish. If Oldar returned to Darkon, of course, Azalin could easily punish him, even kill him and take over his body, but then he would have failed. He would again be trapped in Darkon, now with *no* one he dared trust with his existence the way he trusted Oldar.

Withdrawing from Oldar's mind, Azalin sent his Sight
soaring through the night toward the small farmhouse
where the young man's parents and his brother were
sleeping uneasily, their own dreams troubled by Oldar's
disappearance and the brief, puzzling message he had
apparently left on their door the night before.

*   *   *   *   *

In Oldar's dream, he was his own father, the searing
pain in his chest translating into a wracking cough that
seemed on the verge of tearing his lungs from his body.
But even as he wiped the phlegm and blood from his lips,
the pain faded, first into a faint tickle and then into nothing, and he felt himself drifting back toward sleep, an
image of his father seeming to float in the air before him,
no longer gaunt and pale but filled with the glow of health
and strength Oldar remembered from his childhood.

"Father?" The spoken word brought him briefly closer
to wakefulness, but something still held his body in thrall,
kept his eyes heavy, his thoughts muffled.

"He is healthy once again," a distant voice seemed to
say. "I have seen to that."

And sleep closed in once more, this time dreamless
and peaceful.

*   *   *   *   *

Oldar awakened abruptly from the soundest of sleeps,
his heart suddenly sent racing by the unfamiliar surroundings, by the outlandish sight and luxurious feel of the huge
canopied bed he found himself in. Where was he, anyway?

But then it all came rushing back: his namesake's
grave, the stranger who called himself Balitor, the long

ride through the countryside to this mansion in the highlands overlooking Il Aluk, the fantastical words they had
exchanged on the road and then here at a polished oak
dining table as servants brought them food and refresh-
ment the like of which Oldar had never dreamt.

Throwing the covers back, he leapt from the bed as if
escaping and scrambled into his clothes, which looked as
pitifully out of place in these surroundings now as they had
the night before. He had been a fool to follow the man, a
fool to listen to his nonsensical talk, an even bigger fool to
confide in him about the long-ago nightmares of his namesake and of an impossibly luminescent river guarded by
horrors risen from their graves. But the man had invoked
the name of Lord Azalin, to whom all owed allegiance and
service, none more so than Oldar and his family.

Throwing open the ponderous door, Oldar darted into
the wide marble hallway—and lurched to a stop.

Balitor was approaching a dozen yards down the hall,
accompanied by a man Oldar had never seen before, tall
and mustached, the toes of glistening black boots visible
beneath the hem of a silvery gray cape. Then, as Oldar
blinked, the man seemed to shimmer like a heat ghost
on a hot summer day, and suddenly he was several
inches shorter, the face narrow and hawklike, not handsome, the cape now as black as the boots.

Balitor swallowed nervously as the two men came to a
stop a half dozen yards from Oldar's gaping mouth.

"I am Lord Azalin," the stranger said, and Oldar recognized the voice that had spoken in his mind.

"Is it true?" he blurted out. "About my father?"

The man nodded with a thin smile, ignoring Balitor's
baffled look. "It is. His breath once again comes as easily
and as cleanly as yours, as it will for many years to come.
He is most likely already in the fields this morning."

And Oldar suddenly knew it was true. His breath caught in his throat, and after a moment he blinked and swallowed away the lump.

"I was told you have a chore you wish me to perform," he said, knowing that whatever task Lord Azalin set for him, he would accept without question.

The man nodded again, then turned and motioned for Oldar to follow. "Come, and we will discuss it."

Obediently Oldar followed while Balitor stepped aside nervously, his eyes downcast.

*   *   *   *   *

A moonless and sleepless night had not yet fully given way to a sunless dawn as Balitor and Oldar swung onto their waiting mounts and set out through the streets of Il Aluk toward Avernus at a rapid trot. All night and much of the previous day they had talked, even though, after the first hour, no new thoughts had come forward, only endless rechewings of the same wads of mental cud. Even so, they had not been able to bring themselves to stop, and as the night wore on, Balitor had become more and more convinced that within this Oldar's body lived that other Oldar now more than a century dead. And he could not help but fear that their present journey to Avernus would end even less happily for them than had that other journey a century and a half ago.

But Oldar would not consider going back on his word or refusing Lord Azalin in any way, even to leave behind the sword and scabbard the sorcerer-king had conjured up and was now fastened firmly to the pommel of his saddle. "For one who has never touched a weapon of any kind in all his life," Balitor had protested, "the presence of such a thing is an invitation to disaster."

Oldar had shaken his head at that and a dozen other of Balitor's pleas. "This whole matter is utterly beyond my comprehension," Oldar said grimly, "but I will not question it. My family has been in Lord Azalin's debt for generations, never more so than at this moment. This is a small price to pay, even if it means my life."

Despite the boy's determination, it was obvious to Balitor that he had grown more uneasy with each moment as Avernus, its towers and turrets dark shadows against the leaden sky, loomed ever larger and finally swallowed them up.

Instead of the splendid carriages and peacock-clad nobles that had greeted their arrival a century and a half ago, a score of mounted men in studded leather armor waited in the torchlight that was still required in the deep shadows of the castle and the bailey walls. Barely had the pair cleared the gate than the torch flames whipped as if in a sudden wind, even though the air was still. A moment later a huge translucent image of Lord Azalin's hawklike face wavered into view in front of the castle wall a dozen yards up. Only Oldar gasped at the sight, but few could suppress the chill that swept over them, least of all Balitor, who had been privy to all too many of Lord Azalin's purposely dramatic manifestations over his own unnaturally long life.

The eyes, several inches across, seemed to sweep the assembled group, then fastened on Domran, the Kargat agent who had brought the journal from Falkovnia.

The yard-wide lips moved, and a voice like muffled thunder said, "You shall be their leader, Lieutenant Domran. You will lead these men to the place in Falkovnia where you found the journal."

As the voice spoke, the chest of Domran's studded leather armor shimmered and then darkened to a midnight black. In the center, then, appeared the ruby eye that was Lord Azalin's symbol, while at the same time a jeweled dagger appeared at his waist, a quarter-length cape across his broad shoulders. The others edged their mounts away until their new leader sat alone, eyes wide, in the middle of a growing circle. When the transformation was complete, he looked around, swallowing visibly, then raised his head and nodded his thanks to the frightening image that still loomed above them all.

"I will travel with you," the thunderous voice resumed, "in the person of this man."

All eyes turned toward Oldar as his mount, nudged by an unseen spur, moved out from the shadow of the bailey wall.

"His name is Oldar," the voice continued. "For reasons that concern no one but myself, his family has been under my protection for generations, as he himself is now. Any who harms him or allows harm to come to him will answer to me! On this journey, what he sees, I will see. What he hears, I will hear. When he speaks, the voice will be his but the words will be mine, *and you will heed those words if you value your lives!*"

With that warning, the image vanished in a sudden gust of icy wind that extinguished every torch, leaving the courtyard illuminated only by the gray light that filtered through the low-hanging clouds.

* * * * *

It was obvious to Oldar throughout the dreary day's journey that, despite Lord Azalin's categorical and unequivocal warning, the majority of the men—Kargat, he had quickly learned—were far from happy with the situation. Their occasional hooded looks in his direction betrayed their feelings toward him beyond any doubt, and Oldar wished he dared to explain that he understood their feelings and to declare that he was no happier than they at being required to accompany them. It was galling enough to them, he was certain, that they were commanded not by a proper officer but by a novice no more experienced than any of them. But to then be ordered to defer to the slightest whim of someone who was not a Kargat, not even a warrior of any kind, only a lowly farmer, must be particularly humiliating. And if this interloper did truly serve as eyes and ears for Lord Azalin, that fact only added to the insult. If Lord Azalin needed someone to serve him in this manner, he should have chosen one of them, a Kargat, or at least an officer in some baron's forces, not an untrained and undisciplined outsider who knew only how to grub in the dirt and tend to stables.

And the fact that Oldar and his entire family somehow enjoyed Lord Azalin's protection must only make the hurt worse. Despite their own years of service, neither the Kargat nor their families enjoyed any such protection. If anything, their families were at risk because of their service, for the Kargat, if their identities ever became widely known, were ever the target of malcontents and the like. One such family, according to rumor, had been driven from Oldar's village less than a decade past, and nothing had been done by way of retribution against the offenders.

But there was nothing Oldar could do to alleviate the situation other than to remain as silent and inconspicuous as possible, toward which end he spoke not a word that entire day, only rode silently next to Domran, who, though he cast many an uneasy glance toward his companion, spoke only to his men and then in only the tersest manner. Time and again Oldar wished Balitor had accompanied him so that he would not feel so utterly alone. He even wished for some concrete indication that Lord Azalin was indeed within him, observing, constantly aware of what was happening. In that way, at least, Oldar would feel less adrift and helpless, less fearful that the slightest wrong step could bring disaster upon him.

But there was nothing, no slightest hint that he was anything other than what he had been all his life, no hint that Lord Azalin or anyone else was watching through his eyes or even aware of his existence.

Until that night . . .

They had kept up a brisk pace the entire day and continued until the last vestige of light vanished from the still cloud-filled sky. Where they finally stopped, only miles from where the border between Darkon and Falkovnia vanished into the bottomless pit that some called the Shadow Rift, the forest was thick and tangled, alive with the sounds of a hundred night creatures, unlike the silence that surrounded Avernus. Or so it was while their campfire glowed, while they ate, and while the Kargat cast silent, resentful glances at Oldar and their novice leader. Even as they drifted into uneasy sleep, the cries and clicks and rustlings continued.

But when Oldar awakened and raised his head from the saddle he used as a pillow, he was aware of only silence, the kind of silence he remembered from his dreams of that other Oldar. The others, he saw, were all still sound asleep. Even the one assigned to stand watch and keep the campfire fed was hunkered down next to its dying embers, his back against a gnarled tree trunk, his eyes closed.

Beyond the embers of the fire, something stirred. Leaves rustled as if in a rising wind, and the dozing sentry jerked awake and lurched to his feet.

Take up the sword, a soft voice said in Oldar's mind, sending an icy shock through him, despite its soothing tone.

Without conscious thought, his hands found the weapon's hilt, still in the scabbard attached to the saddle. Lord Azalin's earlier warning suddenly filled his mind:

"*There will be dangers that only this weapon can foil,*" he had said, conjuring the blade and scabbard seemingly out of thin air. "*Keep it close at all times.*"

And as Oldar's fingers now closed about the hilt, it was as if the weapon became an extension of his own arm, even though he had never touched this or any other weapon in all of his life. His heart pounding, he rose to his feet, half wondering if he was once again dreaming, if perhaps everything since his visit to the graveyard had been one long, bizarre dream.

The sentry, seemingly unaware that anything was amiss, was bringing the embers to flickering life with a handful of dry twigs, while in the shadows barely a dozen yards beyond the renewed fire, something was beginning to form: mist at first, swirling like a silent whirlwind, and then something more solid, until . . .

Abruptly a horse whinnied, and then another and yet another, until the night was filled with the sound and all were stamping their hooves and rearing up, straining at their tethers. And when the confusion was at its greatest, as the other Kargat were coming to their feet, hands reaching for hilts of swords and daggers, a nightmare stepped out of the mist into the firelight, a nightmare of decaying flesh wrapped in a muddied burial shroud, its eyes glowing like the embers of the campfire. The Kargat nearest the creature swung his sword wildly, but the creature swatted him aside as if he were a feather and stalked forward through the fire, its feet scattering the burning twigs and embers. Two other Kargat were disposed of with similar ease while the rest formed into a jagged circle about the creature, swords and daggers poised.

"Stand aside!" Oldar heard his own voice shout over the din the horses were still making. Then he heard in his mind: *Your weapon will deal with this horror.*

A nightmare, Oldar thought. This is truly a nightmare. But still he stepped forward, hearing his voice shout again for the others to stand aside, even though it was the last thing in the world that he wanted.

As they hurried to obey, he saw that the creature was almost upon him. He was paralyzed with cold terror and the impossible feeling that he had lived through this same nightmare before, but his sword rose up as if it had a life of its own, and as the creature's skeletal hands reached out for his defenseless throat, his own panic-driven muscles brought the sword down and across.

The blade erupted in a cascade of green phosphorescence as its edge struck the bones in the creature's neck—and continued on. For an instant the embers in the eye sockets burned more brightly and the skeletal fingers scraped at Oldar's throat.

But then, instead of collapsing to the ground, both skull and rotting body dissolved into an even greater shower of greenish phosphorescence that drove the bewildered Kargat back as they covered their eyes. For a moment it hovered in the air, swirling chaotically, and Oldar was certain he saw, in that moment, Azalin's face appear and then another face, that of the tall, mustached man he imagined he had glimpsed in Lord Azalin's stead at their first meeting, but this time there was a look of sadness in the eyes of both.

Even as the images appeared and just as quickly faded, a tendril of the greenish phosphorescence darted out and struck at Oldar's chest like a serpent, then vanished, taking with it all the rest, leaving behind not even a sprinkling of graveyard dust. Oldar gasped, almost screamed, as his chest was seared with burning pain, as if a flaming ember from the campfire had been pressed to his skin, but before he could rip at his shirt to pull it free, the pain was gone.

And a voice said silently in his mind, *Be not afraid, young Oldar, for I am with you.*

His entire body tingled then. A moment later, the horses began, one by one, to still their hooves and fall silent. When finally the silence was complete, his own voice—deeper than it had ever been, and stronger, but still his own—emerged from his lips and addressed the startled and bewildered Kargat: "It is well for you that this one is under my protection, is it not?"

From that point on, Oldar was treated with a mixture of fear and respectful deference. No more hooded, baleful looks were darted at him, no more grumbled complaints exchanged. Instead, at first, whenever Domran gave an order, most eyes darted questioningly toward Oldar, who could only tell them, nervously if plainly, that if Lord Azalin had anything further to say, he would undoubtedly say it. Until such time, Lieutenant Domran was their leader and no one else.

A mile short of the border with Falkovnia, Domran turned to the east along an almost nonexistent trail through the forest, paralleling the border for two or three miles before he turned back to the south toward Falkovnia. To cross into Falkovnia by a main road, he hastily explained when Oldar looked at him questioningly, was not wise. Strangers not obviously engaged in trade of some kind were not always welcome, and the main roads were all too often patrolled by overzealous members of the Falkovnian military. In any event, the area where the journal had been found was far from any road, barely a hundred yards from what had once been the border with G'Henna but which was now the beginning of the bottomless pit that was the Shadow Rift.

 **SEVENTEEN**

Falkovnia
748, Barovian Calendar (continued)

Azalin felt the weakness permeate his being the moment he passed through the mists and emerged into Falkovnia, and once again he had to strengthen the constant hold he maintained on the horses merely to keep them from bolting from his presence.

But at least he *had* been allowed to move out of Darkon and into Falkovnia, just as, eight years ago, he had been allowed to move through the mists and out of Darkon into the Barovia of four centuries past. But what would happen this time when he attempted to free himself from the phylactery and was no longer bodiless? Would his control and his powers be as weak as they had in that long-ago Castle Ravenloft? Or would he, this time, be immediately thrust back into Darkon?

For a moment he thought of turning back to Darkon and sending the Kargat on alone, but he knew it was impossible. The situation Domran had described—and described truthfully, Azalin had determined beyond all doubt—was hopeless for anyone not thoroughly versed and proficient in the sorcerous arts, and there was obviously no such person that

Azalin could trust with such a mission, certainly not among
the Kargat. He therefore had no choice but to resort once
again to this desperate subterfuge and hope that, when he
emerged from his phylactery, he retained enough of his abilities to achieve what had to be achieved.

He had recognized—or hoped he had recognized—the
spells that Domran had run afoul of, spells that, in
Darkon, he would have been able to dispose of easily. It
was no wonder that this Galron had needed the help of
"science" to achieve his ends, if these were the best he
could muster, even after his so-called ascension. And if
this device that Albemarl described had worked for Galron, it would certainly work for Azalin.

If he could gain access to it.

If it could be transported back to Darkon.

If it were not simply part of another trick perpetrated
by his tormentors . . .

But there was nothing to do now but wait and watch
silently through Oldar's eyes.

*   *   *   *   *

As the Balinok foothills were abruptly replaced by the
labyrinthine valleys Domran had described, all of Azalin's
senses came alert, doubtless sending a chill through his
host. *Something* had changed, almost as certainly as it had
changed when he had crossed from Darkon into Falkovnia.

Abruptly Domran's halting description of the landscape
he had passed through to reach the clearing at the edge of
the Shadow Rift filled Azalin's mind. "As if I had crossed
into another land," he had said, and this was the same.

For this was *not* Falkovnia they were traversing now,
any more than the Shadow Rift that lay ahead of them was
the G'Henna it had displaced. This was a small corner of

some other, unnamed land, perhaps the land described in Albemarl's journal.

Azalin reached out with his senses and found, to his utter amazement, that his Sight was once more with him. It was not nearly as powerful or as far-ranging as it had been these last years while he confined himself to the tower room high in Avernus, nor even as powerful as it had been when he had been a mortal sorcerer on Oerth.

But it was far more powerful than it had ever been in Darkon itself, or in Barovia. He felt as if suddenly he had been freed from the phylactery and all its limitations.

But why? How? Did the laws of nature and sorcery that governed this land differ so greatly from those that governed others? It was possible, certainly. His own laws for the rule of Darkon, after all, differed from those by which Strahd governed Barovia, which differed from those by which Von Kharkov ruled Valachan, so why should the laws by which sorcery operated here in this tiny pocket of a world not differ from the laws in the surrounding lands?

Suddenly he wondered, Was *that* why his powers were so greatly enhanced in that tower room in Avernus? Was that room an even tinier pocket of yet another world, where the laws of sorcery were drastically different from those in surrounding Darkon? Or just the *threshold* to another world?

Or was it, his ever-present paranoia insisted on asking, yet another trick by his tormentors, meant only to hold out false hope?

But it didn't matter, not here, not now. What mattered here and now was that his chances for success were, on the face of it, far better than they had been only minutes before.

Experimentally, cautiously, he sent his Sight flowing ahead.

And there, at the very edge of its range was the clearing that Domran had described. The various spells were
easily detectable, but at this distance he could neither
manipulate nor overcome them. He could, however,
observe and, to an extent, analyze them, and he was
relieved to see that the assumptions he had made based
on Domran's descriptions and those in Albemarl's journal were apparently correct. It was fortunate for both
Domran and Azalin himself that the spell that had kept
Albemarl confined to the grounds—essentially the same
spell that had kept Domran from approaching the
palace—had already been nullified, most likely by whatever process had transported the palace to this remote
corner of Falkovnia.

According to Domran, and now according to Azalin's
own Sight, the palace and its grounds were incomplete.
The outer walls that had once enclosed the grounds were
truncated, at one end by the rift, at the other end by
whatever marked the border of the clearing. Both ends of
the compound had been somehow sheared off and—
what? Left behind? Destroyed? Whatever had happened,
it had interfered with the workings of the spell and left the
ruins of Albemarl's school and at least a part of the
grounds open to anyone who cared to enter, sorcerer or
not. Had it still been in place when Domran arrived, the
young Kargat would likely still be confined there, gradually starving.

But there was, he now saw, something else that held
promise to be more difficult to overcome than either the
nullified spell or any of the spells that Domran had
encountered: a cadre of what almost certainly were
guardians of some sort, themselves enclosed in a powerful spell whose purpose he could not fathom. They
appeared to be mortals, not demons or spirits, but unless

there were other protections beyond the ability of his Sight to detect, they were almost certainly responsible for the grisly carpet of bones that Domran had testified literally surrounded the palace.

*　*　*　*　*

The land that had once been part of the foothills of the Balinoks was indeed a maze, one in which Domran became quickly and embarrassingly lost. If not for Lord Azalin's Sight, they would have wandered helplessly until nightfall rather than emerging from the forest at the edge of the seemingly empty clearing before the morning was out. To Domran's relief—and Oldar's—Azalin meted out no punishment nor even gave indication that he was aware of the young Kargat's failure.

As they all dismounted and tethered their animals just short of the line of demarcation between forest and clearing, Oldar felt the distinctive tingle in his chest that he had come to realize meant Lord Azalin was once again active. An instant later, the ruins of what must have been Albemarl's school sprang up before him, and then the marble palace and partial walls beyond. The latter shimmered briefly, then steadied, but all eyes were on the carpet of bones that surrounded the palace. The lack of skulls only made the sight that much more unnerving.

Oldar heard himself saying, "That which we seek is there, beyond that field of death. I will show you the way."

For an instant Oldar instinctively resisted, sending his body lurching to one side rather than stepping forward. A dozen pairs of Kargat eyes darted toward him, then hastily away. With an effort, Oldar forced his muscles to relax and wait for Lord Azalin to once again take control.

Finally his body, instead of taking a step forward, half turned and snatched the sword from the scabbard still attached to his saddle. Somehow Oldar kept himself from resisting, and the sword once more seemed to meld with his hand, becoming a part of his—of Lord Azalin's—body.

Slowly at first, then more rapidly, Oldar's body strode through the knee-high grass, past the granite and marble ruins of the school and on to the second line of demarcation, where the grass ended and was replaced by a tangle of weeds and vines, not unlike a miniature version of the forest that surrounded them.

The now-familiar tingle enveloped his body more strongly than ever as he came to that second border, hesitated briefly, and stepped across. A wave of dizziness momentarily blurred Oldar's vision, but he was not turned back. Whatever the spell that had earlier kept Domran out, it had not stopped Azalin and his host. Behind him, Domran followed, then another and another until all twenty Kargat, swords drawn, stood at his back.

The enveloping tingle grew almost unbearable as Oldar's body began again to move forward. Ahead, the bones stirred, and Oldar feared for a moment they were about to re-form themselves into whatever they had been in life and then rise and attack.

But they did not. Instead, with dry clacking and scraping sounds, they parted like leaves before the wind, leaving a clear path before him, and Oldar knew once again it was Lord Azalin's doing.

The massive palace doors creaked and slowly swung back, revealing a huge room that took up at least half the interior of the building. In the center, towering almost to the remnants of the roof fifty feet above, was what looked like nothing more or less than a gigantic hourglass fashioned from glass and gold, mounted on a broad metal platform covered with intricate and incomprehensible symbols that writhed like blood-red serpents, constantly shifting.

And on the floor around the platform were countless skulls, even more than could be accounted for by the masses of bones they had just passed through. Oldar could not suppress a shiver of revulsion. If this was what Lord Azalin was searching for . . .

And it was.

For one unguarded moment, Oldar felt the wave of triumph and elation that swept through his master and protector, but it did nothing to counter the revulsion that Oldar himself felt. If anything, it was made worse by the contrast.

And then his body was walking forward again, through the doorway, across the marble floor toward the device. This time the bones—the skulls—did not part as he approached, but soon Oldar could see that they were not free to move. Fine gold wires ran from the eye sockets of every skull to the metallic spots on the lower half of the hourglass.

With obvious unease, the Kargat followed until all stood silently behind him.

The metallic sound of swords being withdrawn from scabbards echoed through the room. Azalin spun Oldar's body around, controlling it with a brute force he had not before exhibited. Even as he turned, so did the Kargat, their own weapons raised.

In the broad open door through which they had just entered stood a dozen men in simple warriors' garb not unlike the studded leather the Kargat wore. On either side a dozen more appeared as if out of nowhere, and yet another dozen and another until they ringed the entire room.

For an instant some appeared to hesitate, grimacing in pain, as if their very existence were agony, but soon all were advancing, not with the slow, lurching steps of the walking dead but with the even strides of an advancing army—or an execution squad.

*   *   *   *   *

Azalin cursed his own foolish eagerness. He had *known* these guardians existed, *known* they were wrapped in a spell he had not been able to penetrate, a spell that could well hold a trap, and yet when he had seen the huge device and felt its latent power, he had hesitated hardly at all. He had dissolved the other spells with such childish ease, even in his weakened state, that he had lowered his guard and recklessly plunged ahead, arrogantly trusting in his virtually untested powers to see him through.

Mustering all his strength even as he cursed his blundering arrogance, he called on every battlefield spell he had ever learned, trying desperately to give the Kargat arms greater power, their leather armor greater strength, while at the same time slowing the enemy's advance, making weak their sword strokes, making blind their eyes. Some stumbled, some fell backward, others blinked in puzzlement, all were crippled in at least some small way. He began to hope that his efforts would be enough. Ten of the advancing horde fell for each Kargat defender, and then even more as the attackers' numbers decreased and he could concentrate his spells on those remaining.

But then, just as it seemed that he and the handful of remaining Kargat might win out, the attackers already slain began to rise, their wounds closing, their faces contorted in agony and determination, and he feared he had lost.

Unless . . .

Abandoning all attempts to control them, he instead dived into their minds, probing their memories, probing for weaknesses, probing into the nature of the spells that drove them. At first everything else was blocked by their vivid memories of the unendurable pain they had experienced again and again, almost as great as that which the decayed body of Firan Zal'honan had experienced in the room high in Avernus. A hundred times they had been slain, a hundred times they had been returned to a semblance of life, only to be slain again, either immediately or after an interminable wait whose tedium was almost as intolerable as the brief intervals of death and the agonies of resurrection.

But worst of all, he quickly saw, were not the repeated deaths and resurrections, nor even the relentless monotony they were forced to endure while waiting to be slain again. Worst of all was the nightmarish torture that descended on them if they had the temerity to refuse to do battle at all. For these were neither willing defenders of this place nor mindless automatons who had no choice in their actions. They were living prisoners of the ancient spells that bound them, simple spells cast by someone who had not the talent needed to control their minds and bodies, only the brute strength to inflict unimaginable pain upon them if they refused to take up their swords and go into battle again and again.

As the last Kargat fell and Oldar's body stood defenseless before them, he shouted into their minds: *I can give you the peace you all desire! I can give you final, irreversible death!*

Some stopped, a brief glint of hope appearing in their eyes before it was replaced with new agony. Others hesitated, grimaced, and continued forward, unable to bear the pain that hesitation brought.

I am your only chance to end this torture once and for all! Slay me and your hellish existence goes on forever!

More stopped then, and those who did not were set upon by others, falling only to rise again.

Until finally all were silent and rigidly motionless, the blood of the Kargat and of each other red on their swords, excruciating pain in their eyes.

And Azalin knew he had won.

*   *   *   *   *

He had not the power to completely dissolve the spells by which the transformed Galron had enslaved the guardians for centuries, and even if he had, he would not have used it, not then and there. Instead, he used counterspells to diminish their constant agony to a bearable level, letting them know that if he was himself destroyed, the counterspells would perish with him. Their only hope, he made clear to them, was to return with him to his own land, where his powers were equal to the task of giving them final peace. And to bring with them the object for which he had come, the device Galron had forced them to guard all these centuries.

He was relieved, then, to find that he was still able to wield reasonably powerful versions of most of the same spells that had allowed him to twice embed his phylactery within Oldar's chest. Here, he directed the spells at Albemarl's huge machine, shrinking and folding it and displacing great portions of it into adjoining planes until it was reduced to manageable proportions, though still too large to move through the tangled forest. The only route open to them, he quickly saw, was the narrow corridor of barren rock that ran along the edge of the Shadow Rift itself. It was not a route he favored, nor did any of his new companions, but there were no others, and soon, grudgingly taking turns, a dozen at a time, they were carrying the huge, skull-encrusted, coffin-shaped slab like pallbearers along the cliff's edge. Oldar's horse and those of the Kargat trailed obediently, if nervously, behind.

To his relief, and somewhat to his surprise, the trek was largely uneventful. Occasional wisps of shimmering fog rose up out of the depths of the rift and fluttered near the edge as if to watch, and occasional rumbles could be heard, sometimes accompanied by a slight trembling of the rock beneath their feet, but nothing interfered with their progress, nothing emerged from forest or rift to block their way or send them plunging into the bottomless pit.

Finally they were at the border to Darkon.

As Oldar passed through the mists, it felt to Azalin as if massive weights were being lifted from both his body and his mind. The moment he emerged into Darkon and was therefore no longer dependent on his phylactery, he reached out to the unburied dead and ensconced himself in the nearest body, that of an unwary traveler who had not obeyed swiftly enough a Kargat demand.

Rejoining the group in his new guise, he cautiously unraveled but did not entirely dissolve the spells that still gripped his new companions. He also lightened the spell that inflicted constant pain on them but left enough in place to serve as a constant reminder. With even greater caution, he strengthened as greatly as he could the spells that he had placed on Albemarl's device, reducing the amount of the device that still occupied space in this plane even more, until finally it was a faintly glowing sphere that fit handily into Oldar's saddlebag.

"You have done well, young Oldar," he said. "Now we return to Avernus."

 **EIGHTEEN**

Darkon
748–750, Barovian Calendar

Azalin allowed himself only a moment to revel in the joy of once more being truly alive. The body he had appropriated from its shallow grave the night before had been dead far longer than Gwilym's, and even in life it had not been comparable. But compared to what he had endured for the centuries before Gwilym's, it was, in this room, sheer bliss.

But now was not the time—there *never* was a time—to indulge himself so. Now was the time for decision and action.

A moment later his Sight swooped down into the bowels of Avernus, where the hundred-odd guardians patiently awaited their promised death. One by one, slowly and meticulously, he examined them for even the faintest traces his tormentors might have left behind.

And there were none.

Nor did their memories reveal any such. They did, however, reveal much that confirmed what Albemarl had written in his journal.

Science, in their world, had been, if not a companion to magic, an important adjunct.

Their master Galron had indeed abandoned his body. To that end, over a period of more than a year, they had brought thousands of young, vigorous men and women from hundreds of miles around to Galron's palace, only to see them transformed into dying oldsters in a matter of minutes as their vital energies were somehow drained away. Finally Galron had lowered himself into the device and then conjured up a rainless mage storm of massive proportions, bringing bolt after bolt of blinding lightning crashing down on metal rods he had mounted on the roof of the palace and connected to the device by serpentine cables that glowed and pulsed with each strike, as did the device itself. As the mage storm reached its height, the entire palace was enveloped in a crackling electrical aura, though the device became a pulsating shape of blackness hovering in the center.

And then the mage storm was over.

And Galron—Galron's body—was gone from the device, burned away by the energies involved, some said.

But Galron himself was obviously not gone. His voice thundered silently in every mind as he performed feats he had only dreamed of before.

And there the guardians' memories of that world ended, for that was the point at which Galron had bound them into the spells that had held them prisoner ever since, forcing them to emerge from their timeless limbo again and again, century after century, to protect what Galron had left behind.

Every guardian's mind told essentially the same story.

Finally, satisfied he could learn no more from them, he dissolved the last of the spells that still bound them to life. As their bodies shriveled and their tortured life-forces drained away, their gratitude filled Azalin's mind, but he impatiently brushed it aside. Such things mattered not to him, nor did it matter that their suffering had finally ended. What mattered was that he now possessed what he had set out to retrieve—and that the promise he had made to them had been kept.

*   *   *   *   *

Despite his inability to find any trace of his tormentors on either the guardians or the device itself, Azalin was still not fully convinced they were not in some way involved. He had underestimated their levels of deception and treachery too often in the past and was determined not to do so again. Thus, instead of bringing the device into Avernus, he took it to the Grim Fastness, the Il Aluk head-quarters of the Kargat, where he released it to its original size and shape and shielded it with the most powerful of all his protective spells. In addition, he left his phylactery embedded within Oldar and likewise surrounded the boy with a sturdy shell of protective spells and bade him remain nearby, with Balitor in Il Aluk. In this way, if the device did prove dangerous, a retreat into the phylactery and thence into the mists was at least possible.

Returning to Avernus, he used his Sight to study the device ever more closely, to try to fathom the supposedly scientific principles that had enabled Albemarl to store such massive amounts of life energy. Physically, there was little inside the lower half of the device but thousands of metal plates separated by an odd gelatinous substance. In that respect, it looked rather like the devices a madman had brought to him during the early years of his reign in Knurl.

"It will harness the power of lightning itself!" the fool had claimed, as if anything so grand could be accomplished by mere science! By way of demonstration, the lunatic had produced a bolt of lightning a few inches in length, accompanied by a feeble crackling that was closer to the sound of parchment being crumpled than of the deafening thunder of true lightning.

Each of the plates in Albemarl's device, however, was indelibly inscribed with dozens of seemingly meaningless symbols, though Azalin had little doubt that, in whatever sorcerous languages were native to Albemarl's world, they were far from meaningless. And portions of the constantly writhing blood-red symbols that adorned the lower half of the device itself would occasionally, for just an instant, duplicate the symbols on one or more of the metal plates. It was as if the surface symbols—or whatever power had placed them there—were forever searching for the proper pattern, like a man trying to find the one key out of a million that would fit one particular and very intricate lock.

After several months of futile study, he decided the only way he would ever learn the truth was by observing the device in operation. And then, if it were indeed a trap laid by his tormentors, it would be too late. The trap would have been sprung.

Unless . . .

With greater care and deliberation than he had ever exercised, he used his augmented powers to duplicate the device, but on a scale much less grand. Instead of metal plates two feet square, he shrank them to inches, with the etched-in symbols correspondingly small but no less distinct. Instead of a forty-foot behemoth, the shell of the device was just large enough to accommodate a single body. The outer symbols, no less shrunken, twinkled like blood-red stars as they took up the constant motion of their larger brethren.

And to assure there was no interaction between the devices, no chance that the mage storm needed to bring the one to life would activate the other as well, he removed the lesser one more than threescore miles to Nartok and the Temple of Eternal Order, commandeered for this purpose by the Kargat.

Meanwhile, the hundreds of Kargat who had once scoured the lands for magical knowledge and devices now sought out life. Rather than raise suspicion by having the subjects brought to the temple or the Grim Fastness, only to never be seen again, the Kargat slaughtered them where they were found throughout the lands, their life-force flowing into the very blades with which their lives were taken, blades that Azalin himself had specially prepared for the task.

Finally, he was ready.

Only one question remained: Who would be the one to enter the device?

*　*　*　*　*

His name was Lowellyn Dachine. He was captain of the Kargat given charge of the temple in Nartok when Lord Azalin transferred a mysterious device from Kargat headquarters in Il Aluk to the temple. But he was also— or so he thought of himself—the son of Lord Azalin.

In truth, Lowellyn Dachine was only one of a number of Azalin's failed experiments.

Though born of woman, he had been created, not sired, for no creature of Azalin's nature, regardless of the power of his magic, was capable of producing son or daughter. Decades ago, while Azalin had still been searching desperately for a method whereby he could assimilate new magic, he had hit upon the idea of duplicating himself.

Using variations of the same spells he would later use on Albemarl's device and on his own phylactery, he embedded in the wombs of several women living seeds that should in time have grown to be precise duplicates of Firan Zal'honan, with all the talents and abilities he had possessed in mortal life. Though Azalin himself was prevented by his tormentors from remembering and using even the simplest of new spells, surely these duplicates would not be similarly handicapped. And if they were not, if they could indeed learn new magic, he would find a way to transfer that learning to himself. If all else failed, he reasoned, they could be slain, and one by one their bodies— and their minds and powers—would become his.

But it was not to be. Perhaps his own sorcery was at fault. Perhaps his tormentors intervened, as they had in so many other things. Certainly the results were such that they would have been amused. Many of the would-be duplicates died in their mothers' wombs. Others emerged as monstrosities that, if not destroyed by mother or midwife, did not survive the cradle. Only a handful were born fully human, and none of these bore even a passing physical resemblance to the Firan Zal'honan who had been. The only trait of his that they all shared was a talent for sorcery, which Azalin in all cases mightily encouraged. In the end, however, it was all for naught. Though they all proved marvelously capable learners, his attempts to take into himself the magical knowledge they gained proved as futile as all his other attempts to gain such knowledge. Nor was he then prepared to take the chance of having his own body destroyed in order for him to take up residence in one of theirs.

But Dachine knew none of this. He only knew he had grown up fatherless and Lord Azalin had evinced an interest in him from his earliest years, even brought him to Avernus a number of times to conduct odd experiments that, judging from Lord Azalin's reaction each time, ended unsatisfactorily. Those circumstances, coupled with his natural talent for sorcery and Lord Azalin's repeated urgings to make use of it, had roused Dachine's suspicions from the time he realized, earlier than most, that little in Darkon was as it first seemed. Questions asked of his mother, now long dead, had gone unanswered or were vehemently denied, but her demeanor was never convincing. His one regret was that he had not used his own magic to extract the truth from her, but she had died unexpectedly before he had gained sufficient power and subtlety to do so without her knowledge, and he had not been able to bring himself to do it openly and with force.

But now . . .

Now he had been personally chosen by Lord Azalin to take charge of the temple in Nartok, and it was obvious that something of great import was about to happen. A mysterious device had been transported to the temple from Kargat headquarters in Il Aluk, a device whose purpose—whose very appearance—was known only to Lord Azalin himself. For days it had lain in the rear nave of the temple, protected from all hands, concealed from all eyes by spells cast by Lord Azalin himself, but even he could not prevent rumors and speculation, nor conceal the constant comings and goings of both priests and Kargat with their equally mysterious blades.

But only Dachine, being sorcerer as well as both Kargat and priest, could sense what was contained in the blades: the very life-force of those the blades had slain. Those who fared forth to do the assassinations knew only that Lord Azalin had given them the blades and required the deaths. Only Dachine and others with his abilities could see that the blades, as they were returned one by one to vanish beneath those same spells, literally pulsed with that distinctive energy.

And Lord Azalin was obviously well versed in such matters. How else had he managed to remain not only alive but young and vigorous for the nearly two centuries he had ruled Darkon? Even among the general populace, there were tales of how he had publicly and capriciously demonstrated his abilities, draining decades of life from one who had offended him during a particular evening and bestowing those decades on one who had pleased him.

Coming so close on the heels of the years of forays into other lands to retrieve "anything relating to magic," this device was likely a result of those forays, or so Dachine told himself. It was also obvious to him that whatever the device was, it involved life itself, though he could not imagine what it could be that Lord Azalin's own sorcery could not already accomplish. It must be something truly magnificent, and he could not help but wonder if it were not related to those other unexplained and, to him, incomprehensible experiments for which he had long ago been summoned to Avernus. On those occasions Lord Azalin had greeted him personally, and Dachine, a powerful sorcerer even then, had sensed an eagerness despite Lord Azalin's stoic facade. Each time, then, for a few brief minutes, Lord Azalin had seemed to burrow into the young Dachine's very mind, and once again, even more strongly, Dachine had sensed Azalin's eagerness, but as the minutes and seconds passed, the eagerness always changed to disappointment and finally anger, though it did not seem to be directed at Dachine himself.

And then the experiments—and the summonses—had ended. There had been no further contact of any kind between the two until Dachine, now a captain in the Kargat, had been summoned to command the occupation of the temple in Nartok.

Surely there was significance in that. A new, grander experiment? One Lord Azalin had learned of in another land? One that would not end in the disappointment and anger of all those others?

Dachine didn't know, *couldn't* know for certain, but he could not help but think that perhaps at last his time had come. . . .

* * * * *

In the end, the decision of who was to enter the lesser device was relatively straightforward.

For purely technical reasons, Azalin briefly considered Lowellyn Dachine, and had even put him in charge of the Kargat who commandeered the temple so as to have him immediately available. Despite Dachine's radically different physical appearance, his mind and talents were as close to those of the mortal Firan Zal'honan as any in Darkon, and he would therefore provide a truer test of the effects of the device than any other. What the lesser device would do to Dachine, Albemarl's device would do, to a greater extent, to Azalin. But that very similarity to Azalin's earlier self, manifested most notably in Dachine's sorcerous powers and ruthless ambition, quickly convinced Azalin that he dared not use Dachine. There was no way of knowing how greatly Dachine's power would be multiplied by the device, and Azalin did not relish the possibility that the young sorcerer's power might exceed his own.

The obviously best choice for all other reasons, of course, would have been Oldar, but he was already fulfilling a vital role. There was absolutely no one else Azalin dared trust with the phylactery.

Second choice was almost as obvious: Balitor. Though not as naively trusting and grateful for small favors as Oldar, he had nonetheless always been loyal and, after a few decades as Baron of Il Aluk, almost completely lacking in personal ambition. It had been his own choice, in fact, to step down in favor of another, and he had been largely content ever since in his role as Il Aluk's reclusive elder statesman and Lord Azalin's occasional errand boy.

Or if he was not content, he had never complained nor given the least hint of dissatisfaction.

*   *   *   *   *

It was near midnight when Balitor approached the Temple in Nartok. He had left his horse at a nearby stable and now stood uneasily in the cobblestoned street in front of the massive, ugly building. He had not been anxious to enter even before he saw it, and his reluctance was only intensified by the torch-lit sight of its walls of dull black stone and its gargoyle-surrounded domes of mottled, bone-white tile that resembled nothing more than poisonous fungi. Even the doors, four of them at the head of a flight of wide stone steps, were set in frames carved to make the entrances look like gaping mouths, as if ready to devour any worshipers who dared enter.

As he watched, the doors swung wide and regurgitated a stream of people of all ages, peasant and merchant alike, who scuttled out and down the steps, probably grateful to have survived another of the temple's compulsory services. The sight of their resigned but frightened faces only made Balitor's desire to flee all the greater. But he knew he had no choice in the matter. Lord

Azalin could reach out and take him no matter where he fled, so there was no point in even trying to run. It could only cause irritation, and Lord Azalin was deadly enough when his mood was good.

Balitor had enjoyed the last few weeks with Oldar as much as any he could remember since those long-ago days with the young man's namesake, before either of them had set eyes on Lord Azalin—or Firan Zal'honan, as he had called himself those first few days after he had stumbled out of the mists. In those days, he and Oldar had lived by their wits in the streets and alleys of Il Aluk, and though they often slept in the streets or stables, it seemed to Balitor that their sleep had been sounder, their awakenings brighter than anything he had experienced since. An old man's foolish dreams of youth, he knew, even though, thanks to Lord Azalin's occasional ministrations, he was still physically much the same as he had been then, almost two hundred years ago.

But mentally—that was another matter. No amount of physical rejuvenation could refresh his mind and soul. In those early days, he had had a purpose—to survive, to find food and shelter and an occasional friend, to find enough coin to afford a drink and a song. Now, for all too many decades, his only purpose was to fill his hours until it was time again to sleep, while not allowing himself to think more often than absolutely necessary about those whose lives had been shortened to extend his own. Occasionally one of the barons or some minor functionary would come to pay his respects or, more rarely, to actually ask his advice on some insignificant matter. Even more occasionally, Lord Azalin would send him on an errand, most recently to fetch Oldar.

And now he was on another such errand, one he feared might be even less innocuous than the last.

"Come immediately to the temple in Nartok," a voice unmistakably Lord Azalin's had said, awakening him in the night. "I have a chore that only you can perform." The one standing over his bed, however, had been Oldar, his body obviously under the control of another.

Almost certainly this errand—this "chore"—had to do with whatever had been brought back from Falkovnia, which was something Balitor did not even want to think about. From what Oldar had seen and heard while Lord Azalin was perched in his head during that expedition, the device provided storage for dozens, perhaps hundreds or even thousands of times as much life-force as Balitor himself had had thrust upon him over the years. And that life-force would have to be taken from someone—from many someones—which meant that many would have to die before the device could be filled, a process that Balitor was almost certain was already under way. Rumors of disappearances and unexplained deaths, always common, had reached new heights in the days since the device had been brought back, and Balitor had little doubt why. He only hoped that whatever Azalin's plans were, they did not involve *him*. Over the decades, he had accepted without protest Azalin's gifts of renewed youth, knowing it could be dangerous beyond mere death to refuse, but something of this magnitude . . .

He shuddered, envying Oldar the naiveté that allowed him to hear these same rumors and yet not comprehend their true meaning, nor even suspect that he himself, by aiding Lord Azalin, was in any way involved. But he was not thus blessed. Perhaps this time, though, if his worst suspicions were borne out, he would at least have the courage to refuse, as the original Oldar had had the courage to refuse Lord Azalin's offers.

Finally, the last of the worshipers scurried down the

temple steps and into the night. Bracing himself, for what little good it did, Balitor crossed the cobblestones and climbed the steps to the hideous doors.

To Balitor's relief, Azalin was not there to greet him. Not that he'd expected it, not here, away from Avernus. The one who was waiting to usher him in, however, was scarcely more reassuring than the appearance of the temple itself. An emaciated six-and-a-half feet tall, with jutting cheekbones and dark, sunken eyes, he wore the loose-fitting ash gray robe of the priesthood, and yet he introduced himself as Lowellyn Dachine, a captain of the Kargat, an admission that was as startling as it was uncommon, considering the normally secret nature of the upper echelons of the Kargat. It was their function, after all, to spy out disloyalty and discontent and administer punishment, either secretly by night or openly by day as instructive examples.

And, of course, to do as Lord Azalin bade, be it to search out magical knowledge in other lands or to harvest the life-force of the innocent and not-so-innocent.

The Kargat priest offered no explanation, nor did Balitor ask for one. Balitor knew that when an explanation was to be offered, it would come from Lord Azalin and no one else. Doubtless Dachine knew the same. Instead, Dachine silently led the way through the nave toward the massive stone altar at the far end, beneath the temple's main dome. A bald, skeletal-faced priest still standing behind the altar looked up and scowled as he saw the pair approaching, but almost immediately turned and stalked away. It was Bishop Grimshaw, Balitor realized as he saw the golden sickles embroidered on the sleeves of his otherwise plain gray robe. No wonder he had scowled. Dachine and his Kargat had, after all, essentially stolen the temple from him.

A dozen lesser priests in their own ill-fitting gray robes were scattered about, cleaning up after the hundreds of worshipers who had just left and preparing for the hundreds more who would be subjected to another service the next night. Balitor was not surprised to see one priest on his knees, scrubbing vigorously at a stain that could have been blood. Services in temples of the Eternal Order, while decreed compulsory for most, had never had a reputation for safety. Considering the fact that Lord Azalin himself was the author of the decree, however, Balitor suspected that attendance was safer than the alternative. One of the few rewards of his own unique situation that Balitor had always appreciated was an exemption from that particular decree.

Although, he thought with another shiver as Dachine shepherded him past the altar toward the rear wall and a wide double door half hidden by an ornate wooden screen embossed with images of skeletons rising from their graves, he would perhaps be required tonight to make up for that lifelong exception.

 **NINETEEN**

Darkon
750, Barovian Calendar

Puzzled, Dachine ushered the one called Balitor through the main nave and gestured open the broad double doors at its rear. Who was this fool, and why had Lord Azalin summoned him? He was obviously no sorcerer, nor even a noble of any importance. There was an air of age about him despite his youthful appearance, but . . .

Suddenly Dachine remembered his history. More than a hundred and fifty years ago, this man had been the Baron of Il Aluk, replacing the traitor Aldewaine. He had reigned for a time and then, against all sense, stepped down. Instead of striking the man down for the insult, Lord Azalin had ever since kept him from age and death, infusing him again and again with the life-force of others! The same life-force that the Kargat had been harvesting across the land, bringing here to be infused into Lord Azalin's mysterious machine, just as lesser amounts had been infused into this Balitor!

And Dachine wondered, Was the man a key of some kind? A key to the operation of the machine? Was that why he had been kept alive so long, despite his seeming uselessness? The idea made no sense, since Lord Azalin had not even suspected the existence of such a machine until a few months ago. But there had to be *some* reason. Lord Azalin, after all, had never been known for either charity or forgiveness.

But Dachine of course had no way of knowing. He had not even been able to determine what the machine's function was intended to be, nor what its true appearance was. He had tried every spell he knew in efforts to penetrate the spells Lord Azalin had woven about the device, but to no avail. He knew only that it must by now be filled to bursting with the life-force of countless of the Kargat's victims, and he knew that only from having watched hundreds of Lord Azalin's daggers, each pulsing with stolen life, being absorbed by the machine moments after the returning Kargats offered them up.

Grimacing inwardly with continued frustration, Dachine followed Lord Azalin's orders and gestured Balitor through the doors and along the corridor toward the far end, where it opened out into another, smaller nave, this one beneath the temple's rear dome. As it had been since the machine had appeared, the nave was deserted. No one but Dachine himself and the blade-bearing Kargat had been allowed inside, much to Bishop Grimshaw's fury. Even Grimshaw, however, had not seen fit to protest too vigorously or openly. Like everyone, he doubtless knew the penalties for defying or angering Lord Azalin.

As they approached the spell-obscured machine, squatting directly under the center of the rear dome, the surrounding air shimmered like a distorting lens. Dachine drew in his breath sharply, wondering if he was finally to be vouchsafed a true vision of the device he had been caretaking for all these weeks.

But even as a golden, coffinlike shape began to solidify behind the shimmering air, a second object took shape above it, just below the dome: Lord Azalin's face, its eyes locked on the pair even before its countenance was fully formed.

* * * * *

Somehow Balitor kept from shuddering while Lord Azalin's image spoke, confirming Balitor's worst fears. Lord Azalin wanted *him* to climb into this—this infernal machine he had brought back from the edge of the Shadow Rift! Lord Azalin wanted *him* to be "transformed into something greater" than he was now! There had been no specific mention of innocent people having been slaughtered in order to prepare the machine for operation, but everything pointed to precisely that. Even the machine itself, revealed as a golden coffin now that Lord Azalin's spells had been stripped away, was a grim reminder of what it doubtless contained. How many—in how many lands—had died for this so-called transformation?

"But-but why *me?*" he managed to stammer out, not noticing the scowl that Dachine was directing toward him.

"You question my judgment?" The image's brow furrowed in the beginnings of a frown.

Balitor shook his head. "I question my own worthiness, Lord Azalin," he said, still avoiding the truth, which was that the very thought of absorbing all those stolen lives filled him with stomach-wrenching guilt.

"There is none more worthy, my friend," the image said, the embryonic frown becoming an equally embryonic smile, "except perhaps young Oldar, and he has other responsibilities now."

Dachine, dumbfounded at this talk of friendship and worthiness, could not contain himself any longer. If anyone was worthy of this honor, if anyone was *owed* this honor, it was he, not this spineless leech! "If this one is too lily-livered to accept the danger that accompanies this honor," he grated, "I will offer myself in his place!"

"I would hold my tongue if I were you, Captain Dachine!" the image said, the smile turning instantly to a scowl. "You are present for one reason and one reason only: to see that my wishes are carried out!"

Balitor's stomach lurched as Dachine's eyes flashed with anger for a moment before, with grudging obedience, the Kargat lowered them to stare grimly at the temple floor. So *that* was why the Kargat was here, Balitor thought with a silent shiver. If I try to reject this "honor," Dachine will pitch me into the machine.

For just an instant, Balitor's instincts told him to bolt from this temple of death, but once again his common sense told him it would be utterly useless. Even in the unlikely event that he could elude the Kargat, there was no place in Darkon where he could hide from Lord Azalin.

And then he thought, as if grasping at straws to ease the churning in his gut and salve his own conscience, If this so-called transformation is as great as Lord Azalin seems to expect, perhaps I will then have the ability—the power—to redeem myself for a century and a half of cowardice.

Or even—and the thought came suddenly and unbidden, as if thrust into his mind by another—rid Darkon of Lord Azalin and his depredations!

His heart suddenly pounding, he tried desperately to force the traitorous thought from his mind. If Lord Azalin should somehow become aware . . .

"If it is your wish that I undertake this chore in your name, Lord Azalin," he said hastily, afraid his trembling voice would betray him, "then I am ready to do so."

The image smiled faintly. "It is good that you do this

willingly, for the rewards will almost certainly be beyond anything you can imagine."

Balitor said nothing, only bowed his head and waited.

And felt himself being gently lifted by unseen forces.

*   *   *   *   *

Azalin watched as Dachine reluctantly levitated Balitor and lowered him into the machine, seemingly a massive golden coffin with tiny, ever-shifting blood-red symbols on every surface. The Kargat was obviously, and not surprisingly, envious, almost to the point of rebellion. Azalin didn't think it would reach that point, but even if it did, it wouldn't matter. Once Balitor was within the device, he would be gripped by the same forces that would, when they were fully unleashed, transform him. Until then it would take a greater sorcerer than Lowellyn Dachine to extract him.

And having Dachine in the nave with the device served its own purpose: to see what effect the device's operation would have not only on the being within but on an onlooker, particularly this onlooker, who, in certain significant ways, might serve as a stand-in for Azalin himself.

Finally all was ready, and Azalin began.

*   *   *   *   *

Above Nartok, the few stars that had been visible in the midnight sky faded from view as clouds formed and darkened and boiled in the sky like the witch's brew they were. And as they formed, a wind arose, not blowing across the city but inward from all directions, whipping at the torches in the streets until every open flame in Nartok was bent toward the temple as if in prayer. The air went desert dry and yet bone-chillingly cold, as if a snowless winter had suddenly gripped the city.

Within the temple, despite the closed and barred doors, candelabra flames bent in a chill draft and pointed mutely toward the rear nave while priests paused in their cleansing labors to shiver and clutch their ill-fitting robes more closely about themselves.

Across the city, voices were stilled as eyes turned to follow the wind. Those near enough to the temple could see the mottled domes take on a faint, greenish glow, as if to serve as guides for the unnatural wind.

Then the lightning, dry and rainless, began. First there were only distant rumbles from deep within the clouds, dimly lighting entire sections of the sky like candles behind a gray stained-glass window. Gradually the rumbles grew louder, the flickers brighter, contrasting ever more sharply with the pockets of blackness that still separated them. Throughout Nartok, all eyes except those few still closed in sleep were turned toward the lowering sky as they shivered in the rising wind, wondering what wizards were doing battle this night.

For this, all but the dullest-witted knew, was not a natural storm of lightning and rain but a mage storm, the sort conjured up by the most powerful of wizards to hurl against each other when all else failed. There were many who correctly identified its author as Lord Azalin, for who else in Darkon had the power to bring about a display such as this? And some, who saw the first bolt descend from the clouds and strike the temple domes, were momentarily gratified that finally he had turned against the so-called Eternal Order and its vile priests.

But as bolt after bolt struck the domes and still they remained seemingly untouched except to emit an ever brighter, ever more gangrenous green glow until it lit the billowing bellies of the clouds themselves between strikes, they realized sadly that this was not, after all, likely to be the night that would see the end of the Eternal Order.

*　*　*　*　*

Lowellyn Dachine gritted his teeth as he obediently levitated the usurper Balitor into the coffinlike machine that had finally been revealed. His shattered hopes, his bitter frustrations had turned to boiling anger, but he knew there was nothing he could do. Lord Azalin's powers had time and again been demonstrated to be far superior to his own, indeed to those of any other wizard of Darkon. And even if Azalin's attention were fully occupied with the generation of the mage storm that was necessary to trigger the device, the forces that already bound the fool inside were far too strong for Dachine to break.

But surely there was *something* he could do! He would rather die a thousand deaths than see this idle fool be given what was rightfully Lowellyn Dachine's!

Through the stained-glass windows that ringed the dome overhead, he saw the first flickers of lightning from the coming mage storm. Lord Azalin's image had already faded to transparency and now vanished altogether as the dome itself began to faintly glow. The device—the golden coffin—seemed as yet untouched, and he could see Balitor's terror-stricken face as it was forced to look directly up at the dome.

The fool! To fear a transformation such as this! A transformation that could give even an ordinary mortal like him the power to . . .

The truth came to Dachine in a flash: Azalin was *afraid* of him, afraid of what Lowellyn Dachine might become! This mortal weakling had no powers, no talents of any kind, so that when he was transformed into something much greater, he would *still* be a weakling, hardly a threat to the great Lord Azalin.

But Lowellyn Dachine . . . *he* was already a sorcerer of great power. Given time, he might even eclipse his lord and master. If *he* were to be transformed, he would then and there become the lord and master, to whom Azalin must bow and scrape!

Overhead, the dome was glowing a brighter green, and the rumbles of thunder grew ever more intense. The blood-red symbols on the surface of the golden coffin were pulsing and writhing at an almost blinding pace. Surely Lord Azalin was as fully occupied as he would ever be; mage storms required not only immense power but immense concentration. The slightest lapse could send the lightning and the other unseen powers of the storm back against its creator and . . .

Dachine levitated himself sharply until he hovered over the coffin and its terrified occupant. He felt the power of the forces that confined the man and knew he could not break them. He could not, no matter how hard he tried, displace Balitor from the machine.

But he *could* join him! And when they were both transformed, he could destroy the fool with no more effort than it took to swat a fly. And then he could turn his attention to the great Lord Azalin!

Taking great pleasure in the increasing intensity of the fear in Balitor's eyes, Dachine lowered himself, slowly and deliberately, into the coffinlike apparatus.

A moment later, the dome glowed brightly as the first bolt of lightning struck home, and the coffin itself was enveloped in an even brighter glow.

And Lowellyn Dachine felt new power flowing through him like a cleansing flame. . . .

*   *   *   *   *

Balitor tried desperately to move as he saw the emaciated face and mad eyes of Dachine hovering over him,
slowly descending, but it was as if he were embedded in a
block of transparent granite. Then, as Dachine's face was
almost touching his, the Kargat smiled, and Balitor somehow managed to clamp his eyes tightly shut as a stupen-
dous clap of thunder, followed an instant later by a bolt of
lightning striking the temple itself, almost deafened him.

A moment later, Balitor's entire body erupted in fiery
pain, the like of which he had never before experienced,
and he wondered frantically if the lightning bolt was
passing through his body, scorching and consuming it
from the inside out. He would have screamed had he
been able, but his throat was as frozen as the rest of him.

A second deafening crash of thunder and then a third,
and the brilliance of the lightning seemed to burn
through the lids of his eyes. And then the sound and the
light were continuous, strike following strike, but over it
all he could hear a bubbling hiss so loud it seemed to be
coming from within his head, within his body. At the
same time, the searing pain faded, and he wondered if it
was truly waning or if his nerves had simply been burnt
from out of his flesh.

But, no. As the pain diminished and the lightning continued to send the temple dome through paroxysms of
kaleidoscopic brilliance, he felt his body, felt *parts* of his
body . . . moving.

Beneath his skin, his muscles—his viscera?—writhed
like a nest of snakes, and he wondered with new horror if
that was the source of the grotesque bubbling sound he
could still hear over the crashing thunder.

The sound of his own metamorphosis?

Desperately Balitor tried to raise his head to look down at his body, but he could not, and he was grateful for the paralysis, for his inability to actually *see* what his body was becoming.

He suddenly wondered what had become of Dachine. Was this the Kargat's doing and not the machine's?

As if in answer, a voice spoke in his mind: *You will learn soon enough what is my doing, fool!*

And he felt the same writhing presence in his head now, as if his skull were filled with wriggling graveyard worms.

*   *   *   *   *

Exhausted, Azalin released his hold on the dwindling energies of the mage storm. Never before, even in his mortal days on Oerth, had he been so drained by the performance of any magic, let alone something as straightforward as a mage storm. Such storms drew on the natural energy of the sky and the land. The spells that produced them caused that existing energy to be *released*. He did not himself *create* it.

But this time . . .

This time it was as if the energy of the storm, the energy of the tens and then hundreds of lightning bolts, was being sucked out of the storm and had to be constantly replenished. And his *own* energy was being drained as well, drained out of him as he had drained it out of so many others. But where was it going? Into the storm itself? Into the machine? Into Balitor, or whatever Balitor was becoming? Had it, after all, been a trap? A trap he had at least partially avoided only because he had used this smaller machine? Would he have been completely drained, left utterly helpless, had he attempted to use Albemarl's machine directly?

Or was it all because he was in this room, where his powers were multiplied but where nothing worked quite the way it did outside its confines?

But he had no time for guessing games. What was done was done. Trap or no trap, he needed to see the results, to see what the effect had been on Balitor, inside the machine.

Drawing on all his remaining strength, he sent his Sight flowing weakly toward the temple. But as he did, as his Sight moved farther and farther from where his body stood, his strength began to return, until as he finally hovered above the still-glowing dome of the temple . . .

For a moment he hesitated, but then he sent his Sight darting through the dome. And twitched as his Sight was enveloped in the energies that still crackled silently in the room below, half blinding him. But at the same time, his remaining exhaustion vanished, as if, through his Sight, he was soaking up the energies that still hovered about the machine.

In an instant, then, as his own strength fully returned, the blinding energies in the room vanished and fell silent, and it was as if he were there himself, so clear was his Sight.

And he saw that Balitor's body was gone from the machine, not even a skeleton remaining. But Dachine—Dachine was gone as well! In an instant, Azalin realized what the Kargat must have done, and he cursed himself for an arrogant fool. To not have foreseen that possibility . . .

Above the machine, something came into being.

Shadowy and translucent, like his own son's spirit had been, but darker, the object constantly shifted and writhed, as the symbols on the sides of machine, now frozen and still, had once writhed continuously. One instant, it was Balitor's face that grimaced in pain, but in the next, it was Dachine's glowering in anger and then neither, as if the hundreds of stolen lives that had gone into the machine were momentarily manifesting themselves as well.

And all around the shadowy form was an aura of power beyond anything he had ever encountered, perhaps even more powerful than his own. Right now it was all directed inwardly, as Dachine and Balitor battled for control, but when the Kargat triumphed, as he almost certainly must . . .

Fearful of what he would find but knowing he had no choice, Azalin cautiously took his Sight closer, until . . .

As if a giant hand had grabbed him by the scruff of the neck, he felt himself being dragged into the ever-shifting vortex.

* * * * *

Suddenly all restraints on Balitor's movements vanished. It was like a tightly coiled spring being released as his muscles seemed to respond instantaneously to the increasingly frantic commands he had been bombarding them with for what must have been hours. He found himself leaping free of the coffinlike machine, springing high into the air, almost to the dome, while his hands grasped at his head as if to rip out the *things* that he still felt wriggling and churning inside his skull.

And even as his body seemed to tumble in the air, before it could crash to the floor of the nave, he realized that his fingers had penetrated his skull and were grasping the wormlike things and ripping them free like so many leeches and hurling them from him, and . . .

. . . and the machine and the nave and the temple and the entire city of Nartok were gone. His body thudded not onto a cold stone floor but onto a cushion of knee-high grass and springy soil. Above, the sky was blue and cloud-flecked, the kind of sky one could live a lifetime in Darkon and never see.

Then, without having moved a muscle, he was on his feet, feeling the gentle breeze on his face and wondering, Did I die in that machine? Or am I simply dreaming?

He had dreamt of such places, true enough, had even imagined they existed. The first Oldar, he had often imagined with a tinge of jealousy, had perhaps returned to a place like this when he had turned his back on Lord Azalin and left Il Aluk. But this . . .

He looked down at himself, and he was wearing the same doublet and breeches he had worn when summoned to the temple, the same as when he had been lifted through the air and sealed into the machine, the same as when the Kargat priest had . . .

The air shimmered, and Lowellyn Dachine was standing before him. For a moment the Kargat's skeletal features were blank, his body and ash-gray robe as motionless as a statue, but then a spark of life appeared in the eyes and seemed to flow outward like ripples in a pond, the face taking on an angry scowl, the elongated fingers clenching into fists, the robe undulating in the breeze.

"What nonsense is this?" Dachine exclaimed, sneering. "You are freed of that burden of bones and blood, and all you can think is to create it again?" The Kargat laughed. "Very well. If your thoughts are so limited, so be it. It will only make my task all the easier."

The sky darkened, filled in an instant with thick, low-hanging clouds that flickered with hidden lightning. The grass was stripped from beneath Balitor's feet, which were now sinking into gray-green mud that seemed to have a life of its own as it oozed up his legs.

And suddenly his skull was filled once again with wriggling, squirming *things!*

You think it so easy to be rid of me, fool? The Kargat's silent voice filled his mind, and Balitor's body was wracked with pain as the things in his skull shot tendrils throughout his body.

But once again, as if ruled by some forgotten instinct, Balitor clapped his hands to his head and shuddered as he felt his fingers slip through his skull, as if moving through a congealing curtain of water. Once again he felt countless wormlike things writhing as he closed his fingers about them and hurled them from him, but even as he did, he felt them again, as if he had never hurled them away or they had instantly regrown.

Even as he clapped his hands to his head once again, the Kargat's hollow laugh echoed in his mind.

Again and again the nightmare repeated itself, each time sapping his strength a tiny bit more. And each time, memories not his own seemed to clamor for his attention, memories of a childhood devoted not to fending for himself in the streets of Rivalis but to the learning of sorcery, memories not of a lifetime of acceptance of things as they were but of a virulent resentment that had festered for decades, memories of . . .

Suddenly a figure appeared out of nowhere, just as everything else in this nightmare world, even the world itself, had appeared out of nowhere, and in the bare moment Balitor was distracted, he felt the things in his head growing stronger, felt the tendrils that were constantly spreading and respreading throughout his body become even more painful.

But in that same moment, hope flared within him, for he saw that the figure was that of Lord Azalin. Surely *he* could put an end to this nightmare!

In desperation, Balitor reached out, all previous thoughts of using his newfound power to displace Lord Azalin long since banished from his mind.

And as he reached out, his arm was suddenly a dozen yards long, and his fingers were steely, foot-long talons, and they were closing about Lord Azalin and dragging him forward like a recalcitrant puppy, and . . .

Abruptly the tendrils of pain were gone, the writhing *things* within his skull were gone, but at the same time, it was as if the very ground he seemed to be standing on shivered and began to move. For a moment, the clouds and mud were replaced by the blue sky and grass he had begun to think he would never see again, but the feeling of motion increased as a wind blew up and whipped at him, bringing with it sheets of fog and darkness and . . .

And Lord Azalin, struggling to pull away since the moment Balitor had gripped him, was suddenly yanked free and vanished.

And the fog and darkness closed in completely.

* * * * *

Not yet!

Lowellyn Dachine—the thing that Lowellyn Dachine had become—felt Azalin's presence and knew that he had to escape. He knew he had the power to deal with Azalin— *would have* the power, once he was able to fully control it, once he no longer had to fight this utter fool at every turn, once he no longer had to contend with the naive illusions that seemed to give their creator such strength, even though that creator was obviously not even aware of the very acts of creation, so totally ignorant in the ways of magic was he.

Once he was fully in charge of the powers he had so far only glimpsed, he would be eager to confront Lord

Azalin, but for now . . .

For now he abandoned all his efforts to destroy Balitor's delusions, all efforts to grip his mind. Instead, he concentrated totally, fiercely on one thing: escape.

As if in response, the mists rose up out of nowhere and seemed to beckon to him, and he felt sudden hope. To summon up the mists and travel through them at will, as the Vistani were said to do, had been a dream since Dachine had first cast a spell, but never before had they sprung up like this, not as a barrier or a border but as an uncharted pathway.

Straining mightily, as he had long ago strained to send forth his Sight for the very first time, Dachine flowed into the mists, dragging with him the leaden anchor that was Balitor.

* * * * *

For a few seconds, Azalin's Sight had been engulfed and held prisoner in the world Balitor, all unknowing, had created, and in which he and Dachine battled for dominance of the single, yet still compartmented, creature they had become.

And in those seconds, Azalin had sensed two things: immense power and intense hatred.

For an agonized moment, he had felt the power manifest itself in the imagined talons Balitor had thrust out, not in anger but in desperation, and he realized with horror that it was a power even he could not break. Had the hatred been Balitor's, he would never have broken free, but it was not.

It was Dachine's, and it was directed not only at Azalin but also at Balitor, even though the two were virtually a single being. But a single being at war with itself.

Abruptly that grip had failed of itself—failed as the creature turned on itself and fled . . .

. . . somewhere.

Into the mists? To where Azalin could not go?

But they—*it!*—would be back. The hatred he had sensed left little room for doubt. And when it did return, Dachine would be in full control. The untutored Balitor almost certainly had no chance against a sorcerer of Dachine's power. It would then, Azalin knew, have the power that no other creature had possessed in two centuries: the power to destroy him.

Unless . . .

Briefly his Sight continued to hover over the now depleted machine, and he saw that the once-moving symbols had not only become simple, static markings but had also begun to fade. The entire machine, like an ancient, rusting coat of untended mail, was disintegrating even as he watched, and he wondered abruptly if the original would do the same once *it* was used.

Or if, even now . . .

Quickly he sent his Sight soaring through the night, over dozens of miles of forest and field, until it swooped down over Il Aluk and through the fortresslike walls of the Kargat's Grim Fastness. Finally he hovered directly above Albemarl's device and saw, with relief, that it was untouched and whole beneath the spells in which he had encased it. And even as he watched, a returning Kargat agent briefly bowed his head as he proffered yet another of the life-filled daggers, watched as it vanished into the illusionary spells, and turned to go as, unseen to any but Azalin's Sight, the dagger's life-force was silently absorbed.

And Azalin thought, Tonight. Whether the process is complete or not, I must do it this very night, before Dachine returns.

 **TWENTY**

Somewhere in the mists
750, Barovian Calendar (continued)

Balitor felt that he was moving, being dragged at a terrific pace, but with only darkness all about him, he could not know. He tried to scream, first Lord Azalin's name, then, in utter desperation, the Kargat's, but there was no sound.

Because he had no body. No mouth to scream. No ears to hear. No eyes to see.

Abruptly he was surrounded not by darkness but by billowing whiteness. An instant later a memory leapt into his mind, a memory he would have sworn he had not possessed a moment earlier. He and . . . Oldar? He and Oldar were riding from Il Aluk to Avernus, and almost as suddenly as now, they had been enveloped in rising mists.

The mists.

The same mists that surrounded Darkon and the other lands, the same mists that now and then sprang up without warning and swallowed up unwary travelers. Had he entered them before? Until this moment, he had been certain he had not, but now . . .

Now he was virtually certain that he had, he and Oldar. But that was not all, these newfound memories told him.

Waiting for them in the mists had been a hideous creature of decaying flesh and exposed bone. It had very
nearly killed Oldar, but . . .

Suddenly the grotesque and impossible memory was
driven from his mind as the mists became filled with
voices, hundreds of voices. And he could hear them all—
could not *avoid* hearing them all—as if they were speaking
directly into his mind. Blocking out his terror, he listened,
not just to one voice but to all, hearing them speak in a
thousand tongues, each as incomprehensible as the last,
at least to a mind such as his, totally illiterate in matters
magical. Still he continued listening, hoping that somehow
the seeming gibberish would become words. But it would
not, no matter how hard he concentrated.

Until finally . . .

A single set of voices emerged from the chaos, as if he
had been led through a teeming city to a single window,
from which emerged words whose meaning he could
fathom.

And as he listened, a sinking feeling gripped the body
he no longer possessed, and he knew that somehow he
was going to have to find a way to warn Lord Azalin. . . .

* * * * *

Oldar found himself once again in the fields of his childhood, watching his father work to bring in the crops. As Lord
Azalin had promised, the weakness, the pallor, the bloody
cough were no more. His father, while still not young,
seemed reborn, displaying a vigor Oldar had not seen for
years. His mother, her dark Vistani hair just beginning to
turn gray in the weeks since Oldar had left the farm, worked
at her husband's side with almost equal vigor, and Oldar
longed for the day he could return and work with them.

But until Lord Azalin released him . . .

"Young Oldar."

The familiar voice speaking his name spun him around to face the welcome interloper. "Balitor! Have you returned?"

Balitor's image shook its head. "I bring a message of greatest urgency for Lord Azalin. Unless you can reach him and persuade him to listen to you, Darkon is almost certainly doomed."

"But he is with *you* in Nartok! You were summoned to the temple—"

"He was not there, only his image, as it was in the courtyard the morning you and I were summoned to Avernus. I suspect he is in Avernus still. In any event, *I* am no longer in Nartok. I don't know *where* I am, or even *what* I am!"

"You are Balitor, as you have always been."

The image shook its head again. "I wish it were that simple, but it is not. But none of this matters. All that matters is that you speak to Lord Azalin!"

"Even if I were able—"

"You have no choice, young Oldar!"

"Even if I were able, what would you have me to say to him?"

"That he must not make use of the device you brought from Falkovnia!"

"That is surely Lord Azalin's decision, not ours," Oldar said uneasily, beginning to wonder if this were indeed Balitor or some sorcerous impostor.

Balitor's image scowled with impatience and anger. "Of course it is Lord Azalin's decision! But he does not know what will happen when—"

"I suspect there is little Lord Azalin does not know. You yourself have told me as much."

"He knows what happens in Darkon, yes! But I am

almost certainly not in Darkon! I suspect I am in a place that can be reached only through the mists, a place where Lord Azalin has never been. He may not even know of its existence."

"And yet you are able to speak to me so plainly?" Oldar asked, his suspicions growing.

"Don't ask me for explanations! I have none! I understand none of these terrible things that have happened to me, nor what I am capable of doing! I merely thought deeply of you, and I found myself here—wherever this is. Your own dreams?"

"If you can speak with me in this way, certainly you can speak with Lord Azalin yourself."

"If only I could! But I cannot—or if I can, I have not found the way, no matter how much I have tried. Perhaps a bond is required, a bond that does not exist between Lord Azalin and me. Or perhaps his own magic shields him from me as it shields him from his enemies. But we waste precious time, young Oldar. If I am not mistaken, Azalin is already on his way to Il Aluk."

"But how will I convince him? Surely he will not listen to one such as me. Nor should he."

"Tell him it is *I* who gave you the warning. Tell him I spoke to you from out of the mists, which may even be the truth. Tell him there are creatures there whose very thoughts I overheard, creatures who know him well and who desperately wish him to enter Albemarl's machine and will stop at nothing to achieve that end. Tell him their only goal is to overrun all of Darkon."

"But who *are* these creatures? Why do they—"

"I have told you again and again: I understand none of this! I *want* to understand none of it! I want only to preserve our home, and soon I fear I may not even want that! Now, go! Go before it is too late!"

Before Oldar could speak, Balitor's image shimmered and vanished. A moment later, Oldar's parents and the fields they worked and the sky above vanished as well, and he awakened, as he had known he would.

Without hesitation, he scrambled from Balitor's uncomfortably luxurious bed and into the peasant's clothes he still insisted on wearing. Through the velvet-draped windows, he could see that it was still night, with only a torch flame here and there to punctuate the blackness. A minute later he was racing down the broad, thickly carpeted stairs, through a half dozen richly appointed rooms and out to the stable.

But as he was reaching for a saddle, something tingled deep within his chest. At the same moment, the horses began shifting nervously in their stalls. He turned toward them, hoping to calm them, but as he did, first one and then another began to whinny.

And Lord Azalin—Lord Azalin's image?—stepped out of the shadows.

"What is it you wish, young Oldar?" he asked.

"How did you know—"

Azalin's stern look silenced Oldar. "Do not waste my time. I sensed your need to speak with me, so I am here. What do you wish?"

Oldar swallowed nervously and began. When he stammered to an end, Azalin's expression was grim.

"Return within," Azalin said, gesturing toward Balitor's mansion. "I may have need of you this night, but if the dawn comes and I have not summoned you in some way, you are free to return to your home."

And he was gone, the image shimmering and vanishing in an instant.

*   *   *   *   *

Emerging from the tower room in Avernus, Azalin was forced to a lurching halt as the body he inhabited once again went through its death throes, but even as it did, his mind continued to race. As if the situation were not already ambiguous enough, now he had Balitor's supposed warning to deal with.

Had it truly been Balitor who had entered Oldar's dreams to deliver the warning? Or had it been Dachine, who even as a mortal sorcerer would have had little difficulty in deceiving one such as Oldar? If it was Dachine, it was almost certainly an obvious attempt to keep Azalin from entering Albemarl's device and undergoing the same kind of transformation that Dachine had already undergone. Even if it was indeed Balitor who had spoken to Oldar, there was no way of knowing who or what it was he had overheard. Balitor would have been as easy to fool as Oldar, certainly.

But if Dachine were somehow *not* involved, if the warning were genuine . . .

Who or what, then, could it have been that Balitor had overheard?

Azalin's tormentors? Were they truly lurking in the mists, watching, waiting? He had long assumed they were constantly aware of his every action, perhaps even his thoughts, and what better place for beings who obviously had great control over the mists? But even so, surely they would not be so careless as to allow Balitor or anyone else to be privy to their thoughts.

Unless . . .

Unless, like some novice sorcerers, they were so arrogantly certain of their power that they cared not who overheard their plans. The voices who had spoken to him over the centuries were certainly arrogant enough, but if that were the case, why would they show signs of concern over what Azalin did or did not do? More likely it was all just another part of their game, another way of amusing themselves, to see which way he would jump with each new prodding. But that would mean they knew about Albemarl's device and that it, too, was a part of their game!

Angrily he brought his spiraling thoughts to a halt. It all came down to one question: Should he enter Albemarl's device or not? And the answer to that was obvious.

If he did not, he would remain as he was. He would never escape this land, except perhaps when he was destroyed by Dachine upon his eventual return.

If he did enter the device . . . anything was at least *possible*.

Finally, his body's death once more completed and the attendant pain relegated to memory, Azalin summoned up a jet black stallion with eyes as fiery as his own and set out for Il Aluk.

*   *   *   *   *

Once again Balitor found himself floating in the mists, or so he now assumed this billowing whiteness to be. For a moment an almost intolerable urge to return to Oldar's dream world gripped him, but he resisted. At best, it would be pointless. If his talking to Oldar had been nothing more than his own vivid imagination, imagining it a second time would not make it any more real. If it had been real, returning to speak to Oldar again—if he were able—could only delay Oldar's getting word to Lord Azalin.

And that, unless he had been driven completely insane by this insane experience, was all that really mattered. If there were only a way of being sure without having to . . .

Dachine's image flashed through his mind, but he pushed it aside sharply.

He wondered how much longer he could continue to do so. Dachine's memories continued to invade his mind, appearing in his thoughts like bubbles rising to the surface of a simmering kettle, and with each memory came a flash of intuition, an insight into Dachine's reasons for doing what he did, for being what he was. But those memories and insights were, so far, utterly alien to Balitor. He could not imagine ever acting thus, but if, as Dachine seemed to think, the two of them were destined to become one . . .

His imagined body shuddered at the thought, but somewhere in a dark corner of his mind, something laughed.

And the memories continued to come, the barriers to weaken.

*   *   *   *   *

Impatiently Lowellyn Dachine waited. It was all he *could* do, he had quickly and angrily realized. Trying to do battle with Balitor had only made matters worse. Each time he tried to force his way into Balitor's mind, it had, incredibly, strengthened the other's resistance. Each time he tried to destroy the world that the fool had created—without even realizing he had created it!—made it easier for Balitor to re-create the simplified landscape that seemed to give his peasant's mind some feeling of comfort.

It was only when Dachine had *stopped* doing battle that he saw that, despite Balitor's resistance, without any efforts on his own part, the barriers were beginning to weaken. And they continued to weaken, as if it were part of some natural, inevitable process. Even during those panic-filled moments when Dachine had not been able to sense Balitor's presence, he had felt them weakening, had felt more and more of Balitor's peculiar memories joining his own. The joining, the assimilation, was proceeding.

And now finally it must be nearing completion. The memories stretched back unbroken through nearly two centuries of the simpleton's wasted life. To think that he had been *given* the rule of Il Aluk and then had willingly thrown it away! Even now he still resisted this new gift of even greater power! Sheer madness!

But it didn't matter. All that mattered was for the process to be complete, for Dachine's own will to take complete control. Then—*then* he would leave this temporary haven in the mists and return to Darkon to deal with Azalin and . . .

Were he still possessed of a body, Dachine would have gasped as the last of Balitor's memories bubbled into his mind—memories of the time *since* they had been joined and fled into the mists, memories of the voices and the warning Balitor had tried to relay to Azalin.

Another of the devices existed, those memories shouted to Dachine, this one in the Kargat's Grim Fastness! And Azalin, unless he was stopped, would very soon enter it! If that was allowed to happen, Dachine realized instantly, his own newfound powers would most likely pale in comparison to Azalin's!

In the same moment, a wave of relief swept over Dachine, for he also saw in the final trickle of Balitor's memories that here, for the first time, was something they both agreed on, though for obviously different reasons: Azalin must be stopped from entering the device in the Grim Fastness.

*   *   *   *   *

Azalin barely glanced at the blocky gray edifice that

was the Grim Fastness as he leapt from his fiery-eyed mount and let it vanish in a rush of icy wind. Flowing directly to the huge chamber that housed Albemarl's device, he blocked all entrances with darkly glittering spells. A pair of Kargat agents, having only moments before offered up their daggers, looked over their shoulders, startled, then hurried to the stairs and down. From both above and below came voices and rapid footfalls as word of Azalin's arrival spread. Soon the halls outside the chamber would be filled, but the spells would block any from entering the chamber itself.

One after another, Azalin removed the protective and concealment spells from about the device and saw to his surprise that the hundreds—perhaps thousands—of daggers that had been brought here appeared to have been metamorphosed into faintly glowing translucent skulls, each connected to the device itself by what appeared to be a fine golden wire. This gave him pause—it had not happened with the other device—but only for a moment. Now was not the time to resume the endless second-guessing that had virtually paralyzed him before. He was committed to doing this and doing it quickly.

The grotesque device finally stood before him, all spells removed, looking like nothing more than a gigantic forty-foot-high hourglass of glass and gold. The same blood-red symbols that had, in miniature, swirled about the surface of the device in Nartok were here full size, writhing like crimson serpents. Beneath the golden surface, even Azalin's stunted Sight could discern the thousands of paper-thin metal plates held separated by an oozing, gelatinous substance, the like of which he had seen nowhere else. Here and there tiny points of light glittered and subsided. Though he couldn't be sure, it seemed to him that the symbols engraved on the plates had been altered in some way since last his Sight had inspected them.

Even as he levitated to the top of the device and raised the lid with a gesture, he began to summon up the mage storm. As he sank into the device, the first rumbles of thunder could be heard. At the same moment, Azalin felt *something* gripping his body like a giant, chill hand, holding him motionless, and the now-transparent lid closed.

Outside, the storm clouds had fully gathered. A dry, icy wind was already blowing inward from all directions, gusting so strongly that the few denizens of Il Aluk who dared to be abroad were almost knocked from their feet.

*   *   *   *   *

The thing that was Balitor and Dachine winced mentally as it—as *they*—emerged from the mists within sight of the Grim Fastness and into the midst of a full-blown mage storm. They were too late!

Or were they? Flowing through Azalin's glittering spells as if they were water, they saw that Azalin's body, suspended eerily in the upper half of the device, was still whole. Until that symbol of his mortality was burned away . . .

A gray shadow with a face and form that constantly shifted from Dachine's to Balitor's and back, they flowed to the top of the device and hovered there, looking down. The symbols around the bottom of the device writhed at an ever-increasing pace, while Azalin's fiery red eyes glittered as his contorted face was turned up to them.

Too late! Azalin's triumphant words appeared in their mind, but even as they did, Dachine was reaching out with his newfound powers to wrench free the cover and rip loose the hundreds of delicate wires that . . .

Suddenly they were gripped as if by a giant hand, and Balitor tried to scream that these interfering forces were the same creatures he had overheard in the mists, the ones desperate to have this process carried out, but he could project neither thought nor sound. A moment later they felt themselves being hurled like rag dolls away from the device, and then the mists swallowed them up, and they were so lost that even Dachine realized they would be unable to find their way back to that particular night in Darkon in time.

*   *   *   *   *

A shadowy figure seemed to appear in the thick air above Azalin and the machine, but it was gone almost before it had registered on his distracted senses. He was concentrating as best as he could on the mage storm but was beginning to fear that, away from that tower room in Avernus, he was not going to be able to produce one of sufficient intensity to activate the device. Desperately he focused all his powers on the storm, and yet it was not gaining sufficient power.

But why? Galron had succeeded! And from Albemarl's account, Galron's powers had not come close to matching his own!

But then abruptly, even as his frustration and puzzlement distracted him further, the storm began strengthening once again, this time with explosive speed, as if it had reached a critical threshold and had taken on a life of its own. The clouds thickened and lowered while the inrushing wind neared hurricane speeds, and before Azalin could more than briefly wonder why, a half dozen bolts of lightning smashed into the uppermost reaches of the Grim Fastness and seemed to be funneled directly into the machine. The lower half pulsed, alternating between icy brilliance and a blackness that was darker than the darkest night. The lightning continued to crash repeatedly until the entire building seemed aglow, and the viscous liquid that surrounded and separated the metal plates in the machine bubbled and seethed like a witch's caldron.

Azalin felt power surging—burning!—through him, felt his body char as the liquid flowed up and into the upper chamber, then dissolve layer by layer into nothingness as the liquid bubbled about him like fiery acid, and he was filled with a mixture of terror and anticipation. There was no turning back. Whatever was to happen to him was happening and could not be halted.

He heard a scream. It might have been his own.

*   *   *   *   *

Oldar, still fully dressed, stood, wind-buffeted, on a small balcony of Balitor's mansion, his hands white-knuckled as he gripped the stone railing against the rising wind and watched the unnatural clouds boil and spew out bolt after bolt of lightning. No matter which part of the sky the lightning came from, virtually every stroke lanced jaggedly toward the massive, blocky structure that Balitor had said was the Grim Fastness, the home of the Kargat in Il Aluk. And there was not a drop of rain, only the cold, dry wind that felt as if it could suck the very life out of anything unfortunate enough be abroad in the night.

A mage storm.

Balitor's warning to Lord Azalin had gone unheeded, Oldar knew, and this was the result. It was the only explanation. Only a sorcerer of Lord Azalin's powers could produce a storm such as this, and it was obviously centered on the very spot where sat the machine they had brought from Falkovnia.

Once again he recalled Lord Azalin's final words to him and wondered at their meaning: "I may have need of you this night, but if the dawn comes and I have not summoned you in some way, you are free to return to your home."

He could not imagine how he could be of service here. To serve as Lord Azalin's eyes and ears in places where Lord Azalin could not himself go—that had in a way been understandable, even though he did not understand why or how a sorcerer of Lord Azalin's capabilities could be barred from going *anywhere*.

But here, in the heart of Darkon, only a few short miles from Avernus itself, where Lord Azalin's power was absolute in all things, where he could blanket the city with rainless clouds, fill the sky with lightning and thunder, summon up a wind that made even the sturdiest buildings shudder—how could a lowly peasant like himself be of any aid to someone of Lord Azalin's powers?

And what of the promise—instructions?—to return to his home if he were *not* called upon? Would there *be* a home to return to if Balitor's warning were both true and unheeded? If Darkon were indeed overrun by those nameless, faceless creatures Balitor had overheard in the mists?

Oldar grimaced in puzzlement and fear as the barrage of lightning stabbing again and again at the seemingly defenseless building intensified. In the ever rarer moments between strikes, he could see that the upper reaches of the building were developing a faint glow.

But then, without warning, a searing pain erupted in

his chest. At the same moment, the wind rose to hurricane force and sent him staggering backward, slamming
him against the stone facade of the building next to the
open door to his bedroom. All strength gone from his
limbs, he slid limply downward, despite the force of the
wind, until he was sitting, legs thrust out before him. His
pounding heart only intensified the pain, and he wondered helplessly if he were dying.

But as the pain reached its peak, spreading throughout
the upper half of his body, a jagged streak of lightning,
long and slender as a thread, lanced out, not from the
clouds but from the glowing gray edifice that was the
Grim Fastness. Striking him directly in the chest, it set
his limbs to dancing like a madman's and filled his vision
with a kaleidoscope of sparks.

An instant later the pain was gone. His vision cleared,
and before him, as if suspended on the ribbon of lightning that still persisted, was the huge golden skull of a
dragon.

And then both were gone, the thread of lightning
simply vanishing with a hiss, the golden skull shredding
into a thousand particles that glittered in the flashes of
lightning that still thundered down on the distant building.

And were carried away by the wind.

He sat there, too weak to move. Gradually, as the lightning strokes lessened in both brilliance and frequency,
his strength returned. By the time the storm was gone,
by the time the clouds began, unbelievably, to disperse,
he was able to stand.

And though he knew not how he knew, he knew he
was free to return to his home.

PART III

THE COMING OF
NECROPOLIS

 **TWENTY-ONE**

Darkon
750, Barovian Calendar (continued)

Finally it was over.

The clouds' dark bellies lifted from where they almost touched the rooftops and then thinned. Here and there a star peeped through, as if to see if it were once again safe to emerge. The wind fell to a chill whisper. Everywhere in Il Aluk there was utter silence. The Kargat and the priests in the Grim Fastness stood quivering and silent as they waited for what was yet to come, knowing they had been witness to something far beyond their understanding.

Azalin . . . existed.

His first thought was that he felt very much as he did when he made unhindered use of his Sight: completely free and weightless, able to open his senses to all aspects of the world around him. But he was not now anchored to a body, neither to a living body as once he had been in his mortal days on Oerth, nor to a decaying corpse.

He simply . . . existed.

He looked about himself and saw that he floated, with-out consciously willing it, above the machine that had just transformed him. With no more effort than it would once have taken him to move his head a fraction of an inch, he looked inside the machine and saw that the metal plates were melted and fused, their symbols distorted and frozen. Where moments before it had pulsed with unimaginable energy, now it was a lifeless shell, and he wondered why it had not been similarly depleted and destroyed when Galron had been transformed.

As he had done countless times before, he searched for signs of his tormentors, but this time . . .

This time his search was not limited to one tiny area at a time. Instead, it was as if his Sight could scour all of Il Aluk in no more time than it would have taken him to examine a single room before. And there was nothing, no sign that his tormentors were present or had been present recently.

In an instant he was hovering above Avernus, where the situation was far different. Their spoor was everywhere in the castle, though nowhere more strong than in the room where once his son's spirit had been imprisoned.

In another instant he was hovering at the very border of Darkon, where the mists had always risen up to block him. But now . . .

With little more discomfort than a faint tingle, he passed through, and moments later he was looking down at the crumbling towers of Castle Ravenloft, realizing that he could destroy Strahd in an instant if he wished. But that was not his purpose now—not yet, perhaps not ever. Now he sought the spoor of his tormentors and found it was strong. It overlay virtually everything in the castle, most of all the vampire lord himself. It left no doubt in Azalin's mind. His tormentors were indeed the same beings, the same forces that had trapped Strahd here, had drawn not only him but his entire land into this prison, where it had served as seed and magnet for all that had followed.

And he thought exultantly, They can hold me no longer! Their mists are no longer my prison!

For a moment he hovered there, his mind flashing back across the centuries, back to the first time they had spoken to him, the first deceit they had practiced on him, and then further, to the agonizing day when he had made himself vulnerable to their wiles: the day he had been forced to slay Irik, his only son.

Once again, the vision as painfully vivid as anything he had ever experienced, he watched from the balcony of Castle Galdliesh as the waiting crowd roared in the courtyard and the headsman made his way methodically down the line of traitors, their heads sometimes tumbling down the steps, forcing even that bloodthirsty mob to draw squeamishly back. Once again he saw the headsman halt at the last of the kneeling traitors: Irik, his son, barely nineteen. Once again he raised his hand to stay the axe, and once again he strode forth into the Galdliesh courtyard to take up the axe himself. Once again, as the bloodthirsty crowd first gasped and then roared their approval of their leader's sense of justice, he brought the axe down.

And once again he imagined that he saw Irik's lips form words of forgiveness as the head struck the stone at the base of the chopping block and rolled free.

Though he had no body, Azalin was filled with pain at the sight. Pain, not remorse, for he had done what was right, what was just. Irik's weak and traitorous actions had left him no choice. He could not spare his son when he did not spare others whose guilt was no greater. His only true remorse was that, despite all his powers, he had been prevented from ever restoring Irik to true life and giving him the chance to redeem himself, to erase the traitor's brand from his soul. All else paled beside that, even his own centuries of being taunted by his tormentors, being forced to exist within a lifeless, decaying body that would turn the stomach of the strongest men.

But now . . .

Now that he was no longer a prisoner of the mists, now that he was no longer bound to Darkon or any of the other trapped lands, perhaps he could at last find where Irik's spirit had truly gone when the ghostly simulacrum that now inhabited the boy's tomb had replaced it.

In an instant he was hovering above the sarcophagus in the Avernus tower, and he was now able to see that the sarcophagus was the very one that he himself had brought into being to house the boy's remains on the very spot of his execution in the shadow of Castle Galdliesh. And he could see that the wraith that emerged from the cold stone was indeed a simulacrum, an imitation that had fooled him for decades.

But in the very stone of the sarcophagus was still a trace of the true Irik, a trace that, until now, he had been unable to detect, so faint and ancient was it. And a trail, the same trail he had been able to follow when, by magic alone, he had been briefly transformed. This time he would not lose it.

Though he had no body, Azalin felt a rush of exhilaration unlike anything he had felt since his earliest mortal days.

For a moment he hesitated, paralyzed by a sudden fear of what he might find at the other end of that trail, if indeed he could follow it to its end. But he had no choice. Now that he was able, he had no choice.

Out through the walls and spells of Avernus he soared.

In an instant he was enveloped by the mists. But he was not blinded. Instead, the trail seemed to grow less faint, as if it was preserved better by the mists than by the stone of the sarcophagus.

But where . . . ?

As he continued to flow through the mists, the shimmering trail growing more distinct by the second, a chill crept over his bodiless form, and he slowed cautiously. *Something* lay ahead. The chill, he realized after a moment, was the same as the one fifteen-year-old Firan Zal'honan had felt that night three and a half centuries before when he and Corsalus had summoned up the creature that had destroyed his brother.

But how could that be? That chill had emanated, he had always been virtually certain, from the creature itself and from the nether regions from which it had come. That night they had opened a door into whatever world of darkness those hideous creatures inhabited, and . . .

Suddenly he realized the truth: *That* was where this trail was leading! He was even now approaching those nether regions—through the mists! He had left behind not only Darkon and the other mist-bound lands but that entire plane of existence!

But still the trail of Irik's spirit continued, and he wondered with horror, Was it one of these creatures that had taken him? Did creatures in those dark regions conduct summonings as well, calling spirits *down* from the higher planes in the same manner that *they* were summoned *up* to the planes that held Darkon and Oerth?

He shuddered at the thought of Irik—or anyone!—trapped in a world of such horror. He remembered well the paralyzing aura of the hideous creature he and Corsalus had summoned up, but he could not even imagine what it would be like to be trapped—drowned!—in the constant terror and revulsion of a world inhabited only by such creatures, with no respite no matter which way you turned, for year after endless year!

And even as these thoughts swamped his senses, he saw that, somewhere just ahead, the trail ended!

He stopped, the mists all about him. Far behind him—above him?—but still dimly visible to his senses floated the ghostly, constantly shifting mass that was Darkon and Barovia and Tepest and all the other imprisoned lands. Ahead—below?—the mists thickened until they were almost as impenetrable as they had been before his transformation. It was where they were the thickest, the most impenetrable, that Irik's trail ended.

Slowly, cautiously, he moved forward, every sense extended to its utmost, even though that only intensified the chill and horror he felt. He also felt a growing pressure, as if the mists were solidifying and pressing against him, impeding his forward movement.

Without thinking how it was possible, any more than a human consciously thinks how to move each individual muscle each time he takes a step, Azalin pressed forward more strenuously, and as he did the mists became more and more opaque, until finally he could see virtually nothing.

And all the while the feeling of horror increased until it was almost unbearable.

Finally, barely able to move, he came to the point at which the trail ended—and found that it did not end after all. It continued on, at least a short distance, but Azalin could not follow farther. For him, the mist—or something within it—became at that point a solid barrier, and for a moment he felt relief that he would not be able to continue. Whatever lay beyond this barrier . . .

Then suddenly he felt Irik's presence.

And through that link poured all the years of sheer hell that his son had been subjected to since his spirit had been taken from Darkon and imprisoned here! It was similar to that other Irik's terror as he was absorbed by the creature they had summoned up, but it was multiplied a thousand—a million!—times. Every minute of every year he had been immersed in these horrors, and yet his mind had remained separate, as if to ensure that he never adapted, that his pain and terror would continue forever.

Or until he was released.

Blindly Azalin smashed against the barrier, but it was like a moth against a window, and his anguished mental scream reverberated through the mists and sounded throughout Darkon, bringing thousands awake with a chill and a shiver that sent them to check windows and doors and peer fretfully into the night.

But surely there was a way! If this were indeed the lair of the creatures summoned up again and again to do a sorcerer's bidding, then surely . . .

Of course!

If these creatures could be summoned up, then certainly Irik could be summoned as well! And if his new-found powers were as great as they seemed to be in all other respects . . .

In his mind, he went back to that other night three centuries before and to the dozens of other summonings he had performed since, and he saw that the physical trappings—the mummified *shasheek* he and Corsalus had employed, the circle of their own blood, all of the things they had painstakingly assembled!—were but crutches he and other sorcerers required as long as they were bound to their physical bodies. Physical bodies required physical objects to funnel their mental and magical energies through, but now . . .

Releasing the grip that held him close to the barrier, he flashed back through the mists to Darkon and found himself once again in the Grim Fastness, hovering above the depleted machine. But where he was made no difference. Here was as good a place as any.

In an instant the huge chamber was transformed, the remnants of the machine vanishing as he re-created on a grand scale the setting of that first summoning: the bare wooden floor of Corsalus's hut, planks now nearly a yard wide; the table with Corsalus's outsize magical tomes stacked twice the height of a man; the ring of blood a dozen yards wide, encircling the area where the machine had stood moments before; the mummified *shasheek*, as large as Firan himself had been. None of it was necessary, but for reasons he could not yet understand—penance for his mistakes, mistakes that had led to that other Irik's death?—it pleased him to do it.

He began.

The words of power formed in his mind and were amplified a thousandfold as he shouted them silently into the mists. Chants that had taken Corsalus and he half the night to complete satisfactorily, he projected into the mists with tremendous power in seconds.

And he felt the barrier, far off through the mists, begin to weaken, not slowly and barely perceptibly as it doubtless had in those other summonings that had taken hours to complete, but quickly and with an ominous rumbling, as if of an approaching earthquake. For a moment his attention was distracted as the ring of blood abruptly metamorphosed into a ring of the same blood-red symbols that had swirled and writhed on the surface of the vanished machine, but then the massive wooden planks within the circle twisted and vanished into a growing area of darkness, and he knew that his words had bridged the mists and brought that distant barrier close, that this chill darkness was the very spot where that barrier now touched this world.

As his mind focused once more on the words and the barrier, he felt it weaken and then tear with the sound of a thousand screaming, tortured souls, and he knew that this was more than just a summoning! He was not just bringing these nether regions close and prizing one of its denizens up through the weakened barrier. The barrier was fully breached. The ragged opening was growing greater by the second, and the blackness crackled with points of obsidian light where the two worlds touched. Then the icy, roiling blackness was swirling outward, swallowing up the re-created hovel and lapping at the edges of the huge chamber. Priests and Kargat, peering fearfully in through the wide, spell-shielded doors, gasped and turned and ran as the shimmering darkness rushed at them.

Azalin felt the chilling energy flowing out like a gushing river, and he realized that this was the very stuff of those nether regions, the source of the auras of horror and darkness that saturated the creatures that were summoned up.

The first of the fleeing Kargat lurched and fell, dead before he touched the floor. For a moment Azalin thought the life-force had been sucked out of him, as the daggers had extracted the life-force of the thousands that had filled the machine, but then, as the corpse twitched and writhed blindly, he saw that it was more than that. The Kargat's life-force had not been simply drained away. It still existed, and with it the man's essence, but both had been utterly overwhelmed by the noisome energy that was gushing through the fissure that Azalin had just created.

Just as, he realized grimly, his brother Irik's life-force had been overwhelmed by that creature three centuries ago. He shuddered guiltily to think of what his brother had undergone in those last hours of life.

But the fate of this Kargat was not his concern, nor was the fate of Darkon itself. If it were to be destroyed or overrun, so be it. His only concerns now were his son's spirit, which he had thought lost to him, and his ability to perhaps accomplish what his tormentors had so long kept him from.

He plunged once again into the mists, now roiling and darkening as the black energy poured out through the ever-widening break in the barrier. Steeling himself, he fought his way through that breach like a swimmer battling upstream through death-black, icy rapids, until, finally he grasped his son and . . .

Disbelieving, he recoiled in shock and horror.

The thing that he had touched was *not* his son! It was yet another simulacrum!

From everywhere, in a thousand different voices, came the laughter of his tormentors.

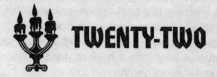 **TWENTY-TWO**

For a long moment, Azalin was stunned into immobility. But then he felt the repellent forces of that other world closing in on him even as the laughter rumbled on, and he pulled back sharply, thrusting from him the thing he had thought was his son, which itself had joined in the laughter. If his tormentors intended to trap him here . . .

But they apparently did not, for there was no resistance as he flowed back the way he had come and emerged high above Il Aluk, weak from even that brief immersion in that domain of horror.

But then his fury at this ultimate deception drove the weakness out, and he saw that the glittering blackness was spreading across Il Aluk. Already the Grim Fastness was entirely within its grasp, and he could see that every Kargat and every priest had been absorbed and lay in a state that would make death seem like paradise.

Focusing once again on the breach he had created in the barrier, he brought all his powers to bear to close it, to seal it off before it absorbed all of Darkon, before his tormentors gained whatever obscene goal they might have in mind.

But he could not. The tear was too great. It was like trying to dam a mighty river even as the torrents battered at him, and all the while he could hear the laughter. But then, as he abandoned his attempts to seal the break and instead concentrated his words and spells on the great bulk of the barrier that still remained, strengthening it and halting the tear, keeping it from spreading even farther, the laughter abruptly halted, and he sensed for the first time in centuries a note of uneasiness, even alarm, in his invisible tormentors.

Another trick? he wondered abruptly, but then he recalled the story that Oldar had told him. Balitor, trapped in the mists, had overheard *something* that had been worried Azalin might not enter Albemarl's machine. Whatever it was had desperately wanted him to enter it and, presumably, be transformed. His tormentors? Had it been Azalin's tormentors Balitor had overheard? Had it been necessary that he be transformed in order for them to play this final cruel jest?

And he saw instantly that it was true. And that it was, this time, far more than a jest.

He had to be transformed in order to be capable of escaping Darkon, of traveling unhindered through the mists. Otherwise he could not have followed the false trail that led to his spurious son. Otherwise he would not have had the power to literally smash a gaping hole in the barrier that isolated those hideous nether regions from the other planes.

From Darkon. From Barovia. Even from Oerth?

But why? Why should they need *him* to smash down that barrier? Certainly creatures of such immense power could do whatever they wished. Except . . .

Except, the only way any such creatures, regardless of their powers, could ever escape their domain was to be summoned up by a skilled and powerful sorcerer. They needed someone on the outside to unlock the door and allow them through.

And if they desired not just a cautiously opened door but the destruction of that door, even of the barrier itself, giving them free and total access to the other planes, they needed a sorcerer capable of wielding unprecedented power.

And they had found that sorcerer: Azalin himself.

They had found the young Firan Zal'honan, had seen in him the raw talent they needed, and, in their grotesque way, groomed and guided him.

Abruptly his entire existence made horrifying sense. And these mist-bound lands, a mismatched patchwork of pieces stolen from other worlds, made an even more horrifying kind of sense, a sense that for the first time gave motive to his tormentors.

If . . .

Plunging once more into the mists, he sped upward, away from the nether regions whose horrors he had unwittingly loosed on Darkon.

And saw that he was right.

For there, as high above the plane in which the mist-bound lands were trapped as the nether regions were below it, was another plane of existence, a plane so vast he could not see the end of it. But he knew without having to see it that this was the plane from which Barovia and Darkon and all the other lands and peoples had been stolen. Stolen and placed here, midway between their plane of origin and that realm of horrors in the depths.

A stepping stone.

The mist-bound lands were nothing more than a stepping stone for the creatures from the depths. Just as Strahd and the other Darklords were confined by unknown laws to their tiny domains, these creatures were confined to theirs. Just as Azalin had found a way to influence but not control events in ancient Barovia, his tormentors had found ways to exert influence in that other plane. Using whatever trickery, lies, or deception that was necessary, they did their work.

Barovia had been the start.

They had been incapable of stealing Barovia themselves and imprisoning it in the mists, so they had worked through Strahd, whose own powers and the unbreakable link he had developed with the land had enabled him—unknowingly!—to transport it here, where it formed a seed and a magnet for all the lands and peoples that followed.

But even with this stepping stone so comparatively near, they were still incapable of smashing through the barrier that isolated their plane. Could it possibly be the fabled Negative Material Plane, said by some to be the source not only of all magic but also of all evil? So they had found on Oerth, in the town of Knurl, a young sorcerer of unparalleled potential, and they had maneuvered him down through the centuries to a point at which he would be capable of smashing down the barrier and setting them free.

That was why he had seen their touch on virtually every aspect of his existence. They had driven him from his home, given him a perverted form of immortality, imprisoned him in Darkon, where his ability to learn new magic was stolen from him, forcing him to search for other ways of accomplishing his goals. They had, he suspected, led him to Albemarl's machine, knowing that if he used it, it would amplify his own natural power to such an extent that he could then break down the barrier and set them free—*if* they could trick him into doing it.

Even now, the thought that these creatures *needed* him,

that he was the only sorcerer of sufficient power to be of
use to them, gave him a perverse sense of pleasure.

It also gave him a plan.

But first he had a responsibility to honor, a promise to
keep.

* * * * *

As soon as his limbs were steady enough for him to
walk, Oldar hurried to the stables and hastily threw
saddle and bridle onto the same placid horse he had rid-
den to Avernus days before. As he emerged onto the
cobblestoned street, the sound of the animal's hooves
echoed in the eerie silence, virtually the only sound in
the city since the storm—a mage storm, he was more
certain than ever—had quieted and a few stars had come
out. He was crossing the Vuchar, trying to get to the main
road to Viaki as quickly as possible, when he glanced
once more toward the beleaguered Kargat headquarters.

A chill ran up his spine as he saw that the blocky
structure, instead of being an almost invisible shadow
against the night sky, now stood out almost as distinctly
as it had during the mage storm as stroke after stroke of
unnatural lightning had lanced into it. It glowed, not with
any form of light Oldar had ever seen, but with an obsidian blackness that stood out against the darkness of the
night the way the sun stood out against a brightly lighted
daytime sky.

But then as he watched, unable to look away, he saw
that it was not the building itself but something that was
flowing from the building, as if oozing out of the very
walls.

And it was spreading, flowing outward in all directions,
molten blackness flowing like lava. Even at this distance,

Oldar could feel the cold that it radiated.

Balitor's warning flashed through his mind again. So this was the result of Lord Azalin's failure to heed it. This was what was meant when Balitor had warned that Darkon would be overrun.

And now it was truly happening.

Gripping the reins tightly, he urged the horse ahead, then urged it again until it was galloping, its shoes striking sparks on the cobblestones. Whatever this was, would it stop at Darkon's borders? If it did, and if he could reach his family in time, he might be able to rouse them and flee across the Tepest border.

For a moment he thought of shouting warnings to every darkened house he passed, but he realized it would be futile. Few would understand his words, and those who did would take him for a madman, which indeed he very likely was. And even if they saw the cold black tide sweeping toward them, they could never outdistance it on foot, and few had any other choice. No, a warning would at best do nothing more than awaken the people so they could spend their last moments anticipating whatever terror awaited them when they were inevitably engulfed.

His stomach knotted as he realized that might very well be all he could do for his family as well.

Finally he emerged from the maze of streets south of the Vuchar and found himself on the road he had been searching for, cobblestones quickly giving way to hard-packed dirt. Long before the road reached Viaki, he hoped he would find the first of the lesser roads and trails that led home, but he half feared it would slide by in the darkness without his notice. He had seen it only in the light of day and had been hard pressed to make note of specific landmarks even then.

He was passing through an unfamiliar, thickly forested region, beginning to fear he had indeed missed the turnoff, when he heard his name spoken out of the night. A moment later the mists sprang up and enveloped him, his mount vanishing as if it had never existed.

This land is coming to an end, young Oldar, Lord Azalin's voice spoke out of the mists. *Before the night is out, it will be a land of the dead, a necropolis, but you and your family, as I long ago promised your namesake, will be kept safe.*

Relief swept through Oldar, but the relief was tinged with anger. "You did not heed Balitor's warning," he said accusingly.

I did not, but I may yet rectify that error.

"And what of Balitor? He was doing your service, and now he is lost in some terrible place!"

The mists seemed to roil for a moment, and then Lord Azalin's voice returned: *That is another error of my own making that I will attempt to rectify. Farewell, young Oldar.*

And Oldar was alone in the mists, but soon, from somewhere in their depths, came faint echoes of his father's voice.

*   *   *   *   *

Balitor longed for death but knew it would not be granted. He wondered if, after what he had undergone in the Nartok temple, he *could* die.

But at least as long as they remained here, lost in the mists, there would be no further depredations in any world by the creature he was shackled to and who was equally shackled to him.

And they *would* remain here. No matter how the creature that called itself Dachine raged and struggled, Balitor would continue to block his efforts to drag them back through the mists to Darkon or any other land, where Balitor's own power would doubtless be less, but where the creature could call on his massive store of sorcery to take control or even cast Balitor out. Here in the mists, that sorcery was apparently of little use to the creature. Here there were other things that determined who was in control, and as their memories merged and the creature tried to exert that control, it became apparent that here Balitor was the stronger of the two. Perhaps it was the fact that he had lived two hundred years, while Dachine had lived less than a quarter of that. Perhaps it was that Dachine had accomplished virtually everything by his sorcery and had never developed the mental strength to deal with the world on its own terms, the way a pampered princeling who is carried everywhere in a velvet-lined litter might never develop the necessary strength in his legs to walk.

But whatever the reason, here in the mists, the Balitor part of this now seemingly inseparable combination retained enough control to keep Dachine—to keep them both—from escaping. And Balitor wondered: Was the merging as complete as it would ever be? Because it was *not* complete. Their memories had merged, yes, but somehow the essence that was Balitor had maintained its integrity. He *remembered* doing the terrible things that Dachine had done, yet he knew that *he* had not done them. And from Dachine's raging about the "insane" things that *he* remembered from Balitor's past, Balitor assumed it was the same for Dachine. Something, if only Balitor's own will, was keeping them separate. He only wished that he had exercised that will long ago, when Lord Azalin had first bestowed someone else's life upon him. Like the original Oldar, he would have been dead for a century, and none of this . . .

Abruptly Balitor felt Lord Azalin's presence, but it was not the same Lord Azalin who had been torn from his imagined grip when Dachine had fled into the mists. He felt himself being gripped, though he knew now he had no body to *be* gripped. A moment later he felt the Dachine memories draining away, and at first he exulted to be free of them, but then he cried out in his mind, *No! You cannot set him free!*

He can cause no more harm to Darkon than I have already caused when I chose to ignore your warning, Lord Azalin's silent voice said in his mind as the Dachine memories continued to fade and Balitor felt the sorcerous creature somehow being peeled away from him.

What of Oldar? Is he—

He is well, as will you be. I have given my word.

And Balitor was alone in the mists. But soon he heard familiar voices, faint in the distance.

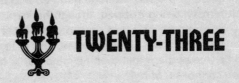

TWENTY-THREE

Oerth
246 CY (397, Barovian Calendar)

As the mists fell away, Azalin knew instantly he had succeeded. The scene before him was precisely as he had visualized it, precisely as he remembered it: a small, log-walled, single-room house, little more than a hut, huddled in the shadow of the city wall of Knurl, the alley-wide street in front of it rutted and littered with refuse.

Inside, at a rough wooden table, sat Corsalus, a young man in coarse peasant's clothes, poring over one of a stack of ancient tomes in the flickering light of a half-burned candle. In one corner, a ragged pallet leaked straw onto the heavily scarred plank floor. The only object in the room that did not bear unmistakable marks of age and neglect was an ornately carved ebony box tucked safely away in one corner.

Outside, two brothers of fifteen and twelve, dark cloaks concealing richly made clothes, stood at the door, the fifteen-year-old's hand raised to trace the symbols that would, combined with whispered words of power, gain them entrance.

This was where and when, for him, it had begun.

This was where and when, for him, it must be stopped.

This was the night fifteen-year-old Firan Zal'honan botched a Grand Summoning and thus caused his brother Irik's tortured death. This was the night that locked the young sorcerer onto the tortuous path that his tormentors never allowed him to leave until he had accomplished for them what they could not accomplish for themselves.

He had already failed once to foil them, when he had tried to kill Strahd and keep Barovia from being drawn into the mists, but he would not fail now.

But it would not be easy. His newfound powers had enabled him to draw himself through the mists to this time and place, just as other powers had taken him to that terrible night in Barovia. But even as he descended and entered the hut with his younger self, he felt those powers fade almost to nothingness even more rapidly than his powers had faded as he had emerged from the mists into the shadow of Castle Ravenloft. He was reduced to little more than a disembodied spirit, and for one terrible moment, he wondered if he were going to fade from existence entirely this time. That other time he had retained some small part of his powers, but then he had also been protected by his phylactery. That other time, he had been in Barovia, a land about to be taken prisoner by the mists, while this was Oerth, which had no link to Darkon or any of the mist-bound lands except through him. That other time, he had been in a land in which he himself had never existed, at a time when he would not yet exist *anywhere* for another thirty years. But here . . .

Here the situation was far more precarious. Here there was no phylactery to protect him. Here he was coexisting with, almost touching, his younger self, as that younger self went through the remembered actions of that fateful night. And Azalin wondered, If he *did* touch that younger self, even inadvertently . . .

The urge was almost overpowering, as if by becoming that younger self he could regain all that he had lost. Only his burning hatred of his tormentors and the fear that he would be trapped in that younger self, then forced to relive all the losses—his brother, his home, his very world—kept him from succumbing.

With a painful effort, he pulled back and hovered, invisible, high in the rafters, where later the shadows from that other world would gather.

And he watched, his mind going over and over the events of that night in excruciating detail and seeing that each and every action was being replayed precisely as he remembered. Could he, in his weakened form, affect those actions enough to change the final outcome? If he retained only a thousandth of the power that had allowed him to come to this place, he could easily block their spells, causing the summoning to fail. He could keep the Opening from appearing in the midst of the circle of blood. He could keep the mummified *shasheek* from vanishing, only to be replaced by the horror that the three naive would-be sorcerers could not control. Most of all, he could keep Irik, utterly innocent in all ways, from being possessed by that creature and being slain by his own father.

He could do that or any of a hundred other things . . . *if* he had the power.

But did he?

Tentatively, as the three youths dabbed each other's faces and breasts with supposedly magical ointment and cast the minor preliminary enchantments that accompanied the ointments, he drew close and murmured the counterspells that should, in an instant, nullify any enchantments cast not only in the here and now but any time since the setting sun.

But they did not. He could feel the spells, particularly those of his own younger self, as they continued to turn the protective patterns of ointment on their skins into symbols of power that penetrated not only their bodies but also their minds and souls.

Briefly he tried the reverse, tried to strengthen the spells, hoping that the added power of the protective symbols would then be enough to tip the balance in Irik's favor. But again there was no effect. The symbols remained only as powerful as the three had been able to make them, no more and no less.

And then it was time for the bloodletting. The mummified *shasheek*, taken from the ebony box that had rested in one corner of the room, already lay in the center of the floor. A knife, held only long enough to draw blood from forearm, was passed from hand to hand as the chants continued and the blood dripped to form a confining pattern about the long-dead creature. Azalin could already sense the chill that suggested the other world was drawing near.

Time was growing short.

Flowing down to hover above the *shasheek* within the blood circle, Azalin discarded all caution and mentally shouted, again and again, the most powerful of counterspells he could muster.

The room only grew more chill, the wavering shadows more solid. To the three who had arranged themselves about the circle and continued their increasingly frenetic chants, it was as if he did not exist.

Except . . .

Occasionally, when there was a rare moment of silence between chants or a moment of exhausted immobility between series of gestures, young Firan's eyes would flick sideways, sometimes dart about the room, as if he heard or felt something the others did not. Could the boy be aware of his infinitely older counterpart's presence?

Pulling back, Azalin tried to remember that night in even more detail. Had he darted similar looks about the room? If so, for what reasons other than sheer nervousness? Or were those actions a first tiny departure from what had been? He couldn't be positive, not of every single detail, not after more than three centuries.

Azalin moved down again, hovering closely over young Firan's head, and once again the urge to touch that other self was almost overwhelming. But in that same moment, the boy darted a look toward him—not around the room but directly toward the spot where he hovered invisibly.

And a frown of puzzlement briefly creased the boy's brow, beaded with sweat from his exertions. Even that slight movement drew an angry glance from Corsalus, and young Firan, ashamed to have been so shaken by nothing more than a sudden chill, lowered his eyes to the *shasheek* and waited for Corsalus to resume the chant.

And then it was time to continue, to again pick up the chant with Corsalus while the air continued to grow increasingly chill, turning the beads of sweat on his brow to ice. The candles flickered in an unseen breeze.

And Azalin wondered, Was his younger self the key? Azalin himself obviously could not, in this time and this place, directly affect the spells they were casting, no matter how hard he tried. But his younger self . . . Could he have an effect *through him?*

Was that why, from the moment he had looked down on the boy, the urge to move closer, to actually touch his

younger self, had been so great? Was it his own instinct
telling him, *This is your only chance?*

It would take so little, so very little to grossly alter that
night's terrible outcome. It would not be necessary to
force the boy to cast a different spell at the critical
moment, for the words he had spoken had been letter
perfect. It had been the thoughts, the panicked thoughts
of an inexperienced and frightened fifteen-year-old, that
had warped and changed the spell and set the creature
onto the defenseless Irik. If he could somehow *calm* the
boy, build his confidence, so that when the time came,
when Corsalus lost his tenuous grip on the creature and
young Firan had to step into the breach, he would be in
complete control of himself, his thoughts and his words
not at odds with each other but in perfect unison . . .

He had no choice. He had to try. If he did not, the night
would inevitably play out as he remembered it. He would
be forced to be helpless witness to his brother's tortured
death a second time, and his centuries of torment would
begin anew.

Ever so cautiously, waiting until another pause in the
increasingly frenetic ritual, Azalin crept closer, ever
closer. Once again the boy looked around, his eyes
seeming to stare directly at the invisible, insubstantial
Azalin.

And as the chants continued, Azalin remained close,
not attempting counterspells but concentrating all his
thoughts on his younger self, like an unseen, unheard
mentor, cheering him on, echoing the words of the
chants, willing confidence and tranquility upon the boy.

And he *was* being heard. He was virtually certain of it.
Time and again the boy's eyes flickered in Azalin's direction, and gradually, instead of apprehension, those eyes
began to reflect a growing confidence, even a calmness,

the very calmness that Azalin so desperately hoped to engender.

Then, in the space of a heartbeat, that other world broke through.

The air became so frigid their breaths were suddenly turned to steaming clouds, as if their very words had become visible. In the same moment, the *shasheek*'s mummified corpse vanished, and the Opening appeared where it had lain.

And the young Firan, as Azalin so vividly remembered, was both exultant and terrified. Exultant that his sorcery had *worked*, yet terrified of what was beyond the Opening, terrified that the shield that flickered upward from the circle of blood like translucent gray flames would not be capable of containing whatever emerged.

Redoubling his concentration, Azalin crowded even closer to his younger self as the chanting took up again, louder and more insistent than ever, with Azalin confirming every syllable, every intonation, every thought.

Then the room was filled with a great ripping sound, as if the fabric of reality itself were being torn asunder by monstrous talons. Azalin himself was shaken by the noise and the intensity of the cold that filled the room. And then the shadows began to descend from the rafters, closing in on the three.

And the creature appeared, a deeper shadow within the other shadows, forming above the Opening. Even in his weakened form, Azalin could feel the foul aura of malevolence and hatred the thing radiated.

Shutting out everything but young Firan, pulling so close he was almost touching the boy, Azalin concentrated as he had never concentrated before, for *now* was the moment! Now was when Corsalus lost control! Now was when the creature broke through the shimmering

gray barrier, and Firan's mental blunder sent it not back
through the Opening but into his terrified brother, who
even now bravely stood his ground despite the terror in
his young eyes.

Now . . .

Now Azalin could feel in memory the fearful pressure
of the creature against his own chest while young Firan
felt it in reality and shivered in terror. In Firan's memory
and his own, Azalin found the words of the spell that
would banish the creature, and he pressed even closer to
the boy as they together began to utter the words of the
incantation. He felt the boy's steadiness, and he knew,
even as he crept still closer to tighten their bond even
further, that this time Firan was going to succeed and Irik
would be saved.

But then, as the words flowed from them as if from a
single mouth, he felt himself touch his younger self. He
recoiled in shock, but it was too late: He was caught!

Like a man who had approached too close to a deadly
whirlpool, he was sucked in violently and was instantly
submerged in the mind of his younger self. He felt the
boy's panic at this sudden intrusion, thinking it must be
the creature itself, or another of its kind, and . . .

In that instant, he lost.

In that careless moment, Azalin condemned both his
brother and himself.

Cursing himself, he struggled violently to pull back
and was once again floating, looking down. The creature
was lunging at the barrier, belling it out to double its size,
and would in another instant break through. In that same
instant, Azalin's soul screamed for him to retreat into the
mists so as not to be witness to this horror once again.

But he could not.

Blindly, knowing the gesture was futile but unable to

stop himself, he plunged directly at the creature itself, now solidifying into the horror of scales and claws that Azalin could never wipe from his mind. He was batted aside as if he were a mayfly, and from somewhere he heard the laughter of his tormentors.

And then he remembered with a surge of hope: Years ago, when he had followed his own lifeline back to this time and place, it had been not only his tormentors whose presence he had sensed. He had also sensed the presence of those others, those who seemed to be opposed to his tormentors.

With all his strength, a pale shadow of what it had been, Azalin called out to them, *Show yourselves! Declare yourselves! Hide in the shadows no more! If ever you would openly fight these creatures, do it now!*

But even as he screamed silently, he saw Irik hunch over, saw the gray pallor come to his skin, saw the grimace of terror distort his innocent features.

And finally a distant voice said silently, *We have not the power to openly oppose them, not here. Our only hope is in those like yourself, who are also* their *hope.*

And he felt himself, the insubstantial spirit that he had become, being pushed away, being pushed toward the source of the laughter of moments before.

Being pushed toward his tormentors!

He struggled against it, but to no avail, and even as Irik was being possessed by the creature that had been set loose upon him, Azalin felt the shadowy fingers of his tormentors closing about him.

* * * * *

They were neither Azalin's friends nor his allies. They were only the enemies of his enemies, the foes of those he called his tormentors. For as long as any of them could remember, they had watched from their vantage point in the upper reaches of the mists. Now they watched with a growing sense of hope as more and more disjointed fragments of this insubstantial creature's memories of what was to them the future darted briefly to the surface of his agitated mind.

When he had called to them with such urgency, they had been both startled and puzzled. But in that same instant, they had seen the astonishing truth standing out in his thoughts like a beacon: Here was someone who had not only returned to the Prime Material Plane from the demiplanes—the stepping-stone worlds brought into existence by their foes—but had returned to his own past on the very world he had been taken from. They had long suspected that such feats were possible within the mists, but never before had they seen proof.

And then, as they concentrated on this odd interloper more intensely than they had ever concentrated on any-one from any plane or demiplane, they realized with a terrible shock that this being, now little more than a dis-embodied spirit, had very nearly—*would* very nearly, three centuries in the future—brought about the very dis-aster they themselves had been working to avoid for as long as they could remember: the total destruction of the barrier that was all that kept those creatures sealed in their own vile plane. Such power, which their foes were constantly seeking out, constantly encouraging, was heretofore unparalleled.

But they also saw he had, in the end, seen through their foes' deception and had averted total disaster, though they suspected that, despite his final efforts to set right what he had been tricked into doing, the demiplane itself was doomed. Without complete access, their foes would not be able to use it as the long-sought stepping stone to the Prime Material Plane, but even the relatively small break in the barrier meant that the demiplane itself would never be the same, would never again be habitable by anything approaching normal life.

But that was of little importance to them. What *was* important was what this creature who called himself Azalin had done next. He had plunged into the mists and navigated through them with more skill than they themselves had ever dreamt possible. And he had returned here, to his own childhood, in an effort to literally change his past.

But though it was *his* past, it was *their* future, and they immediately found themselves thinking, He failed because, out of his own time, the powers he had achieved were almost completely lost to him. But he had not lost the mental strength, the obsessive determination that appeared to have driven him throughout his existence.

And then they wondered, What would be the result if this remarkable creature were to be absorbed by their foes, as so many others had been? Would he be lost like a grain of sand dropped into the sea? Or would he retain even there the strength he had exhibited—*would* exhibit—throughout his existence? Would he, against all odds, be able to exert an influence?

They didn't know. They could only push him toward their foes and watch and wait.

*　*　*　*　*

Finally it was over.

Irik lay dead, beheaded by his own father. Firan lay unconscious on the floor.

Even so, Azalin, trapped within the massive *gestalt*

that would be his tormentors, was beginning to feel faint stirrings of hope. He knew he would have to watch the anguish of his own existence through his tormentors' eyes, exactly as he had just now had to watch the possession and destruction of his brother.

But his tormentors were not omnipotent. Far from it, in fact. They had needed *him*, someone with *his* powers to break through the barrier that had for as long as they could remember held them in check. They had needed him so badly that they had spent three centuries constantly watching and manipulating and tricking him, every act designed to lead him to precisely the point he had very nearly come to, the point at which he would use his powers to unwittingly set their plane loose on Darkon and all the other mist-bound lands. They had needed someone like him so badly, they had watched and manipulated and tricked several generations of his ancestors in order that he be born.

But now . . .

Now they were barely aware of his presence within their *gestalt*, certainly not aware of who and what he was. They fed on such insubstantial spirits and so far had paid him no more attention than any other minor morsel.

But they would, he vowed.

They would . . .

 **EPILOGUE**

Oerth
588 CY (739 Barovian Calendar)

The night before his eighteenth birthday, Oldar came awake drenched in icy sweat and gasping for breath. Images of a terrifying landscape populated by creatures hideous beyond imagining were still so vivid before his eyes that it was not until he had lighted a lamp and looked upon the sleeping faces of his parents that he could be positive they were nightmares rather than memories.

Even so, he shivered as he remembered his new friend Balitor, a middle-aged city dweller who had settled on a nearby farm a few weeks ago. Balitor had suffered through a similar siege not long after, but it had passed quickly enough. In fact, Oldar told himself as he returned to bed and tried to regain his lost sleep, Balitor's tales of his own nightmares were probably responsible for this night's imagined horrors. Why else would he dream of a land where the dead were less likely to find peace in their graves than to rise from them and stalk the night, decayed flesh falling from their skeletal bodies as they walked, their eyes glowing red in the darkness? Such things were too terrible even for the tales parents traditionally used to frighten their children. Certainly they were too horrendous for his own mind to have manufactured on its own.

No, they were only nightmares, spawned by his new friend's fanciful descriptions of his own. Eventually he drifted back to sleep, thinking with a smile that he would have to tell Balitor about the contagious nature of his dreams.

If you enjoyed reading *Lord of the Necropolis*, you may also be interested in the following books, all set in the grim gothic world of the RAVENLOFT® campaign setting.

Lord Azalin makes an appearance in *Tower of Doom*, by Mark Anthony. The book also concerns a hunch-backed bell ringer and a personal agent of Azalin's, as well as a certain monster who occupies the bell tower. . . .

Azalin is featured in *King of the Dead*, also by Gene DeWeese, which together with this book comprises the tragic story of Azalin's life—and unlife. With virtually unlimited powers, Azalin still cannot find peace. Tortured by the death of his son, the unwilling ruler has come to despise the world of darkness and horror over which he reigns. The tale traces the course of his life from a powerful wizard to King of the Dead.

For more about Strahd von Zarovich, be sure to pick up P. N. Elrod's *I, Strahd*, the autobiography of the vampire lord of Ravenloft. Strahd also plays an important role in *Vampire of the Mists*, by Christie Golden, in which a golden elf lost in Barovia searches for a mysterious woman.

Ask for these and other exciting titles from TSR, Inc., at fine book and hobby stores everywhere.